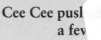

Cee Cee push

a few

"STEP UP, SAVOIE. Ta

if you can." She sho   , but this time his
feet stayed planted. He had her wrists in his hands,
but let go when she tugged. "Coward," she threw at
him. "Come *on*."

She pushed again, and this time, he dragged her
up against his chest, holding her there with his superior strength, with the intensity of his gaze.

She smiled. "Come on, big, bad mobster boy.
King of the Beasts." Her gaze was heavy lidded, her
mouth pursed and ripe. "If you want to put your
mark on me, you're going to work for it."

Her elbow hammered into his ribs, giving her
just enough time to slip away and put the couch
between them.

And just like that, he changed. His posture
altered, becoming sleek and fluid. His gaze gleamed,
centering on her with a focus that was preternatural
in its stillness. Danger oozed from him in palpable
waves.

This was what he was when she wasn't watching.
This was the deadly predator whose name created
fear in men who let nothing scare them. Quick. Terrifying. Brutal beyond belief.

And hers, if she had the courage to claim him.

ALSO BY NANCY GIDEON

Masked by Moonlight
Chased by Moonlight

Available from Pocket Books

NANCY GIDEON

Captured by Moonlight

POCKET BOOKS

New York   London   Toronto   Sydney

Pocket Books
A Division of Simon & Schuster, Inc.
1230 Avenue of the Americas
New York, NY 10020

This book is a work of fiction. Names, characters, places, and incidents either are products of the author's imagination or are used fictitiously. Any resemblance to actual events or locales or persons, living or dead, is entirely coincidental.

First Pocket Books paperback edition August 2010

POCKET and colophon are registered trademarks of Simon & Schuster, Inc.

For information about special discounts for bulk purchases, please contact Simon & Schuster Special Sales at 1-866-506-1949 or business@simonandschuster.com.

The Simon & Schuster Speakers Bureau can bring authors to your live event. For more information or to book an event, contact the Simon & Schuster Speakers Bureau at 1-866-248-3049 or visit our website at www.simonspeakers.com.

Cover design by Min Choi
Cover art by Craig White

Manufactured in the United States of America

10 9   8 7 6 5 4 3 2

ISBN 978-1-4391-4965-2
ISBN 978-1-4391-5542-4 (ebook)

For Dr. E.
Thanks for the insights and honesty!

Captured
by Moonlight

Prologue

THEY FOLLOWED HIM like ghosts.

Quick. Silent. Gliding almost invisibly along the damp dock. Hunting like dark, deadly pack animals through the mist rising off the river.

He ran, a man already consigned to death. They were slick and stealthy as they cut through the shadows like moonlight. He stumbled, knocking into crates, falling to his hands and knees, struggling for the strength to drag himself toward refuge. Lights danced ahead, burning like fireflies in the fog. Distant music teased above the raw tear of his breathing. If he could get to one of those places where humans gathered, he just might survive his colossal stupidity.

If it looks too good to be true . . .

He watched the edge of darkness for movement, gathering for a sprint across open space—though they'd be on him in a second. His legs shook so weakly, he'd be lucky if he made it a few yards.

Why hadn't he taken his brother's advice to proceed with care? Because along with that colossal stupidity came spiteful pride. He didn't want to be like his big brother, owned and obedient, leashed like those who worked the docks. Those who groveled to the lethally elegant Max Savoie. So he took a risk on a deal that seemed so sweet. And now his brother would be tearfully murmuring, "I told you so," over a casket probably paid for out of Savoie's deep pockets.

It wasn't loyalty toward Savoie as much as it was ignorance that kept him silent while they'd pounded him with their questions. Silent except for the screams, while they were breaking his fingers and more. At first he hadn't understood, through the pain and the choke of his vomit, what they wanted to know. But when he tried to tell them that, it only got worse.

He should have guessed it was Savoie they were after. They had the same sleek strength, that same arrogant grace that set Savoie apart from the dockside clan. But by the time he realized what name would put an end to his suffering, he couldn't say it through his split lips and broken jaw.

Then a careless moment of theirs put a gun close to his nearly crippled hand. He held them off, keeping them at bay, with their red-gold eyes and quicksilver movements, until he'd escaped.

Or had he?

At some point in his uncoordinated stagger down the wharf, it occurred to him that there was no way he'd gotten the drop on these lean, merciless killers. If he'd managed to escape, it was because they'd let him.

For all his scathing criticism, after refusing to humble himself to ask for a job, he had to run to Savoie. He was the only power in New Orleans who could stand up to these brutal demons.

But he had to reach Max, before he could plead for sanctuary.

And that's where they wanted him to lead them.

Part of him, the part that was battered and smashed and moaning in agony, urged that he take them wherever they wanted. He didn't owe Savoie anything. There was a world of difference between the minute-to-minute existence he eked out on the streets and that sprawling mansion where Savoie lived in mobster luxury. Savoie, with his designer suits, thick bankroll, and wet dream of a human girlfriend. Savoie, who made his brother and those like him stand taller, prouder, for once acting like men instead of beasts as they rallied around him.

So, maybe he owed him something after all.

He crouched, his blood dripping on the concrete as he scanned the swirling shadows. Through his swollen lids, he saw wolven silhouettes slink low between the cargo crates and metal bins, shapes that stretched and bunched and rose upright to walk on two legs instead of four. Stalking him as if he were some kind of trembling rabbit.

Well, this rabbit was going out with a roar.

He swayed to his feet. Instead of trying to reach the distant sheltering lights, he backed up against the river, gripping the gun in his mangled hands. Realizing that he wasn't going to run, they emerged from the curtains of mist, eyes glittering, sharp teeth gleaming. He pointed the pistol at the nearest one and screamed out with the effort of pulling the trigger.

Nothing. Just an impotent click.

They moved in, aggressive and fearless, closing off every direction except one. He looked behind him—such a long way down to the black surface of the water. But he was a strong swimmer, he thought with a feral smile. It was better than letting them tear him apart, leaving his pieces for his brother to put together. He turned and stepped into the darkness.

And in the middle of that long, cool fall, as the water rushed up to embrace him, something inside his head blew apart with a sudden shock, like being shot.

He hit the water and sank without a sound.

One

MAX SMELLED HER perfume. *Voodoo Love.*

The scent drifted to him on the balmy night air long before he heard the sound of a big block engine rumble through the security gates. He inhaled deeply, drinking it in, letting it tease his senses as Charlotte came closer, up the driveway, into the house, then her footsteps in the front hall, and up the curving stairs. Slow, weary steps. He lay in the darkness, letting her come to him.

She moved quietly about his room, fumbling without the lights. He watched her undress, the efficient movements not as quick as they usually were. Her gun, her shield, her ankle piece, her cuffs, her cell, laid out along the dresser top in a no-nonsense row. She paused with a sigh, then began to lever out of her boots.

"I'd planned to meet your flight."

She gave a slight hop of surprise, and was silent for a moment too long. No sassy reprimand for startling her?

"I had a change of plans at the last minute. I left

a message for you." Defensive and cool. Not exactly the reunion he was expecting.

"I got it." Short and uninformative: *Change of plans. I'll be back late.* "I wanted to pick you up, but I didn't know what time you were getting in."

"I took a cab. No big deal." She started down the buttons of her shirt. *His* shirt. She'd said the feel of silk against her skin would make him seem closer while she was away.

"I was looking forward to welcoming you home."

"Sorry." Still prickly.

"No big deal." His reply was inflectionless, as if it really wasn't.

"I was only gone four days."

"They were very long days. And very lonely nights."

"It's not like I didn't call you." Defensive and now almost irritated, she turned her back on him.

Yes, and their conversations had been as brief and impersonal as her message. He'd learned more from the tone of her voice than from her Spartan words.

She let the shirt slide off her slumped shoulders, then shimmied out of her jeans, leaving both on the floor. He'd missed the unintentional mess she left in her wake, unthinkingly rather than thoughtlessly. She made a long, tough silhouette. Lean muscle, dangerous curves, and sleek bronze skin. The need to touch her, to have her, spiked like a fever, but her cool mood made him careful.

"It's not the same thing, talking across time zones." He thought that sounded reasonable enough to slip in a little gruff emotion behind it. "I like you here, with me."

"I'm here now." There was just enough bite in that to make him frown.

"No," he corrected, his voice low and seducingly soft. "You're over there." He patted the bed beside him. "Come over here to me."

She hesitated, then approached the sheets they shared more often than not. Her walk was full of prideful, independent attitude, which made him smile. If she made things easy for him, he wouldn't crave her quite so desperately.

She paused at the side of the bed, fists on her hips, her tone confrontational. "Close enough?"

"No." He put out his hand. "Down here so I can welcome you properly."

Whatever had her so edgy didn't keep her from seeking him out in the darkness. Her fingers slid across his palm. He enfolded them gently, bringing them to his lips before tugging on them. She sank down onto the mattress into a kiss that greeted her with sweet familiarity, wooing her into temporary compliance. He didn't try to stop her when she straightened. If she needed the separating space, he'd let her have it. For the moment.

"I missed you, *sha*. I wish I could have gone with you."

"It's no—"

"Big deal. So you said. Still, I wanted to be there for you. I would have canceled my meetings if you'd asked me to. I was worried about you being alone."

"Is that why you sent an emissary in your place?" Her question jabbed like a thin, sharp blade between the ribs. Then she let her temper slip. "How *dare* you, Max? How dare you send someone to spy on me? If you can't trust me out of your sight—"

He touched his fingertips to her lips. "That's not why. I just wanted to make sure you were safe."

"So you sent some clumsy goon to follow me? I was on to him before the plane left the ground. Give me some credit, please."

"I do, detective. I wanted you to know he was there. Just in case."

"In case *what*? I was mugged during the funeral?" She tunneled a hand through her short, spiky hair in exasperation. "It's warm and fuzzy of you to be so paranoid, but totally unnecessary. Stop it. Okay?"

"Okay."

His mild reply didn't convince her for an instant. "I can take care of myself. I don't need or want you to handle things for me."

"Can I just handle *you*, then?"

A soft laugh, an improvement. "You drive me crazy, Savoie."

"And you love that about me."

Her hand squeezed his. "Yes, I do." She glanced

around the dark room curiously. "What's that smell? It's really nice."

He snapped on the light, and she stared at the spectacular bouquet of deep crimson roses mixed with other tiny fragrant blossoms on the nightstand.

"Are these for me?" Her voice was small and a bit shaky.

As she reached out to touch the velvety petals, a sudden tightness filled his chest. He cleared his throat and tried for nonchalance. "I was going to give them to you at the airport, and probably would've gotten all misty and emotional. Thank you for saving me from that embarrassment."

She glanced at him, all misty. "No one's ever given me flowers before."

Trying to keep from getting what she cynically called gooey, he shrugged. "I've never given them. I wasn't sure if you'd like them." Her arms whipped about his neck, her face burrowing into his shoulder, and he held her. "I guess you do." He breathed her in on a satisfied sigh. "Welcome home, Charlotte."

"I'm so glad to be here." Her shoulders gave a suspicious hitch.

He drew her in closer, his cheek rubbing against her hair. He figured she was ready to let it out, and started gently. "Was it very difficult?"

"I hadn't seen or heard from her in over twenty years."

Twenty years since her alcoholic mother had abandoned her child and her cop husband. It took a fatal heart attack to bring them back together—a little too late.

"That's not what I asked."

She squirmed but still answered. "I didn't expect to feel anything except maybe anger. I don't know what I would have said to her if I'd made it there in time. She had another family. A husband in insurance sales, stepkids, grandkids." She choked a little. "I met them. They were nice. They wanted me to stay at their house, but . . . it felt a little too strange. I wish I'd asked you to go with me."

That reluctant admission came hard, and there was no way he was going to let her regret it. He kissed her brow tenderly.

"Next time you won't have to."

"I've run out of family to bury, Max." She took an unsteady breath and he could feel her reining in her amazing control. Not quite managing. "I'm so tired." And finally, the extremely gratifying, "I missed you."

He turned off the light, then cradled her against him. He'd thought of nothing for days but a passionate homecoming, had hungered for it and for her. But that would have to wait now. She was a tough, tightly wrapped woman, not one to let go of very much. So when she buckled, even slightly, he was quick to console her. Just being there for her, having her arms curled about him and her breath feathering against his throat, was enough. He'd waited twelve years to have her the first time. He could wait a few more hours.

"Close your eyes. I've got you." As she relaxed, he kissed the top of her head, whispering, "Sleep well."

And as she slept deeply and dreamlessly, he lay awake and alert, dividing his concentration between the feel of her beside him and the sounds of the night.

Because his caution was much more necessary than Detective Charlotte Caissie knew.

If coming home was falling into Max Savoie's arms, returning to work was her grounding back to reality. A grim, often brutal reality, but the only one she'd ever known. Charlotte endured all her colleagues' condolences, then focused gratefully on work. She understood death a lot better than she related to the living, which was why she was so good at her job. The New Orleans Police Department had somehow managed to get through four days without her, and she didn't know whether to be relieved or a bit insulted. The city was only slightly less demanding than her lover, and she was fiercely possessive of both.

Leaving Max asleep under the covers was a sacrifice she hoped the Eighth District appreciated.

Her desk was buried under an avalanche of

paperwork and a sad little plant someone had left with a sympathy card but no water. Before her butt even hit her chair, her phone was ringing.

"Caissie."

"Charlotte, it's Dovion. I've got something down here that might interest you."

Welcome back.

FROM DEVLIN DOVION'S intriguing John Doe, whose brain seemed to have exploded without any physiological cause, Cee Cee was drawn into a parade of nonpressing but time-consuming matters. She touched base with several informants, talked to the team that had taken the call on Dovion's gray-matter scramble, and stopped into her commander's office to get the all-clear for firing two rounds into an escaping murderer. She was meeting her partner, Alain Babineau, after lunch to shuffle through their caseload, then her only goal was to slide under those soft sheets again and get naked with a certain criminal element.

As she entered the squad room, she was so surprised to see Max Savoie sitting on the corner of her desk that she simply stood there, her jaw hanging open.

"Looks like you got company, Caissie." Junior Hammond, who was always snapping at her heels in search of a grade raise, bumped her in passing. "I'm on my way to check for outstandings, to see if he's wanted for anything other than some afternoon delight. Might as well take advantage of a bird in the hand."

"I'm gonna take my hand upside your head, Junior. Besides, I don't think you're his type."

A slow, close-lipped smile spread across Max's face, warming his expression. Aware that every eye in the place, from glowering watch commander to beat cops passing through, was on her and her unlikely visitor, Charlotte moved casually toward her desk. But her gaze devoured him.

With hard, angular features and a long slant of cool green eyes, he wasn't attractive so much as wickedly compelling. Danger always stirred behind his steady stare. He was the genuine article, as terrifying an individual as one could imagine. He'd killed for the first time when he was just a child, with an instinctual viciousness that earned him a place growing up behind one of the Crescent City's most infamous mobsters, Jimmy Legere. After Jimmy's violent death he'd gone from knee breaker to deal maker, taking over the vast criminal empire to become a powerful influence in his own right. And because he was more interested in her than he was in his mentor's ill-gotten gains, most of those endeavors leaned toward legal now.

But that's not all he was.

He wore her black tactical vest emblazoned NOPD, probably to keep himself from getting shot here in the station, over a white tee shirt and jeans. A red high-topped foot swung indolently. Sleek, dark, and controlled . . . and hers. She wanted to latch on to that smugly smiling mouth in the worst way, which made her tone testy.

"What are you doing here, Max?"

"Just thought I'd see if you wanted to have lunch. Since we missed a chance for breakfast." His stare smoldered, intimating what he was hungry for.

"You should have called."

"I was in the neighborhood." He ran his fingertip across the framed photos on her desk. Her father. Charlotte and her best friend, Mary Kate Malone. "Why don't you have a picture of me?"

"I suppose I could pick the most flattering from your mug shot collection to display. No new ones since I've been gone, are there?"

He continued to smile. "Muffuletta from the Central Grocery sound good? Or is there something else you'd rather sink your teeth into?"

"I'm busy, Savoie."

"I've missed you, detective." His hand skimmed the curve of her waist, and she brushed it away. "If you're not hungry, we could go to an interrogation room and close the blinds. I think Two is open. That's always been my favorite; such an intimate, coming-home feeling about it. Surely you can spare five minutes from your busy schedule. I managed to fit you into mine." His voice lowered to a husky rumble. "And now I want to fit myself into you."

Her gaze flew about to see who might have overheard, but everyone nearby was pretending to be occupied. Her face flamed. Her body grew hot and moist. "I'm at work here," she growled.

"I love to watch you work, detective. I could sit here all day."

Sighing, she jerked out her chair. "All right. Let me make a call first." She lifted the receiver, then eyed him pointedly.

"I'll just go over there and see if anyone I know is posted on the Most Wanted board."

She watched him stroll through the room as if oblivious to the fact that every officer there was measuring his wrist size for handcuffs. A bold, aggravating man, a wolf stalking through the hen house as if he didn't know he was going to cause feathers to fly.

"You make me hot, Savoie," she whispered softly.

Across the room, he paused, she didn't have to see his face to know he was grinning.

Standing by the wall with a relaxed posture, pretending not to feel a dozen barbed glares, Max waited for Cee Cee to finish up and join him. The sweat slicking his palms had nothing to do with the hostility bristling around him and everything to do with the woman he couldn't wait to spend time with.

He'd taken a huge risk bracing her in her lair, and he knew it. Her professional world was off-limits. She'd invited him into every other aspect of her life but that one. He was too smart to push, but too honest to pretend the exclusion didn't bother him.

"Savoie?"

He glanced up to see Alain Babineau with a lovely young woman at his side. He and Cee Cee's cover-boy-pretty partner had a wary tolerance for one another. "Detective. So surprised? It's not like you've never seen me here before."

"Not without restraints. Waiting for your attorney?"

"Waiting to take Detective Caissie to lunch."

He didn't imagine the sudden pique of interest in the petite brunette's eyes. She smiled at him rather shyly. "Are you a friend of Cee Cee's?"

"I'm her boyfriend." He grinned because Babineau had suddenly gone rigid. He put out his hand. "Max Savoie."

She placed hers into it with a lack of hesitation that proved she had no idea who he was. "Tina Babineau."

"Ah. I should apologize for keeping your husband away from home so much." At her confusion, he lifted her hand to touch a light kiss to her knuckles. "I'll let him explain."

She blushed prettily, not drawing her hand away until he released it. "Alain and I were just stepping out for a bite. Would you two like to join us?"

It would almost have been worth saying yes, just to enjoy Babineau's glare of irritation a bit longer.

But the temptation of possibly getting very up close and personal with Charlotte was too great.

"Maybe another time, Mrs. Babineau. I appreciate the offer." And he did, surprisingly enough.

"How about Saturday? We're having a house-warming party. Cee Cee has the address." She smiled with genuine pleasure at Charlotte, who had just arrived. "Cee Cee, I was just telling Max he was more than welcome to come with you on Saturday."

"Really?" She exchanged a look with Alain. "To your house?"

Tina touched Max's sleeve hopefully. "Say yes. We spouses and significant others rarely get a chance to mingle socially."

There was a slight catch in her voice, an unexpected plea that touched him as delicately as her small hand, because he recognized it for what it was. Loneliness.

"I'd be happy to, if Charlotte doesn't have any objection."

He glanced at her, seeing objection aplenty in her narrowed eyes. "Sure. If you really want to." Implying he'd be a fool if he did. When he continued to smile, she gripped his arm. "Let's go. Nice to see you again, Tina."

"I look forward to seeing you both on Saturday."

Max sauntered leisurely at her side, letting her fume silently until they exited the building. She shrugged off the arm he tried to drape about her shoulders with a quarrelsome, "Not here."

"Let me know when we leave the 'Hands Off' zone, detective."

"Max, are you aware that everyone at that party will have either arrested you or wanted to kill you at one time or another?"

"So have you, darlin'—but I don't let that stop me from wanting to suck that frown off your face." She looked alarmed, as if he might attempt it right on the steps of the station. "Don't worry, I'll behave. It'll make for an entertaining afternoon."

Charlotte continued to scowl as they walked down the busy sidewalk, trying to hang on to her annoyance with him, because she was so aware of him next to her that her whole body was humming. Every seemingly innocent touch deepened that urgent vibration. The brush of his hand against hers. The nudge of his hip. The stroke of his fingertips on the small of her back when they stepped aside to let a tourist family pass. Calculated torture, after four very long days and lonely nights.

"So," he began, "what exactly does one do at these events? Make shoptalk?"

"You'll be terribly bored. And most likely, the topic of conversation."

"How flattering. How could I find that boring?"

"Mostly there's eating, drinking, and softball."

"I know how to eat without using my fingers,

so I won't embarrass you there. I don't drink, so I won't make a fool out of myself. I've never played a team sport. I think I might enjoy it."

"We already have teams."

Because her tone was stingy and uninviting, he merely smiled. "Then I'll sit on the sidelines with the spouses and significant others to cheer you on and talk, what, knitting and child rearing?"

She almost smiled back, imagining him wedged in between the cop wives. "Like you know anything about those things."

"I can learn. I'm very open-minded. Unlike you, detective."

She glanced up at him in surprise. "What do you mean?"

"Nothing."

They walked in silence until Max stopped before one of the Quarter's exclusive hotels in the heart of the old district. Pale rose-colored stucco and wrought-iron charm sat above a busy café. "What do you think?"

"About what? You want to eat here?"

He smiled. "We could order off the menu, or you could let me get lucky with some à la carte upstairs."

A bolt of pure desire shot to her loins. "You got a room?"

The key dangled. "I'm an optimist, detective." He stepped closer, the heat of his nearness burning like a thousand suns.

"Can I have a sandwich, too?" Her hands slipped

under the vest, curving around to the back pockets of his jeans to tug him against her.

"You can have anything you want."

"I want you, Savoie. Right now."

He grinned. "We might want to step off the sidewalk first."

Two

THEIR ROOM WAS on the second floor facing the courtyard, where jovial diners drank Hurricanes and listened to a wailing Doug Kershaw tune. The sound filtered up through the open balcony doors to mingle with cool shadows.

"This is nice."

Max's arms slipped about her waist. "It *is* nice. Dance with me."

He didn't have to coax her to lean into him. With her head on his shoulder and her eyes closed, Charlotte let herself be moved by the music and Max Savoie.

After a few minutes he tipped her chin up for a long, very thorough kiss while never missing a beat. Her heart was pounding by the time he eased back into soft, searching nibbles.

When she started to reach for him, he caught her wrists and held them down at her sides. "Hands off, detective," he murmured against her mouth. "Just stand there and let me work."

She closed her eyes, trusting him the way she could no other, wanting him the way she would no other.

His tongue slid across her parted lips, teasing lightly until she moaned. When he eased her shirt over her head she offered him the curve of her throat, shivering when his mouth moved down to the valley of her collarbone, chasing along those tempting contours with the sweep of his lips as his clever fingers worked the hooks of her bra. Then that barrier was gone, as well.

His touch was maddeningly light, skimming her ribs, tracing the underswell of her breasts, thumbs buffing her nipples until they were tight and achy. Her hands shook, fisting with the need to grab onto him.

"You're all I could think about," he confided softly. "The feel of you. The scent of you. The taste of you."

She toed out of her boots and tore down her zipper. His hands covered hers, warm, effortlessly controlling.

"Let me do that, *sha*."

He peeled down her jeans, kneeling to pull them free. His strong fingers massaged the tops of her feet, around her slender ankles, stroking up the sleek muscle of her calves, kneading the tight curve of her thighs. Working out the tension, building up the anticipation. His tongue joined in, licking up the silkiness of her skin and she bucked when he tasted her heat. Replacing it with his hand, he rose to assess her flushed features.

"How much did you miss me, *cher*?"

She struggled to hang onto control, breathing

hard as he plunged his fingers inside her again and again. With a ragged cry, she held onto him as she came apart, her knees giving out. The scoop of his arm about her waist was the only thing keeping her on her feet.

When her mind finally cleared from its sensory daze, she sighed. "I missed you like air. Like light. Like sound."

"Yeah?" He smoothed her hair back with a tender touch.

"You rock my world, Savoie."

"And I'm about to do it again."

THEY WERE STRETCHED out atop the crisp sheets, letting the sweat dry on their skin beneath the lazy loops of the ceiling fan.

Cee Cee gave his neck an affectionate nuzzle. "Do I still get my sandwich?"

"Absolutely."

She chuckled softly. "I'm surprised I still have an appetite, after listening to Dovion go on about his latest mystery."

Max trailed his fingertips up and down her back, feeling ridiculously relaxed and content. "What's he got under the sheet now? Nothing quite as interesting as me, I presume."

"You're always interesting under the sheets." She nipped his shoulder playfully, then settled her cheek against his chest. "Some floater with an exploded brain."

Max's expression froze. " 'Cuse me?"

"Massive hemorrhage with no sign of medical cause or trauma. Like it just blew apart. How does something like that happen, I wonder?"

Max was very afraid he knew.

As he'd been taught so severely and well, he swallowed down the panic and pushed away the knowledge of his world possibly crashing down atop his head. He took a slow, deep breath and let it out. Until he knew for certain, there was no reason to alert the precious woman in his arms. Once he knew, he'd have to figure out when and what to tell her. Even as his insides trembled, his hand was steady as he drew her in for a soft kiss.

"I suppose I have to return you to work so they don't think I've kidnapped you."

She smiled at him. "Would you? I think I'd like you to abscond with me."

As his fingertips traced the line of her jaw, she saw a sudden seriousness on his face. "I love you, Charlotte. You are being very, very careful, aren't you?"

"As in crossing the street and checking the expiration dates on the milk?" she teased. When he didn't smile, she took his hand in hers. "I'm a cop. I'm suspicious of everything and everyone. But I have to be out there doing my job. You know that, Max. You know that's who I am, and what I do."

His eyes darkened with something rare enough to alarm her. Fear. A fear so great he wasn't able to hide it from her—he, the master of concealment. His voice rumbled with emotion. "I simply can't go on without you. I can't."

Something was very, very wrong to have him so unexpectedly vulnerable. Instead of pushing for an answer he wasn't ready to give, she heaved an aggravated sigh.

"Oh, dammit."

"What?"

"I'm afraid I simply have to have you again."

She slid her knee across his thighs, straddling him, moving against him with illicit intention as she murmured, "If you're up for it." A moment later, she chuckled huskily. "I guess that answers my question. And quite nicely, too."

She eased back, taking him slowly, by delicious increments, until they were both tense with the effort of restraint. And when he filled her the way nothing else could, she whispered fiercely against his mouth, "You're mine, Savoie. I will never give you up. Remember that."

She was rough, demanding, excited by her control over this wild, dangerous creature who was so much more than just a man. Thrilled and just a bit terrified that she could humble him so completely with her kiss, with her touch, with the hoarse whisper of his name. More than a little afraid of how desperately she desired him, needed him, every moment. Like air. Like light. Like sound.

And when he rolled over her, claiming her with deep, forceful strokes, she answered with an equal abandon, urging their hot, sweaty mating to its shattering conclusion. Then she held him close, luxuriating in the heavy weight of him, in the harsh sound of his breathing, in the rapid beat of his heart.

"I'll be careful if you'll do the same," she promised softly. "Because I simply can't go on without you, either."

MAX INSISTED ON walking her inside the station, and perhaps because she was still a bit wobbly, she didn't argue. Though he was well behaved, keeping an impersonal distance as he escorted her to her desk, she knew they fooled no one. He was swaggering and wearing a smug smile, and she was wearing the tac vest and carrying her untouched sandwich.

As she pulled back her chair, he said her name. She looked up and almost fell over the casters in her hurry to avoid the downward swoop of his mouth.

"Max," she hissed, her gaze flying frantically toward her coworkers. "What are you *doing*?"

"Thanking you. Lunch was tasty and satisfying, as always."

"Step back, Savoie. Thank me later, when we're a little less conspicuous."

An annoyed, arrogant light glittered beneath his heavy-lidded stare. "Afraid we'll shock them senseless?" He looked around and asked loudly, "Is there anyone here who doesn't know Detective Caissie and I are having sex?"

Silence. Everyone stared at them for a long moment, then they gradually all went back to work.

Max grinned at her horrified face. "Whoops. Guess the cat's out of the bag. You can thank me now, Charlotte." He tapped two fingers to the smirky curve of his mouth. When she continued to stare at him, aghast, furious, her body frozen in denial, his amusement fled.

"I shouldn't have embarrassed you," he said coolly. "I'm sorry. I won't make that mistake again."

He stepped back, then turned to stride rapidly toward the exit.

She watched him go. Taking a breath. Then another. "Oh, for fuck's sake," she muttered.

He'd almost reached the door when she called his name, making him look around. She was on him so hard and fast, he staggered as her mouth crushed his. She poured herself into the kiss, holding absolutely nothing back until they were both breathless and slightly dazed. Still clinging to his shoulders for balance, she saw the surprise melt into pleasure in his eyes. And that made the risk worth it.

"Thank you for lunch."

His grin flashed quick and wide. "You are very welcome."

She returned to her desk, feeling rather smug herself. As she settled in behind her pile of paperwork, she glanced at the photographs of those she loved. She needed to get another frame.

A glimpse to her right caught the detectives at the next bank of desks staring at her.

"What are you looking at?" she snarled. "It's not like you've never seen me take a lunch hour before."

Then she unwrapped her sandwich and got to work, a satisfied smile playing about her lips.

DEVLIN DOVION LOOKED up from his slide, surprised to see Max, then smiling. "Looking for Charlotte?"

"Just had her for lunch."

Dovion grinned. Of all of Cee Cee's coworkers, the burly medical examiner was the only one who seemed to have no problem with Savoie and his mobster attachments. The big man, who looked like Jerry Garcia might if he were still on that eternal tour, had a soft spot for his friend's daughter and a curious interest in her first and only choice for a love affair. Because Charlotte trusted Dovion so implicitly, Max had lowered his guard a notch to get to know this man who'd proven to be an ally. "What can I do for you, Max?"

"She mentioned you had a rather strange case laid out on your table."

Dovion leapt on Max's interest with glee. He loved an audience, and most of those who arrived down here were lacking in the interactive department. When Charlotte had mentioned that Max might enjoy learning about his cases, Dev had been thrilled. He also figured it would be a good way to get a sense of the fella without being too obvious.

"Yes, indeed." He wheeled his chair to an adjacent counter where he had arranged several pictures. "Strange isn't the word. I've seen plenty of strange. This just defies explanation." When Max leaned over, Dovion was alerted by his tension. "You're not going to throw up, are you?"

Max leveled a cool stare at him, then examined the photos. "What am I looking at?"

Dovion identified various sectors of the brain on a normal specimen, then did a comparison with the splatter in the cranial cavity of his John Doe.

"The damage appears to be from the inside outward, instead of the other way around," Max noted.

Dovion beamed. "Exactly."

"What could have caused something like that?" Max asked, mirroring Dev's own intrigue.

"Short of having an explosive charge detonated inside his frontal lobe, I have no idea. No traces of any foreign residue. Fascinating. Just fascinating."

Being around death all day gave Dovion a different slant on life, so he abruptly changed the subject. No sense wasting any time beating around the bush.

"Charlotte is very fond of you," he began.

"Is that right?" Max's gaze followed him as he went over to one of the many sinks, peeled off his gloves, and scrubbed up with quick efficiency.

"That's not big news to you, but it is to anyone who knows her. It hasn't been easy for her to trust anyone enough to spend personal time with them. Most fellas don't have the patience or the sense to find out why, but there's a reason for it."

"I know."

Dovion studied Max intently. "She's told you about her past?"

"We don't have any secrets."

Now, that was news. Dovion had taken her home from the hospital when she was just a seventeen-year-old kid, beaten and abused in ways that sickened him. Her father had been out on a case, and Dev had been as close as a brother to Tommy Caissie until that moment. What kind of father sent someone else to bring home his injured child? Cee Cee had pretended that hadn't hurt her almost as much as the shattered bones.

"You break her heart, we'll tangle," he told Max.

"Duly warned."

"You're shaking in your sneakers, I'm sure."

"Right down to the laces." A faint smile, completely innocent of any mockery.

Damned if he didn't like the boy for that bit of respect.

"Good." He gave Savoie another long look, then ventured, "I don't have an ID on the vic yet, but I think he's one of yours."

Max's pulse gave a nasty jump. "One of mine?"

"He was armed and found floating down by

the docks. There were signs of more conventional trauma to the body. He'd been worked over pretty thoroughly."

Tension beat a fierce tattoo in Max's head. "That doesn't make him my employee."

"That doesn't make him an altar boy, either." Dovion shrugged. "Want to see if you recognize him? We're waiting for a print match, but it would speed things up if you could come up with a name." He pulled out a drawer, then dragged down the zipper on the plastic bag inside.

Max's anxiety tightened; his temples thundered with the beginning of a headache, one of the many he'd had this week after having never suffered one before in his life.

At the first glimpse of red hair, his stomach turned over. His gaze shifted away until he got a grip on his gut, until he was certain his expression would reveal nothing.

Tito Tibideaux had been pale in life, and death had bleached his skin to a skim-milk transparency. Against that pallor, the bruises stood out starkly on Philo's younger brother's face, detailing the brutality he'd endured. Someone had beaten him into an almost unrecognizable pulp before he'd succumbed to that final energy pulse that blew his brain apart.

"Anyone you know?"

"No. Sorry. Can't help you."

The zipper was tugged back up with a quick,

impersonal pull, then Dovion glanced up at his smooth, blank expression.

"I guess I'll see you Saturday." At Max's blink of surprise, Dovion smiled. "News travels fast when it involves someone of your . . . affiliations. Not afraid of stepping into that social lion's den for Charlotte's sake?"

"Not many things frighten me."

One of those things was the sight of Philo Tibideaux's baby brother under plastic. Because Max suspected that he'd inadvertently put him there.

He left the morgue on the lower level. In the shadows of the overhead doors, with the pain in his head so intense it skewed his vision, he leaned against one of the city vehicles, buckling under the sudden surge of sickness that boiled up to spew out on the asphalt. He sagged against the fender until the hot and cold shivers subsided, then finally straightened to face a harsh, killing fact.

His time was up.

"MAX, GOT A minute?"

He looked up from the stack of mail he'd been staring at sightlessly for the last half hour. A minute was more than he wanted to give Francis Petitjohn. Francis, with his sly smile and furtive eyes, who'd happily kill him and step over his warm corpse to his cousin Jimmy's position. The position Jimmy Legere had given to a wild card like Max Savoie, instead of keeping it in the family, stunning the criminal underworld of New Orleans. Max still hadn't decided whether to thank or curse his mentor for that overwhelming responsibility. On this dreary afternoon, he was leaning toward the latter.

"What is it, T-John?"

"Have you had time to look over those prospectus sheets Cummings's people sent over? They need an okay on the costs so they can present the package to the zoning and building commission folks."

Max blinked his eyes into focus and pushed the papers around on his desktop until he unearthed the proper documents. He tried to concentrate on the long list of figures and codes, but the headache that had been building like a low-pressure front for what seemed like days prevented him from zeroing in on them.

"I haven't had a chance to. Have you gone over them?"

Francis recovered quickly from his surprise. "Sure. I've overseen a couple of projects like this for Jimmy."

"Does everything look all right?"

He shrugged. "Yeah. Had McCracken and his people go over every decimal point and board foot. Don't have a lot of confidence in Simon Cummings's honesty, and I suspect the feeling is mutual. This is just the preliminary round, no big deal, but I don't want them to think they can get away with anything. I'd stack Jimmy's bean counters against Cummings's swindlers any day. I can explain it line by line to you, if you'd like."

He drew himself up to enjoy the sense of superiority. It was rarely that Max, with his massive ego, deferred to him on anything. Trust had been broken between them long before Jimmy's blood had been spilled by T-John's hand. He watched Max rub his eyes, saw the slump of his shoulders, and was quick to snap up the advantage. Careful not to appear too eager, he said, "Or I can just take care of it for you, if you want. Doesn't matter to me."

Max looked up, his gaze assessing T-John with an instinctual caution. "I know McCracken. He's a good man. Take him with you."

"You bet. You want I should bring the final draft back for you to read over?"

"I've got some things I need to do now, and I probably won't be back in until tomorrow."

"Okay. I'll see to things. I'll leave a copy in your box." He hesitated, not wanting to push it too far by asking, then went ahead. "You all right?"

Max's gaze narrowed, but instead of the suspicion T-John feared, there was dull weariness. And gratitude.

"Fine. Thank you."

"No need to thank me, Max." No, indeed. Not when he was being handed the opportunity he'd been waiting for, like a submerged alligator watching for someone to carelessly get too close to shore. With a smile, Francis's jaws snapped tight on the means to destroy the man standing in the way of what should have been his.

Cheveux du Chien. Hair of the Dog. A barred door led down a shadowed hall into a soaring, dark warehouse club with an unnatural clientele. Among them, Max Savoie usually felt right at home.

But not tonight. Not with the news he carried.

A few months ago, he had no idea this place existed, no idea these strange beings existed. He thought he was alone. The only one who moved through the human world with a secret so dark and deep, his life depended upon its being kept. A secret his mother taught him to hide. A secret Jimmy Legere had trained him to exploit. A secret that now targeted him for danger and brought that threat to those who'd opened up their world to him and looked to him to lead them.

Because although he was the same, he was also amazingly different. He was a pureblood: His centuries-old lineage knew no weakness from human intermingling. His skills knew no boundaries except the imagination.

They were shape-shifters, and he'd just begun to understand what that meant. There was so much for him to learn—but no one to teach him, now that his father was dead. There had to be someone else who held the key to the knowledge of his past. But now killers were on their way to make sure he didn't have the chance to find that truth.

He walked between the crowded tables, his own presence shielded while he swept the room for anything unusual. He could read his clansmen with the ease of a glance across a boldly printed page. There was no mystery to these basic beings. Herd animals, his father Rollo had called them with contempt. Creatures with no subtlety or stealth. Recognizing them by individual scent and psychic signature came easily to Max now. His clan. His family.

But sometimes he saw more; a shimmer of their thoughts occasionally teased him. And every once in a while, when he met their gazes, he'd see images moving across the black screen of their pupils. He always quickly looked away. These were things none of them spoke of being able to do, so he kept them to himself. He was no stranger to secrets.

As he passed them by, he felt the shock of their awareness when they saw him, the fear and awe that came with it. Though he didn't relish their homage the way Rollo would have, he didn't underestimate its power. Or its obligations.

"Where y'at, Savoie?" Jacques LaRoche, the club's owner, bellowed from across the room. He was a huge, bald mountain of aggressive muscle and fierce loyalty. Max had never had a friend, so he was hesitant to attach that name to their relationship, but he liked the bold LaRoche. And more than that, he trusted him. Another unfamiliar and vaguely distressing emotion he was trying to adjust to.

Seated on the other side of the big bar was Philo Tibideaux, Jacques's second on the docks, where they ran the workers for Max. Workers that filled this club after hours to be what they couldn't be where human eyes could see. Beings with unnatural quickness, with abnormal senses, with the ability to take a fierce animal form that would have had them hunted to extinction if they were discovered. Because humans destroyed what frightened them. That was the first harsh lesson Max had ever learned.

Gesturing to the two of them and the office, Max continued through the noisy cluster of tables as the hard beat of the techno spin reverberated between his temples. It was with relief that he closed the soundproof door and gave his ears a rest. But the headache continued with almost eye-watering intensity.

Then the tall, lanky redhead entered a step ahead of LaRoche. The minute the door closed, Max got right to it.

"I was asked to identify a body at the morgue today. I told the ME I didn't know who it was, but that wasn't true." He turned to the younger man, his stare steady and unblinking. "I'm sorry. It was your brother."

Philo took a staggering step backward. "Tito? No. You must be mistaken."

LaRoche gripped both his friend's arms when his knees failed him. His intense gaze was on Max, his voice was low and somber. "Are you sure?"

"Yes. I'm sorry. I wish I wasn't."

Too stunned to feel grief, Philo dropped into the chair LaRoche steered him to. "Tito can't be dead.

He's going to meet me here in an hour. He was starting a new job yesterday. I was gonna buy him some drinks and we were gonna close the place down. He can't be dead." He looked to Max, his eyes swimming. "He *can't* be."

"Who was he going to work for?" Max kept his voice firm, needing Philo to concentrate on something other than his loss.

"He didn't say."

"What kind of job was it? On the docks? In the city? Think."

Philo blinked, tears spilling down his drawn face. "I doan know. Let me think. Some kinda delivery job, he said. He was gonna work third shift last night for training, then tomorrow he was gonna start on second."

"Who gave him this job? How did he find it? In the paper? Through a friend?"

"No. No. I thought it was kinda strange, but Tito, he called it good fortune." A crazy laugh escaped him, filled with irony and disbelief. "Some fellas not from around here started making talk with him, at a rib joint down in the warehouse district. They was looking for a fella who knew his way around town, who was familiar with the business, the players, and the neighborhoods, who had a way with people. He told them he was their man. He told them there wasn't nobody he didn't know in the Big Easy."

And that confident boast had gotten him killed.

As Philo began to weep into his hands, Jacques asked, "What happened, Max?"

"Somebody beat him pretty good. They found him floating this morning. Did he ever carry a gun?"

"Tito?" Philo answered with a choked laugh. "No. Never. He was afraid he'd shoot his own foot off."

"He had one on him. Maybe he took it off of whoever killed him."

"How did he die? Tell me how he died."

"He was killed by a pulse. A sort of psychic explosion in the brain."

Both of them simply stared at him until finally Philo said, "I've never heard of that. Who can do that sort of thing?"

"I have," LaRoche said grimly. "It's something only a pureblood can do. Why would Trackers be after your brother?"

Philo shook his head, mystified.

"They weren't after Tito," Max told them quietly. "They were looking for me."

Three

MAX WAS STANDING on the side porch, leaning against one of the faded pillars while he looked toward the river. Cee Cee just watched for a moment, letting her love for him sweep her away like the current of that powerful water, not struggling against the fear of drowning the way she used to.

Soft rain blew against him, dampening his gorgeous grey linen shirt so that it clung to the long, hard line of him, almost transparent. Moisture dotted his short black hair, which was bristled from restless finger combing.

He didn't notice the dampness. Nor did he appear to notice her, which made her frown slightly as she approached him in his lonely vigil. Then he reached back for her hand without looking around, and she smiled as she slipped her fingers across his palm. He drew her into the curve of his side.

"You're all wet, Savoie."

"So you tell me, detective—more often than I enjoy hearing." He brought her hand up to his lips for a light kiss, then held her palm over his heart.

She wasn't fooled by his mood. Beneath the glassy surface calm, his waters ran deep and troubled.

"I like it when it rains at night." His voice was low, wistful. "You want to think that when you wake up in the morning, all the grime will be washed away and the world starts over clean."

"If only it worked that way."

"With the world. And with people."

Because she sensed he needed to be calmed more than he needed to be questioned, she teased, "Any particularly dirty thoughts you need to have rinsed clean?"

A small smile. "A few."

"Care to share them with me?"

He nuzzled her hair. She felt him inhale deeply, breathing her in. "One involves rose petals, those new shoes you just bought, and your handcuffs."

"You leave my flowers alone."

A chuckle vibrated beneath her cheek.

"How about a long shower and a soft bed?" she suggested.

"Hmmm, that could work. And you wearing nothing but those shoes." A pause. "And the handcuffs."

"Deal."

He glanced over her head before she was aware of movement behind them.

"Is there anything else you need this evening, Mr. Savoie? Detective?"

"No, thank you, Helen," he told his housekeeper softly. "We've got everything right here."

MAX COULDN'T REST, so after Cee Cee had fallen asleep, he slipped outside to run the night. A low, dark shape skimming through shadows, the taste of freedom filled his nose, a bouquet still so exquisitely new, it intoxicated him. The sense of his own tremendous power, now unchecked, exhilarated him. Wild things that usually roamed the darkness gave him a wide berth, sensing a superior predator and afraid to draw his notice.

Max was out on a hunt, but not for prey. His was a different mission: a search of the far corners of the city, seeking a sign that someone or something had breeched his territory. He found no clues, nothing unusual, until he ended up where Tito Tibideaux died.

He trotted along the docks, nostrils flaring wide at the scent of blood and death, picking up vague impressions of other beings like him. The traces had been nearly washed away by rain, but enough remained to disturb him. *Intruders.* A dangerous rumble sounded low in his chest as he recognized the faint markings on the ground. Paw prints elongating, abruptly changing to bare human feet. Shifters. Trackers. Deadly hunters trained from birth in cunning and savagery.

At a disadvantage, because he'd had no one to teach him how to channel his unique talents, he had no more time to lament his shortcomings. It was time to prepare.

They might have greater numbers and more developed skills, but they were underestimating one thing. This was *his* city, filled with those he would protect to the death.

And in New Orleans, Max Savoie was king.

IT WAS VERY late or very early. A ripple of the sheet, and he was back beside her. She wouldn't have known he was gone except for the chill of his bare toes and the ragged sound of his breathing.

He lay flat on his back, staring up at the ceiling, denying himself her warmth and comfort. Why?

His silence stirred up a hive of insecurities. Where could he have gone in the middle of the night without waking her, with his stealth suggesting secrets? Illegal secrets? Dangerous secrets?

What was he involved in? And was it something she should be worried about professionally or personally? There were so many worrisome areas in his life that could get inflamed without warning. Dark, deadly niches in his past and present, concerning who he was, what he'd been . . . and *what* he was.

Threatening situations didn't frighten her; she was a cop. Give her a tough spot and she'd go up against it without hesitation. But give her a sticky emotional circumstance, and her back was against the wall.

For almost twenty-nine years she had let only a fisted handful of people get close to her, and the other two she'd loved were already gone. She'd zealously guarded the part of her that could be hurt, that could distract her from doing the job she revered. She'd been so careful, so wary. Until Max. The most inappropriate man she could imagine.

He'd cleverly stalked her affections with his lazy smile and red tennis shoes, pushing himself into her thoughts, into her life, into her heart until her resistance crumpled. Until she couldn't imagine a moment without him. She accepted his criminal background, his unnatural heritage, his strange mix of violence and naïveté for one unshakable reason: He'd sacrificed everything he loved for her. Everything. He'd become rescuer, lover, and protector. Against all odds and logic, he loved her, unflinchingly, unfailingly. How could she do less?

He gave a slight start when her fingertips curved about his jaw. She could feel his tension, yet he didn't resist when she turned his face toward her, when she fit her lips softly to his.

"Come here, baby. Let me hold you."

He rolled up against her, over her, around her, curling into her as he began to shiver. A protective anxiety rose as she clutched his dark head and kissed his brow.

"It's all right. I've got you. Let go, Max. You're safe. Let go."

All the stress and torments of the day poured from him like life's blood. Afterwards, he lay trustingly limp and weary, and finally closed his eyes.

Just before he drifted off, she felt his slight smile as he murmured, "Thank you, *sha*."

"You are very welcome."

CHARLOTTE DIDN'T EXPECT him to be up before her, but his shoes were gone and the bathroom smelled deliciously of his shaving soap and shampoo. She dressed quickly, hoping he hadn't already left for the city. As she came down the sweep of the stairs she saw Giles St. Clair, Max's Mack truck of a bodyguard, flirting determinedly with Helen's daughter, Jasmine. She relaxed, knowing Giles wouldn't let Max go anywhere without him. Though Max was more than capable of taking care of himself, Giles insisted, saying someone of Max's position needed someone at his back. And because Max had been at Jimmy Legere's back almost since he could tie his shoes, he allowed Giles to proudly assume that role.

Giles greeted her with a grin and a cup of coffee. "He's out on the side porch, detective. Good to have you home."

Who would have thought the plantation-house hideout of one of the city's most nefarious mobsters would ever welcome her, or that she'd feel a sudden twist about her heart to hear it called her home?

Or that she'd want to settle into it with the dark-souled man who'd taken his predecessor's place? Reading the *Wall Street Journal* at the wicker patio set off his office, he wore his sleek, black Armani suit and an open-collared white shirt, looking both elegant and ruthless.

She tunneled her fingers into his hair and pulled his head back, her tongue was in his mouth before he could say hello. He gave a rumbling purr, and when she straightened he was smiling.

"Morning, baby. You looked far too fine for me not to grab a quick taste of you to get the day started." She dropped into the chair across from his. "Want some coffee?"

He licked his lips, his eyes crinkling with amusement. "Just had some, thanks."

"If I'm not careful, I could get as addicted to you as I am to caffeine."

"And that would be a bad thing?"

"Can't think of a downside at the moment." She sipped her coffee and let her eyes close contentedly. She loved the deep silence of Legere's rambling estate. No hurry-up-and-get-going traffic and city sounds.

"Charlotte."

His sober tone alerting her to a serious shift in topic, Cee Cee opened her eyes. "What?"

"I should have told you this yesterday, but it threw me so hard, I just couldn't get on top of it. I've been sitting here trying to work up the right words."

Her heart hopscotched in alarm. "What is it?"

He raked his fingers through his hair. "The John Doe at Dovion's—did you get a look at him?"

"Only the eight-by-tens. Not much left to look at

after they were done with him. Why? Oh, Max—is it someone you know?" Her hand slipped over the top of his. Her voice softened. "Someone I know?"

"Philo—"

"Oh, Max. No."

"No, not Philo. His little brother, Tito. I had to take him the news just after the club opened. Put a bit of a damper on the evening, as you might imagine."

She automatically went into cop mode. "Does anyone know what happened to him? Was he working for you?"

"No, and no. Philo said he was doing small stuff to stay off the docks, looking for a place to fit in without trading on his connections. He was just a kid who must have stepped on some powerful toes."

"You know how he was killed, don't you? Dovion is totally in the dark."

"And he needs to stay that way." Max's tone toughened as his instinct for self-preservation slowly overcame the grief. He hesitated, debating on what to share with her. "It's called a pulse," he said at last.

"A pulse. Like an EMP weapon of some sort?" Great. High-tech weapons loose on her streets. As if they didn't have enough to do trying to control the regular stuff?

"No. It's a mental weapon, one my father showed me. It's a concentration of psychic energy. Only a very controlled pureblood could direct it with that kind of killing force. It's like heating an egg in the microwave without poking holes first."

She shuddered, then studied Max carefully. "Is this something you can do?"

"I don't know. It's not exactly something you can practice until you get it right."

She sat back, musing out loud. "What was he involved in that would bring out a big gun of that caliber without you being aware of it?"

"I don't know. A pureblood doesn't give off signs unless he wants to, and whoever killed Tito didn't want to."

"A warning? Who and why?"

"Again, I don't know. He, or they, must have been trying to find out something, the way the boy was worked over. But what he said and about what, I just don't know."

And that was worrying him.

Charlotte could tell there was more. Something else was building behind the shut-down expression, something she wasn't going to like or he wouldn't let it drag out so long. She squeezed is hand and gently coaxed, "Just say it, Max."

"Tito's like most of us. He doesn't have any official paperwork behind him. Your boys might come up with his name if they're lucky but not much else. And since we don't want to stir up questions to get folks curious, no one will step forward to identify him—not even Philo."

She couldn't imagine that. Knowing his brother lay unclaimed and unnamed under plastic, just out of reach.

"But Philo wants his brother buried, Charlotte. Not in a pauper's grave on the city's dime, with no one around to mourn him."

"What can I do?"

His gaze lifted, dark and intense. "Get Dovion to release the body to Father Furness, before he does any more testing. Before he finds something that'll make him more suspicious than he already is. No one can know who claimed the body or where to find it. I'll have it brought here for burial. There's a plot of consecrated ground that hasn't been used for generations. Tito should rest easy there."

"So you want me to do what, exactly? Sneak a body out for a hush-hush burial behind high walls? Am I allowed to ask why?"

He never blinked. "You can ask." But he wasn't going to tell her.

She pushed out of her chair and walked to the porch rail. In the back of her mind, she could hear a taunting sneer. *Now that he's got a cop in his pocket.* "Dammit, Max, we weren't going to do this. We weren't going to ask for on-the-job favors."

A pause, then his quiet, "Forget I asked. I'm sorry. I shouldn't have."

There was no bitterness in his voice, and when she turned there was no blame in his expression. But she still felt it from her own conscience. "It's not that I don't want to. But these things always start out with small requests and before you know it, you're hiding evidence and turning your back on things you shouldn't."

"I know how it works, detective. That's not what this is about. I'm not trying to back you into a corner. I wouldn't put you in that kind of position. Like I said, forget I asked. I just . . . I just . . ." His gaze slipped away.

"I didn't think you were. I just didn't want anyone else to get the idea that because you and I . . ." Cursing her cautions, she crossed to him, hugging his dark head to her briefly. "I've got to go. Can I give you a ride in?"

"No. I need to make some calls." He leaned back when she released him but didn't look up at her. His features were heavy with fatigue and sadness, and she lifted his chin so that his dull gaze met hers.

"Don't do anything right away."

"Charlotte, I don't want you to—"

She cut him off with a soft kiss. "I'll call you in a bit."

He watched her travel the length of the porch in her long, determined stride, admiring the way she worked the back pockets of her jeans, even as he wondered how different her response might have been if he'd told her he was in danger. He suspected she would have bristled up in possessive fury, smothering him to keep him from harm. No one harmed what was hers. There was no one he trusted more to protect him, to the limit of her life.

And that was the problem.

The longer he could keep her out of it, the safer she'd be. When it became more dangerous for her not to know than to be privy to everything, he'd tell her. But for now, when it was so vital that he stay under the radar, it wouldn't do to have her slapping up a defensive wall around him as if battening down for a hurricane. She was a force of nature, one that was impossible to ignore.

"What time you wantin' to leave, boss man?"

"I'm ready now, Giles." Now that she was gone, he had no desire to linger.

So he let Giles take him into New Orleans, let his secretary Marissa bring him a stack of correspondence he didn't know how to handle, and looked at a long line of appointments he didn't want to keep. All the while, the image of Tito Tibideaux's battered face haunted his thoughts.

What had he said before his violent death?

Max pinched the bridge of his nose, then rubbed his eyes, trying to urge the headache behind them to go away. He had so much to do, so many claims upon his time and energy, yet he couldn't summon the strength of will to handle any of it. He was restless, anxious, constantly provoked by a sense of urgency he didn't understand. His nervous system crawled with it.

His sensory awareness was overloaded with fine-tuned details. The slightly burnt scent of coffee, the petulant ringing of the phones and fax machine, the rhythm of motion all around him were distracting and even distressing. He was aware of Francis Petit-john creeping about on the other side of his closed door.

A glance told him that the promised details of the Cummings project were in his box, awaiting his inspection. He didn't know anything about construction and, for the moment, was too tired to learn. Jimmy had expected too much of him—had expected him to be capable of more than any one man. And this morning, he wasn't. For the moment, he was shamefully willing to let Francis handle the areas of LEI that he understood well.

He would call McCracken in soon for an accounting of T-John's actions. After all, he wasn't a fool. He would pull up the slack in the reins of control when he felt stronger and focused, and then he would be everything Jimmy wanted. But not this morning. Not with the pain pounding through his head and heaviness hanging on his heart.

So he sat behind the big desk and spent the morning watching the clock hands move inexorably toward the end of the promising life he'd just begun to live.

"Max?"

He glanced up to see Charlotte in the doorway, and all the raw, panicked edges he'd been picking at all morning were forgotten. He managed a weak smile.

"Detective. This is a surprise. Here to take me to lunch?" He put out his hand and she crossed over to take it. It was a struggle not to clutch at her as he would a life raft. He brought her fingertips to his lips as she settled the taut curve of her hip on the edge of his desk.

"Can't. Too much to do. Just wanted to bring you up to speed."

"On what, *sha*?"

"The matter we were discussing this morning."

The light went out of his eyes. "What about it?"

"At 2:00, Dovion's releasing the body of a vagrant who died of natural causes while going through the Dumpsters over on Basin. Father Furness has filled out the paperwork and is supposed to be taking him to the sad little cemetery behind St. Bart's. Teddy and Giles will back an unmarked van in at 2:30, while Dev shares some coffee and chitchat with a favorite police detective of his." She smiled thinly. "They'll pick up Tito instead—a mix-up in toe tags. They'll give him a tour of the city to make sure no one's the wiser, then bring him to the house.

"*Cheveux du Chien* will have an unexpected power failure around 6:00 and shut down for the night, and all the employees will be sent home. We'll start getting company about 7:00. Full security checks. A quick, respectful ceremony that Father offered to perform, then Helen and Jasmine will set out a big spread and LaRoche will provide free liquor and music. The place should be shaking for the better part of the night. I think Tito would approve of the send-off."

Max blinked at her. "You've been busy."

"Look, I'm really sorry about this morning. An old cautious cop habit."

"And yet you did all this for someone you don't even know."

"No. For someone I love."

When she touched his cheek, words failed him. Calm deserted him. He couldn't swallow, couldn't breathe. His gaze filled up until her image shimmered like a reflection on a clear pond. Finally, he simply rested his cheek against her denim-clad thigh and let his wonder shiver out through a soft exhalation. All the disquieting worries were soothed by the gentle stroke of her hand over his hair, by the rub of her knuckles down the side of his face.

"Are you feeling all right, Max?" Her palm pressed to his brow. "You're really warm."

"You usually tell me I'm hot. Is there a reason I've been demoted?" He sat back and dragged her across the desk onto his lap. "Some manly business I haven't taken care of to your satisfaction, perhaps?"

She laughed, her arms looping about his neck, fingers rumpling his hair. "If I were any more satisfied, I wouldn't be able to walk. You don't need to fish for compliments, Savoie. You know I'm crazy about you."

"But my fragile ego still needs to hear it occasionally."

Another low, full-bodied laugh. "There's nothing the least bit delicate about your ego, oh mighty King of the Beasts. Flattery only makes you more insufferable."

"Is that all it's been? Flattery?"

She started to chuckle until she caught a glimpse of something desperate in his gaze. Her tone grew tender. "You know better than that."

"Sometimes I do. And sometimes I haven't the slightest idea why you would care for me."

"Let me remind you then."

She tipped his face up, filling her hands with his strong jaw, her mouth with the sweet taste of him. "You make me feel invulnerable, Savoie."

Not the right thing to say. Panic arrowed shift and sharp through his heart, and he instinctively clutched her tight.

"Move in with me, Charlotte," he said urgently. "Come live with me, stay with me, be with me. I've been alone all my life, and now I can hardly bear it."

In spite of her assurances and the passionate way she'd been nibbling his lower lip, there was no mistaking the quick objection in her eyes. "I'm practically there all the time already."

"Then what's the problem?"

"I need to be close to the city."

A bitter twist of temper got a hold on him. "It's less than a twenty-minute drive, detective. It's not like it's on the moon. There's a telephone and even e-mail, now that you've managed to break into Jimmy's computer."

Her eyes narrowed slightly at the jab and her

tone toughened. "Maybe it wouldn't be a good idea to have me underfoot, since I'm so untrustworthy."

"Isn't that the other way around, *cher*? Are you sure it's not because you like knowing you have someplace to run, should your job frown on you keeping house with a criminal?"

"That's not fair, Max."

"But it's also not untrue. Is it, detective?" His stare grew hard and cold. "Or is it because you only want to roll about with me when it suits you and doesn't interfere with work? Would having me underfoot be too big an inconvenience? Too much of a drain on your precious time?"

When she finally spoke, her words were like shards of ice. "We're not going to talk about this anymore, Max. Obviously we've got a few too many issues to settle before we can take that big a step. Or maybe any steps for the time being." She shoved off his knees into a combative stance. "I have to go back to that all-consuming job that seems to threaten your delicate ego. I'll see you later. After I go home to my place and change, I'll come by as your guest—if you still want me to be here."

"That's your choice, detective. You prefer to come and go as you please. Far be it from me to make a claim on your freedom."

"Don't even think of trying, Savoie. But don't worry, I'll play hostess for you. And if the mood hits me, I might even want to roll around with you afterwards. *If* you're not full of quite so much shit by then."

His sudden laugh startled her, a big boom of sound that never failed to make her jump when it lunged out from his stillness like an unexpected "boo!"

Her eyes darkened with fury until they were as deadly as the bore of her weapon. "You think this is funny?"

He tried not to grin. "I think this is ridiculous in a purely terrifying way. Charlotte, come here."

Her gaze grew suspicious. "Why?"

"Because I want to hold you while I beg for your forgiveness."

"Well, in that case."

His arms banded her hips, tugging her in tight so he could rest his head just below her breasts. After a second, she threaded her fingers through his hair.

"My apology, please."

"I'm sorry, *sha*. I've no cause to say such things to you. I don't mean to push, and I don't blame you for being reluctant to commit to me. It's all right—it really is. I haven't been myself for these past few days. I couldn't rest while you were away, and now I've got this headache that's beating at my brain as meanly as you've been kicking me in the ass. Seeing Philo's brother in that drawer has me so scared of losing you, I'm bleeding from the ears."

"That's a delightful visual." She bent to kiss the top of his head. "Max, you're not going to lose me, because I don't want to be gone. I want to be with you. I don't have any doubts about that or about you. I just need for us to go slow. We're going in the same direction, only I'm traveling the speed limit and you're in warp drive. I'll catch up. You just have to be patient."

"Twelve years is a lot of patience, Charlotte. I've been ready for you since that first time I saw you."

"I know, baby. But just think of how long it took for civilization to go from the Dark Ages to the Industrial Revolution. Then once we got there, things progressed at a pretty fast clip."

"You'll stay with me tonight?"

"And every night I can. I sleep better when I'm not alone, too. And you never know when I might get the urge to roll about with you."

His hands slid down to cup the firm contours of her rump for a fond squeeze. "Like now?"

His intercom crackled, then Marissa's efficient voice said, "Excuse me, Mr. Savoie. You have a meeting with the planning board in fifteen minutes."

He freed one hand to press a button. "Have Pete bring the car around. Thank you, Marissa."

He leaned back in his chair, pulling Cee Cee between his knees and trapping her with the press of his thighs. "You are going to find me so very, very grateful tonight. This will mean a lot to Philo. And it means everything to me."

She bent down until her breath caressed his lips. "You're so hot, Savoie. I want you right now. You think about that for the rest of the day, and hopefully that'll keep anything else from leaking out of your ears." She gave him a quick kiss, then strode out of the room.

It took him a long moment to exhale. Then he was smiling, this thoughts prowling ahead to having Charlotte Caissie naked beneath him, on top of him, or in any creative combination between the two.

"Marissa, tell Francis I'd like him to ride along with me."

He grinned wickedly as he gathered up the necessary papers to stack neatly in his briefcase. A big, healthy dose of ego had him looking forward to tangling with the conservative members of Cummings's committee.

He would devour them.

Four

*H*EY, LaRoche, there's a cop here to see you!"

Jacques LaRoche looked up from his clipboard, annoyance, then surprise crossing his heavy features. He set his work aside and leaned back against the stair railing that led up into the trailer he used for an office. In his own rugged element, with his bare arms bulging with muscle, he exuded raw, brutal power. His smile was wide.

"Detective, I understand you've been instrumental in getting my friend a proper burial. I appreciate that."

Because she'd come straight from her manipulation of Devlin Dovion, Cee Cee brushed aside his gratitude. "It was no big deal."

His smile faded slightly. "What can I do for you this afternoon? Here for a professional or a personal courtesy?"

"A bit of both, I think, at least for now."

"Come on in. I think I have some coffee burning in the bottom of the pot."

She followed him up the narrow stairs into an office as different as day to night from the one he had at the club. Here it was all about work, with no flash or sophistication. Heavy-duty file cabinets, a rickety table covered with cup-stained manifests, and a couch strewn with stacks of rather potent dirty clothes.

Seeing her gaze land there, Jacques winced. "Sorry. Missed laundry day." He cleared the cushions with a sweep of a bulky arm, shoving the clothes onto the floor. "I live here," he explained gruffly.

That, she didn't expect, but she made no comment about his obvious poverty. "Ever think of hiring a maid?"

He grinned. "The females I bring here aren't interested in cleaning my house."

She raised a brow. "You'd probably have to hold them at gunpoint if you brought it up. Ever consider just setting fire to it and moving someplace else?"

"Every morning, detective. I've got one of those apartments reserved in that fancy place Max is putting up with Cummings. That should raise the quality of my potential companions a bit. Now, I'm guessing you're not here to discuss my social life. What do you want, Charlotte?" He dropped down on the saggy couch, while she brushed the crumbs off one of the chairs before taking a seat.

"I'm here officially looking into the death of Tito Tibideaux."

Though he was still smiling, an unmistakable curtain of caution drew across LaRoche's face. "And why does the NOPD give a damn about some no-named corpse no longer in their possession? Why do they care what happened to him?"

"I care. I asked for the assignment." She'd had to practically beg for it, with man-hours at a premium and an unidentified body low on the priority list. She'd been given a narrow window to find evidence or let it go.

"You didn't even know him, detective. He wasn't one of your kind, not one of your tax-paying citizens. Who would miss him?"

"You do. His brother does. So I give a damn."

A slight crook of his brow. "That would make you a minority."

"I'm used to it. Tell me about him, Jacques. He have any bad habits that would bring this kind of trouble to his door?"

A flash of fury and regret crossed his expression. "Tito was a good kid. He wasn't like a lot of us, content with what we have, figuring it was all we deserve. He had big dreams. He wanted to live in your world. He wouldn't let Philo make it easy for him by getting him a job on one of the crews. He was going to make it on his own. And he would have; he had that fire. That I'm-going-to-burn-up-the-world fire."

Her heart ached for the boy she'd never met. "I'm sorry."

"Yeah," LaRoche sighed. "Me, too. Whatcha gonna do? We bury a lot of our kind without any fanfare. We're used to our lives having little or no value or impact on how you Uprights go about your day. He was a good kid. It was a sad thing. Maybe you should just let it go at that."

"Maybe I should. But I'm not going to."

"This about Max?" His tone suggested she wouldn't give a damn otherwise.

"This is about a good kid who won't get a chance to go after a dream. That pisses me off, Jacques, and it makes me want to kick somebody's ass. Feel like helping me?"

"Yeah, maybe I do." Then, that caution was back. "Max know about this?"

"Not unless you tell him. I don't clear my work schedule with my lover."

Jacques grinned, imagining how the Big Dog would like hearing his mate relegating his authority to the bedroom. Probably not much. About as much as he'd like Jacques encouraging her. And that made him chuckle. "Where do we start?"

After LaRoche clocked out, he led her down to the rib joint where Tito had been offered his last job. It was a greasy dive, not the kind of place CEOs came to for employment recruiting. Outside the door that boasted plastic and duct tape rather than glass, LaRoche gave her an assessing look. She was wearing tight jeans and a tighter tank top under a baggy sweat jacket. Still, he frowned.

"Think you could look a little less like a cop, darlin'?"

She took off the coat and tied it about her waist. No member of any male species would see anything but spectacular boobs, lovingly cupped by stretch knit. Just in case they managed to tear their stares away from her chest, she rubbed her eyes and lips until her makeup smudged into blowsy indifference. For a final touch, she pulled out one of her bra straps to dangle negligently down her arm. Bright purple.

"How's this?"

LaRoche grinned. "You slut up real nice, detective. I like that about you." He held open the door to let her saunter in. The up-and-down sweep of every man in the place provided a hormonally charged silence for a long beat. Until she wrapped her arm about LaRoche's thick waist and dipped her hand into the back pocket of his jeans for a healthy squeeze of his butt. He gave a slight jump, then chuckled. "Careful, *cher*. Try to remember that I'm just an animal."

They approached the counter, where LaRoche nodded to the stringy fellow working the place alone.

"Hey, bro. You back there a couple of days ago?"

"I'm here every day. I can't afford no other help. What can I get you?"

Cee Cee slid a twenty across the sticky counter. "Some information. And a half rack to go."

The twenty disappeared. "The ribs'll be extra. I don't throw in no lagniappe."

"Make that a whole rack," she said.

"How are you with faces, friend?"

The owner glanced from Charlotte's cleavage up to LaRoche. "I'd remember yours."

"How 'bout a kid, fresh-faced, red hair, probably wearing some god-awful Hawaiian shirt, woulda come in alone. Started talkin' about a job with some strangers."

Cee Cee slid another twenty over. "Extra sauce, please."

"Doan so much remember the boy, but those fellas, yeah, I remember them good. Got an eye for folks that doan belong. There was two of 'em, dark suits, accent from up north, all business—maybe Federal business, and none of mine."

"Federal? Why would you think that?"

The guy put a dirty hand to his scrawny neck. "You know, strangling on their ties. And cold. Woowee, there was frost in them boys' eyes. They'd been hanging around all day, scaring my customers off. Noses for the law, you know." He winked at Cee Cee and she smiled back. "But the kid, he was too green to notice. They got to talking, bought him his meal, gave him a card."

"Did you hear what they were talking about?"

He gave LaRoche an insulted look. "I mind my own affairs, mister."

"Right. You seen these fellas since?"

"Nope. Once they chatted up the kid, they was gone. Didn't even leave no tip, cheap bastards." He glanced at Cee Cee hopefully when he passed her the dripping sack of ribs.

She gave him exact change.

LaRoche drove, keeping a careful eye on the seat of his Caddy while Cee Cee sucked sauce from bone.

"Don't you go spilling none of that."

"And waste great sauce? Not a chance."

"Where to?"

"Where did Tito live? Would he have given strangers his home address?"

"Not likely. We Shifters tend to be careful about who we invite in. My guess is the boy told them he'd contact them. Then if things worked out, he'd play it a little looser."

"He live by himself?"

"Off and on with a girlfriend."

"Your kind or mine?"

"Yours."

"That bother you?"

LaRoche shrugged. "Not so much as some." He caught the subtle edge in her tone and shot her a quick look. "You wonderin' how I feel about you with Max?"

"Maybe."

He grinned. "Can't say I cared for it at first, but you kinda grew on me, detective. And I remember those kinda feelings that put that punch-drunk look in his eyes."

Cee Cee wondered what had put the sudden melancholy in his. "Are you mated, Jacques?" She hadn't planned to get personal with him, and she wasn't sure she should get that involved with any of Max's preternatural pals. It only pulled her in deeper. As if it could get deeper than body snatching, false statements, and tampering with evidence. But she liked LaRoche for his bold courage and for his protective position at Max's back. And she was curious about these . . . creatures who so resembled men.

"Once," he told her softly. "Long time ago. Things were different then. A lot a things."

"I thought you mated for life."

"We do, detective. We do."

She was silent. His mate was dead. There was nothing to say.

Sensing her discomfort, he quickly changed the subject. "You wanting to poke around in his place?"

"We need something more to go on. Something about who these men are, and what they wanted from him." And what, if anything, that might have to do with Max. She dropped the last rib into the bag and folded it up tight. "And what if Tito's problems turn out to be Max's? Will that be a problem of loyalty for you?"

"I've pledged myself to Max. We all have."

She turned to look at him with puzzlement. "Why is that, Jacques? You don't know him. You don't owe him anything. Why this allegiance, this willingness to follow him?"

"It's because of who he is. He's the Promised, *cher*. We've been waiting for him. He can give us that dream Tito was after: freedom. Dignity. A future for our young. None of us has ever had a chance for that until now."

Jacques pointed to the lurid row of businesses crowded close to the street, promising fulfillment of any weakness in bright blinking lights. The overcast sky spread a frowning darkness over the area, the moralistic pall somehow suited to these streets and to those skulking about for purposes best left to the night.

"Tito's place is up there," he said.

LaRoche swung the big car into a tight alley where there was scarcely enough room to open the doors. He stuck to the shadows away from the street, and entered through a back door. Cee Cee followed.

Tito Tibideaux lived above a tattoo parlor. Not the kind of place that promised colorful artwork, but a seedy spot to stamp the skin with mean prison tats that spoke of gang affiliations. Tito's two-room flop overflowed with the things that had meant the most to him: family, music, and leftovers. Glaring neon from the bar across the street sent a cool blue and red glow across what little of the carpet wasn't covered by loose sheet music and take-out boxes. The gaudy Hawaiian shirts he favored were spread over the furniture like exotic foliage.

His trumpet case was open, the gleaming horn resting on the sofa, waiting for him to pick it up to wail out notes he'd never play again. Photos masked blemishes in the wallpaper. Cee Cee recognized Philo in many of them, along with a pretty black-haired girl—the girlfriend, who conveniently slung beer mugs across the street. No sign of cohabitation, she noted.

She spent a few minutes poking around. New carton of milk in the ancient fridge. Bills on the table, stamped and ready to be mailed. The TV viewer face down. No indication that he'd been in trouble; none that he was looking for trouble or expected it to find him. But it had. She frowned at the sadness of a life half-lived.

Several business cards were wedged under beer-opener magnets on the refrigerator door, and she looked them over without touching them. Take-out places, mostly. And one with just a phone number—an out-of-state area code. She removed it, careful not to compromise any potential prints. Was this the card passed to a kid anxious for a break? Would it lead to a job he hadn't been able to finish? Or maybe he had, and he just hadn't been given the job description that concluded with his death.

With card between thumb and index finger, she started toward the bedroom. Standing at the window keeping a watchful eye, LaRoche cast a huge shadow across the floor. A handy guy. Smiling slightly, she stepped into the bedroom, stopping short when she recognized the smell.

The room was a gory splatterhouse, courtesy of the black-haired girl tied spread-eagle upon the bed. The evidence of deliberate and lengthy torture stunned Cee Cee into an almost fatal moment of hesitation.

She never heard anything. Intuition prickled along her neck, urged her gaze to lift away from the gruesome distraction on the bed.

She had just called out Jacques's name in warning and started to reach for her gun when they moved on her. Two of them, dressed in dark suits that had miraculously escaped most of the arterial spray. She didn't know who they were, but she knew *what* they were as they came at her lightning fast, striking twice before she could draw her weapon. She only had time to close her hand around the card to protect it from discovery.

Pain shattered through her face, and the force threw her all the way to the kitchen, making her crash against the old refrigerator. She rolled onto hands and knees, her vision fogging as she swayed to her feet. In the living room, Jacques LaRoche sailed weightlessly through the front of the console television. He pushed out of the smashed frame with a roar, plowing into the closest adversary, who neatly caught him by the shoulders and flung him through the café table.

The other creature stood motionless, with the

same stillness as Max's that froze time, as he focused on the gun in her hand: her ankle piece loaded with silver slugs. But she had questions, and he couldn't answer them if he were dead.

"Don't you move," she ordered through the numbing ache in her cheek.

He didn't. But the other one hit her low, like a defensive lineman, driving the wind from her with the force of a Gray Line bus. She fell hard, pistol spinning away as she wedged her palm up under his chin to keep the sudden sharpness of his teeth together, then used her feet to toss him over her head.

Before she could get her knees under her and search for her pistol, the statue lunged with jaws wide and eyes flaming. He would have torn out her throat but for Jacques's to-the-moon swing of Tito's trumpet. The rim of the metal bell connected with nose cartilage with a sharp crack, followed by a howl and a hot fountain of blood. Then Jacques had her by the arm, hauling her out of reach of the rapidly appearing fangs and claws.

There was no way they were getting out of the room alive.

They were silent killers. No snarling, no posturing, no mercy as they crouched to attack shoulder-to-shoulder, their features impassive, eyes glowing with that unnatural fire. Cold, deadly animals determined to rip their futures from them.

And Max would be left to sort through their pieces.

"No way, you sons of bitches," she vowed beneath her breath as she went for her service piece and fired. Each took a round to the center of the chest. The impact staggered them, but Cee Cee knew it wouldn't stop them. What would, she wondered furiously, as she knocked off two more shots apiece. They went down this time, but their eyes never blinked as they struggled to stand.

LaRoche's huge arm cinched about her waist, powering her off her feet. In three long strides he was across the room, and with a jump was through the window in a spray of glass. They plunged two stories with LaRoche landing on his feet on top of his Caddy. The roof buckled but held. He bent to shove her through the open passenger window heels first, then swung in under the wheel.

Through the cracked windshield, Cee Cee could see the two creatures at the window above, and without hesitation, they jumped as well. The Caddy's tires smoked in reverse as one landed on all fours in the alley in front of the car, and the other on the dented roof. LaRoche shifted into drive, his foot mashing to the floor. Their rider rolled off the back as the huge grill hit the other head on. The car shuddered to a stop and Jacques threw the shift lever again. Cee Cee braced, staring out the back glass as the second creature leapt up over the trunk onto the roof as the vehicle barreled out onto the street.

Cee Cee whipped around as head and shoulders appeared in her open window, and sharp teeth snapped for her neck. She jammed her gun into the gaping maw and pulled the trigger. He flew back from the window into a trio of garbage cans. As the big vehicle sped down the street, Cee Cee hugged the back of the seat rest, sweeping the pavement behind them for pursuit. After they'd gone four blocks without sign of any, she dropped onto the worn leather to let her breath out in a rush.

"Who are they, Jacques?"

"Trackers. Mostly they leave us alone, but once in a while they'll come down here on a blood hunt and we just stay the hell out of their way."

"Who sends them? What do they want? What do they have to do with Tito?"

"I don't know."

"Don't tell me you don't know! Dammit, those were the monsters who killed him!"

"I know that. But that's all I know." His gaze met hers, filled with anguish and frustration. "They let us go, detective—but they don't let us remember."

IN THE COOL serenity of Jacques's office at the club, Cee Cee accepted an ice pack for her rapidly swelling face. She winced as she pressed it to her cheek, her attention on Jacques LaRoche as he paced with powerful agitation.

"We're a disposable workforce, detective. We fill a need. Men like Vantour make a request and our kind arrives to meet it. We have no pasts, no history, no families, nothing to run back to. We exist to do what we're told. Mindless beasts of burden."

"Slaves," she concluded quietly.

"Not even that. None of us know where we came from. We live in shadows. We hide from rumors and superstitious nonsense. And we dream of something better, of someone who'll break our chains of helplessness."

"And you think Max is your answer?"

"Maybe. He's the closest we've come to it so far. The things he can do, Charlotte—he has no idea, does he?"

"I don't think so. Not completely. And because he doesn't, he'll let you use him. Be careful of him, Jacques. He's not invulnerable, no matter what you might think."

And both of them were thinking the same thing. Could Max take on those two from Tito's room and be victorious? Or would they destroy him?

"I need to make a call," she said.

"Why?" The sudden suspicion was back in his eyes.

"I need to report that poor girl's death." She shook her head regretfully. "Why kill *her*?"

"She was one of your kind, detective. They couldn't let her go after what she must have seen. But there's no reason for you to go back there now."

"It's a crime scene!"

"Charlotte," he said gently, "there will be nothing left to even prove that girl existed. If there's one thing they know how to do well, it's how to cover their tracks. She's gone and will soon be forgotten. And in a while, no one will remember Tito Tibideaux, either. We're just shadows, detective, scattered by a breeze and the sweep of a light. There's nothing more you can do. It's over. They're gone."

She stared at him, seeing the poignant signs of a life abandoned, the death of a girl left unresolved. Objection tasted bitter in the aftermath of their escape. "I'm not going to give this up, Jacques. They're not going to get away with what they've done."

"They already have, detective. They don't care about you or your laws. No good can come of what you have in mind."

"You don't want to see them punished for what they did?"

His features twisted in an agony of fury and fear, and his voice was raw with it. "I want them to go back where they came from, and they won't if you provoke them. This is not your world, Charlotte. It's not your fight. You have no idea what you're dealing with."

"Then *tell* me. Tell me so I can help you."

She saw in the tightening of his jaw that he wouldn't tell her anything. It wasn't because she wasn't like them; it was dark, soul-deep terror that kept him silent.

What had they done to him? What could be so terrible that he'd willingly turn a blind eye to the murder of his best friend's brother?

"You saw what they are and what they can do," he told her with quiet ferocity. "If you go after them, they'll kill you. And if they kill you, who will have Max's back?"

That was the one argument he knew would give her pause. For a long moment they regarded one another with wary respect, until she finally asked, "How are we going to keep him safe, Jacques, if they've come here for him?"

"I don't know, detective." He glanced over her shoulder. "But you might want to start thinking now about what you're going to tell him."

She swiveled to stare through the one-way glass into the dim club. Max was standing at his table, his hand on the back of his chair, his eyes fixed upon the mirrored surface that concealed her.

He knew she was there.

She cursed softly as he came striding toward the office. He opened the door without a knock but didn't step inside. His stare went between the two of them.

"What's this?" he asked flatly.

"The detective took a fall trying to stop a purse snatcher," Jacques explained easily. "Unfortunately, it's probably as bad as it looks."

"Let me see."

Cee Cee lowered the ice pack to reveal a fresh bruise from cheekbone to jawline.

Max's teeth clenched as if he could feel the blow, but he kept his distance and his tone carefully neutral. "It looks like someone hit you."

"I took a knee on my way down. All part of the job. It's a good thing Jacques scared them off."

Max looked from one to the other. They were lying to him. The fact that neither betrayed even the slightest twitch of guilt wounded him worse than any truth could have.

He could smell blood and gunplay on them. Very smoothly he asked, "He or they? Which is it?"

"One on foot and one waiting in the car." Cee Cee never blinked.

What could she be afraid to share with him? He couldn't let it go.

"Did you get it back?"

"What?"

"The purse."

She stared at him, then it clicked. "Oh. Yes. But they got away."

"So whoever put that mark on your face goes unpunished. I don't think I like that, detective."

"I don't like it either, but sometimes it happens. I've gotten bashed up before and I'll probably get bashed up again. You'll have to get used to it."

"No," he told her. "I don't think I will."

He crossed over to her, watching her stare darken

with secrets, her expression firm into that tough-cop facade, which shut him out from whatever she was doing that she knew he wouldn't like.

But there were other ways to get answers.

Her body stiffened slightly when he reached out to her, skimming his fingertips along her stubborn jaw. He let his curled knuckles brush up the soft curve of her cheek toward the worst of the damage. Fury toward whomever had hurt her boiled in his blood, but he was careful to keep that rage from venting outward.

As he bent down she tipped her face up to him, her lashes fluttering, her lips parting for his kiss. Instead of accepting that offer he passed it by, letting his mouth graze just below her ear, where he lingered to breathe in all the smells that clung to her. Jacques LaRoche's musky scent, spicy ribs, death, a vague odor of Tito Tibideaux and two unfamiliar presences. He snuffled them up the way one of her team might dust for fingerprints, and the instant she knew what he was doing, her palms flattened against his shoulder to push him away.

"I've got paperwork to get to," she said flatly.

He straightened, a tide of hot, fierce anger rising with him. The mean, dangerous mood scared him because it came from no place he recognized within himself, because it swamped his cool, controlled responses to shake through him in waves of violent demand. That he compel the truth from her by grabbing her up in rough hands. That he beat it from Jacques with a blind determination. Because he would never think to do such things ordinarily, he backed away from them, alarmed and appalled.

"I'll leave you to it, then. I'll see you at the house."

Cee Cee let him walk out the door filled with frustration and suspicion and hurt. Because she had that card in her pocket, the phone that she had to trace, and until she knew more about what they were facing, she'd rather he not know anything.

So she let him return to his table, to sit with his back straight and unyielding toward the glass. Sooner or later she'd have to figure out a way to deal with him, but not with so much already on the platter tonight.

"Shit," she muttered. Then she was all business. "Jacques, I need to get back to my car."

"I'll have someone drive you. And I'll watch over him."

She found the strength to leave the club by holding on to one icy fear.

She'd felt the power of the Trackers sent after Max, their fierceness, their unstoppable determination. And she wasn't sure Max could take them. So she got her car and returned to her work to run a trace of the number she'd found on Tito's refrigerator.

And she found a dead end. A government block she couldn't get around.

So she called the number.

One ring, and then it was answered by silence. A cold, calculating silence that pissed her off.

"I know who you are, and what you are," she said, her tone hard as that fist she could still feel pounding in her face. "Back the fuck off."

There was no response. Then just the dial tone.

Five

TITO TIBIDEAUX WAS laid to rest on a cool, clear
evening before a gathering of family and friends.
Cee Cee stood at Max's side. She hadn't known
Tito, but she deeply understood the grief and sense
of loss swelling about her. She clung to the warmth
of Max's hand as sorrow wailed through her: for
the father she still mourned, for the best friend she
missed like the loss of herself, for the mother she'd
never had the chance to love. As words of comfort
were spoken over a stranger, she tried to take them
into her broken heart but failed.

Max found her tucked into shadows on the side
steps, hugging her knees to her chest, weeping into
the lonely comfort of her arms. Never in his life
had he felt so inadequate as when faced with her
private pain. She was such a strong, fierce woman
who fought displays of weakness, even when they
were tearing her apart. Perhaps she wouldn't want
him witnessing this slip in her control—they hadn't
parted on the best of terms. Awkward and uncertain, he hung back while the sound of her misery ate
at the hardened edges of his own heart. And then he

remembered her whisper to him on the night she'd returned. *I wish I'd asked you to go with me.*

He knelt down and placed his hands lightly on her arms. Without even looking up she rocked forward, burrowing instinctively into the protective circle of his embrace. Then he simply held her, remaining silent while her weeping wound down into soft sniffles. Her arms finally stopped trying to contain her sadness and opened to include him.

He smiled slightly as he felt her gathering her formidable strength about her, grateful she'd allowed him to tend to her sorrows. And of course, her first words weren't about her own needs.

"You should be with your guests."

"I'm where I want to be." *Where you need me to be, whether you'd admit it or not.*

"I didn't mean to pull you away."

"There's free food and drink. What do they need me for?"

A soft chuckle. Her hands rubbed up his back to his shoulders beneath his black coat. Her head lifted from his chest to nestle under his chin. And she sighed.

"I got a little caught up in things for a minute. It kind of blindsided me. I didn't expect you to—" She floundered for a moment, then murmured, "Thank you, Max."

"I'm just in it for the hope of gratitude sex."

She pushed away, laughing raggedly. Her fingertips grazed his cheek and her smile grew tender. "I think you can safely plan on plenty of that. But I should get back to things. I'm supposed to be your hostess, and here I am blubbering when I should be—"

His kiss silenced her, a tender slide of his mouth over hers that melted the need for apologies. She eased back, smiling as she promised, "Lots and lots of sex."

His gaze smoldered. "We could start now. They won't miss us."

There was a quiet throat clearing as Helen announced herself. "Mr. Savoie, should we open up the house for your friends?"

Max looked at her over his shoulder. "There's a fine moon out tonight. We can howl under it."

"Ms. Charlotte, I could use your help."

With a task at hand, Cee Cee was quick to pull herself together. "I'll be right there, Helen." She wiped her checks, muttering, "I must look a mess."

Max wet his fingers to rub the smudges from beneath her eyes, careful not to disturb the artful makeup over her bruise. "There," he proclaimed. "Beautiful. Define lots, detective."

"More than you can imagine, Savoie."

She stood, his hands skimming down her body until they curved around the back of her calves. He kissed her knees beneath the hem of her sedate black dress and looked up at her, murmuring with a lusty rumble, "Oh, I doubt that very much."

She chuckled and patted him on the head. "Go play nice with your friends."

He leaned his elbows back on the top step to watch her move down the porch. For the somber occasion, she'd chosen an unadorned sleeveless dress of supple knit. The high collar and long, sleek line gave her an air of elegance right down to her shiny black patent-leather sling-back heels. She made a powerful impression with her strong stride, with the way the artificial lighting delineated the muscle tone under bronze skin down bare arms and long legs, the way she carried her head at an arrogant angle and her shoulders with that invisible chip on them. His smile played out slow and smug, thinking how lucky he was that she scared the hell out of most men, leaving the field wide open for him to claim her. Not an easy challenge, but one he found infinitely rewarding. Desire couldn't come anywhere close to describing what filled his heart when she paused to blow a kiss at him, then went inside.

He released his breath with a slow shiver, and surged off the porch to join his company.

AFTER LAROCHE HAD tapped the kegs and the tables were licked clean, the music started and Tito's wake got into full swing. Sensing the uncertainty of the house staff, Cee Cee remained up on the porch, a buffer between them and the strange group of revelers dancing on the lawn. Cee Cee understood their unnamed alarm because she felt it every time she stepped into *Cheveux du Chien*. In their funeral finery, standing humble before God, they could pass for ordinary men and women. But when the coats and shoes came off and the inhibitions let down, a glimpse of what lay beneath those tame, glossy surfaces began to show. With their glowing eyes and quick movements, with what could have been a trick of moonlight but wasn't, making their teeth seem sharp and their features feral, they looked like what they were . . . not quite human.

Everyone who'd worked for Jimmy Legere had heard stories about Max Savoie, about the strange, silent boy he'd brought with him out of the swamps to live among them, though not really one of them. By the time he was a withdrawn, soft-spoken teen, rumors flew in hushed whispers of the things he'd done, and how. Sheer nonsense, of course, those tales of shape-shifting viciousness right out of folklore, spread just to make Legere's enemies nervous. Rumors Max propagated simply by not denying that they were true. He kept to himself, at Jimmy's beck and call, still, intense, dangerous without ever having to prove anything. And by the time he was an adult, just being in the same room with him could make stalwart men break into a sweat.

But no matter how much Jimmy's staff feared Max Savoie, they adored Jimmy and loathed his sneaky cousin Francis Petitjohn. Jimmy treated all his employees like family, taking a genuine interest in their concerns and cares, making it a point to remember birthdays and anniversaries, and slipping them an extra something in their pay whenever there was a need. His relationship with Max was more father to son than master and servant, though Max was blindly obedient to his every wish. And Max had loved him to the very limit of his life, ready to sacrifice it, it was said, when his involvement with police detective Charlotte Caissie led to a fracture of trust between them.

When it came to choosing between Francis Petitjohn, who had seen the chance to slay Jimmy Legere as his means of seizing control of an empire, or backing the lost and despondent Max, they'd pushed aside their caution to take Savoie's hand. And not one of them regretted doing so, no matter what Max Savoie might be. Because he took care of his own, when Petitjohn would have taken advantage of them.

But tonight, as he circled through the gathering on the moon-drenched grass, it was clear that Max was among his own kind, with those fierce, bright-eyed beings masquerading as human. And they were afraid—of the quicksilver creatures and of Savoie.

Aware that the men who served Max without question that morning now milled about, muttering worriedly, Cee Cee wondered if Max knew what was stirring up on his porch. She felt that prickly fear that he'd often described as flaming torches and windmills as the townsfolk gathered to attack what was unlike them.

And Max wasn't making things easier.

He was behaving differently, aggressive, tense,

and fierce as he stalked through his clan. The men gave him room. The women gave him their undivided attention. Cee Cee watched him dance with them, the way he moved, so sleek and graceful, inviting the touch of their hands, the brief sway and rub of their bodies against him. Enjoying their overtures a bit too much, seemingly indifferent to the fact that she was observing him from the porch of the home he'd asked her to share with him.

Enough.

She left the house staff to fend for themselves, storming down the steps, striding across the grass with one destination in mind. Until her arm was gripped and she was spun into Jacques LaRoche's firm embrace. He overcame her instinctive resistance to being handled by simply hanging on until she calmed and accepted his closeness, following his lead stiffly through the steps of a dance.

"I wanted to thank you again for all you've done, detective. Max tells me you planned everything."

Everything except her boyfriend sniffing up every skirt.

"I was happy to do it for . . . Philo."

LaRoche laughed. "Put your claws in, detective. You've got nothing to worry about. He's just testing his boundaries a little."

"What he's testing is my patience."

He chuckled at her temper. "He can't help it, Charlotte. It's what he is, and they know it."

"What *is* he?"

"Coming into mating season, and they all want to make it with the Big Dog. They can smell it on him—the sweat and aggression."

"I—I beg your pardon?"

"Don't get all riled up about it. It's our nature to seek out a strong and compatible mate to breed with, to test all the wells, so to speak, before deciding to plunge in." A chuckle. "Now I've shocked you."

She glared over at the pretty woman dancing with Max, at the way her eyes teased and invited. Irritation bristled up the back of her neck. "But isn't that Philo's girlfriend? If he knows what's going on, why does he put up with it?"

"The same reason we all do. Max is stronger. He'd kill anyone who interfered. This is the only time in our life cycle when we're not quite in control. Instinct controls us. It's his right, and the women's, until he's bonded. He can take whomever he chooses and none of us would get in his way. It's not personal, Charlotte. It's biology."

"Not personal," she sputtered. "What are you saying? That if Philo objected, Max would kill him over a woman he's not even interested in? That's crazy!"

"It's the strongest behavior bred into us, and it's impossible to break from. Don't take it lightly, Charlotte," LaRoche warned. "And don't hold him accountable. He can't stop it, any more than he could stop the phases of the moon."

She was horrified. She was furious. "So I'm supposed to look the other way while he plows his way through this field of potential mates? I don't think so."

LaRoche sighed, his patient sympathy almost as disturbing as Max's behavior. "We're not talking promiscuity or flirtations here. This is a *need* ingrained in him from birth. It's a chain reaction that begins the minute we males have sex for the first time." He made an amused sound. "I wouldn't have figured Max for this late a bloomer, but I guess he's got you to thank for that. He can't *not* act on it, Charlotte. He's not making a conscious choice. You're his choice. We all know that."

"So I'm supposed to just humor him until he gets it out of his system? Exactly how long will that take?"

"It's not a casual phase, I'm afraid. It'll last until he bonds. Until then, it might be easier if you didn't see him."

"No," she said instantly. "No way. These are your ridiculous rules. I don't have to play by them and I don't have to tolerate them." She spun away and right into Max.

His hands gripped her upper arms with a pressure that made her wince as he looked not at her startled face, but at LaRoche. A low, threatening vibration started up from his chest, and Cee Cee was immediately aware of what a deadly and direct creature he'd become.

"Max. I was just explaining things to her so she could understand," LaRoche began.

"What things?"

That harsh growl wasn't like Max. Nor were the high flush of color and hot glitter of his eyes.

LaRoche shrugged nonchalantly. "That you're not yourself. That you feel like your head's about to explode. Like you want to rip mine off right now without knowing why. I'm not stepping in, Max. She's yours. I'm not challenging you."

"Walk away, Jacques. Now."

"Anything you say, Max." He slid a look to Cee Cee. "Be careful. Don't provoke him."

"Don't provoke him," she muttered, casting a sour glance up at the dark, compelling features. "Well, oh King of the Beasts, have you been enjoying yourself provoking *me*?"

"I don't know what you're talking about," he replied gruffly.

Cee Cee gave him a closer study. He was breathing hard and fast. His eyes were wild, glazed. Almost like he was on a roaring drunk, only she hadn't seen him take a sip all night. Her hands ran up and down his chest until he began to focus on her, then his gaze flared bright and hot.

"Why don't you dance with me, Savoie, and maybe I won't be so disagreeable."

He reeled her in until their bodies pressed close but he could still watch her through those strangely lit eyes. He smiled but it wasn't Max's smug smirk of conquest. It was a baring of teeth. Beneath her palm, his heart hammered as if trying to break through his rib cage. Though his movements were fluid, his body was tensile steel wound to snapping.

"You're scaring your friends, baby. I want you to stop it."

"They're not my friends. I pay them to tolerate me." He never blinked. "Am I scaring you?"

"I'm not afraid of you, Max."

"Maybe you should be." He moved so fast. One instant he was staring down into her eyes, and the next his teeth scraped her throat.

She forced herself not to flinch as he lightly licked and nibbled her neck. Her hand lifted to stroke through his hair, soothing, calming.

"If you frighten me," she explained casually, "we won't be having great sex later."

"I can have all the great sex I want." He was nuzzling her collarbone, snuffling up her scent. "With anyone I want. A perk of being King of the Beasts."

"Really? How nice for you. Is that what you want? To have great sex with all these panting females? Would you rather I just went home so as not to spoil your fun?"

He regarded her through fever-bright eyes. "You'd do that? You'd do that for me?"

"Sure, Max," she purred. Then she snarled. "In your dreams." Her elbow socked into his rock-hard middle, but he didn't even flinch.

Grinning that fierce primal smile, he pulled her

in tighter, continuing to move to the tempo of the music, but his movements were blatantly controlling and sexual.

As furious as she was, Cee Cee was also aroused. Heat pooled at the apex of her thighs, pounding with its own primitive beat. And because she wasn't afraid of him, his ferociousness excited her almost as much as it angered her.

"Let's get this straight," she bit out. "There is no way in hell I am going to stand for you working your way through those twenty-odd flavors. No way, Savoie. You are mine, and I don't pass around free samples."

"Yours?" Something dark and unpleasant fired in his eyes. She could practically see their conversation at his office replaying in his head. Could feel him stiffening as he recalled finding her and Jacques together at the club, keeping secrets from him.

"How quickly you fling commitment into my face when it's to your advantage. And what are you going to do about it, detective? Threaten to run away? Hide in your safe little apartment and lock me out? Cower there like your little rodent friends? As if you could keep me away so easily."

His arrogance grated against her temper and she got right into his face. "No. No running. No hiding. You step out of line and I'll beat the crap out of you."

She hoped he'd smile at her audaciousness, and he almost did. Then his mouth thinned and twisted.

"I let you do that once. I won't let you again. Just like I'm not going to let you dictate what I choose to do. I'm not on your leash, detective. And this is my yard. You don't get to pee in it."

Her elbow flashed up, clipping him under the chin. Max saw stars but his grip on her never lessened. With a brisk shake of his head, he fixed his stare upon her again and Cee Cee realized her mistake. She was angry almost to the point of abandoning rational behavior. Max—cool, reasonable, restrained Max—had just slipped beyond it.

He leaned into her face to growl softly, "Let's take this someplace a bit more private."

He cuffed her wrist within his strong fingers, forcing her to keep up or be half dragged as he strode toward the shadows of the untended garden. Though fuming and humiliated, she was also aware that some here would step to her aid if they thought she was reluctant, which would endanger them. So she trotted at his side without a struggle, staggering on the high heels as they caught in the soft earth.

Out of sight of their company, he tossed her down onto one of the stone benches beneath a winter-barren arbor. Before she could scramble up he slid one leg across her thighs, straddling the bench, trapping her beneath him. His arms braced on either side of her, forming an effective cage. She shoved him, squirming, but her wriggling only made the light in his eyes burn brighter, hotter.

"Let me go, Max. Now."

"If you wanted me to let you go, you wouldn't keep coming back to me."

His vanity made her want to howl. She settled for punching him in the gut hard enough to earn a surprised, "Oof."

"To *Max,* yes. But not to you, you—"

"Mobster, killer, monster. You forgot lover, detective. I'm that, too. What are you afraid of, Charlotte? Afraid I won't come back to you? Afraid I might find one of them more to my liking?"

That's exactly what she was afraid of.

"Why are you acting like this? There's no way in hell I'm going to put up with it and you know it. Let me go, you conceited bastard. If you go ahead and roll around with them, I hope you find one who suits you. Because I won't take you back. I will *not* take you back."

He went completely still. Even his breathing stopped. Then he moved in, leaning closer until she could see the frantic patches of gold and crimson swirling in his stare.

"Liar," he whispered against her mouth.

She tried to hit him, but he had her pinned between the brace of his arms, his intrusive size containing her easily.

"What are you trying to prove, Savoie?" she snarled up at him. "You're bigger, you're stronger. I can't take you. I can't stop you from taking me, if that's what you want to do. But I'm not going to like it, and I'm going to hate you for doing it."

He stared at her for a moment, then laughed, a soft indulgent sound. "I don't believe you."

He buried his face against her neck, his tongue making a slow, wet sweep along that taut curve where he would taste the hurried race of her heartbeat. Angry, wanting; mostly wanting. She wrestled one hand loose, grabbing a fistful of his hair to twist, then to knead fitfully as she whispered, "Max."

She sought his mouth and ravaged it. Her fingers closed about his wrist, directing his hand under her dress where he began tearing at her stockings, his movements rough, impatient. He invaded her with a quick thrust of his fingers as her body arched, channeling his aggression into desire until her breath came in hard, hurried gulps as he brought her to a powerful climax.

While she hung on him, dazed and gasping, he told her with low, gruff certainty, "You won't ever leave me, Charlotte, and you'll let me do whatever I want to do. Because you need this. You need me. Because you have nowhere else to go."

The surprising cruelty of his words slapped the lingering pleasure away. All she could do was stare at him, eyes wounded and welling for a brief instant, before her fist connected forcefully with his cheekbone. She flung him off her and scrambled shakily to her feet. While he lay unmoving on his back, hand to his eye, she kicked out of her shoes and headed for the house.

"You can't run from me, Charlotte," he shouted after her.

Then, alone in the darkness, he whispered with desperate urgency, "Run, Charlotte. Run far and fast, and don't look back."

Six

IT ROSE LIKE a fever all day, burning through Max's veins, searing his thoughts, feeding the headache that throbbed relentlessly, dry kindling to the flame. Strange sensations. Hot and surging, swamping his control with sudden harsh urges. Violent. Sexual. Frightening and exciting. Concentration was gone, burnt in the firestorm of compulsive desires.

He struggled with it, alarmed and repulsed by the visceral rips and ebbs of mood that spiked when he'd found Cee Cee and LaRoche together. He had almost convinced himself he had it conquered. While holding Charlotte in his arms as she wept, it receded, forced into abeyance by the sheer magnitude of his feelings for her. But then the music had started and something in the beat, something woven almost subliminally beneath the tempo, moved to the same compelling pulse in his temples. Then it was in his blood, that hard, urgent hammering, so hot he could barely breathe as he moved among those who seemed to understand better than he did why he was not himself.

The women. His awareness of them rose in subtle, dizzying waves until he was drowning. Scent and heat fed the voracious hunger, building a blinding rage of need. This greedy, desperate drive had nothing to do with his mind, nothing to do with his will or his wishes. The animal inside him distilled down to a raw, basic compulsion to mate. Not just with the woman he'd chosen in his heart and soul. But with every nameless, faceless female that crossed his primitive radar. He wanted them all. And he wanted them now.

And why not?

He was the King of Beasts. Their Shifter King. Who would stop him?

Who, indeed. And with a very tasty right hook.

Max got to his feet slowly, off balance. With his first step he stumbled, tripping over Cee Cee's discarded shoes. He gave one an ill-tempered kick before he could stop himself, and knew a sullen satisfaction as it flew into one of the fountains. He picked up the other one, turning the patent leather with its lethal spiked heel in his hand, slipping his fingers down into the wickedly pointed toes where her warmth was still held in the insole. Her scent clung to him, heavy and exotic, and the beast within him growled back to life with a new focus. A small bit of reason in the back of his brain hoped frantically that she had hopped into her muscle car and roared back into the city, where she would be safe from him.

But the minute he emerged from the darkness, he saw he was wrong.

She was up on the porch, standing tall and fiercely proud with her bruised arms akimbo and bare legs set in a combative stance. Her dark eyes flashed to his, conveying an unspoken dare. *Just try to make it up to me, Savoie. Coward.*

That pitch-black glare, so steady, so penetrating in its blame, held him at bay, kept him circling like something wild and wary. She stood on *his* porch, with her greatest enemy's people at her back in silent support of her right to be there, her right to take him to task. His pride and his own clan's scrutiny kept him from going to her. That and the warring shame and umbrage chafing his already raw restraint.

He prowled through the revelers, darkly dangerous. And while he nuzzled a willing neck or ran his hands along a pliant form, his gaze never left her.

Charlotte.

The scent of her, the feel of her, the taste of her swirled about his sharpened senses, consuming him with hot madness. The others who would cling and coo at him were nothing. Cool, bland moons compared to the volatile gravitation of her sun. And he couldn't resist the pull.

Charlotte.

Wanting her shivered icy cold over the burning pump of his blood until she filled every hard, reckless beat.

Agitation quickened his light steps and had him tacking back and forth like a graceful sloop pushing against a gale-force blow. Closing in on her with calculated purpose, he finally strode toward the porch with stalking intensity.

A big hand closed on his arm, jerking him from that self-destructive path. He rounded on Jacques LaRoche with a cold snarl. "You're in my way."

"You planning on making rough with your lady and putting more of them bruises on her?"

Max reared back, eyes glittering, unable to believe he was being challenged. "She's mine to do with as I want."

"She's not one of us, Max. You'll hurt her. You might even kill her. Is that what you want to do?"

He paced, a wild thing in a small cage, his movements tightly controlled as his breath shook from him in harsh bursts. He slowly lifted his gaze to the porch and that hot twist of desire fisted in his groin, the pain unbearable.

"Get out of my way, Jacques."

"Max, *think*. Think of Charlotte. She's going to fight you, and you're going to hurt her. You won't mean to, but you won't be able to stop yourself."

Max bent over, panting hard against the violence pounding through him, his face dripping sweat. His voice was deep, hoarse. "Don't let me hurt her. Please, Jacques. I don't know what I'm doing. I can't think. I don't know what to do. I can't stop myself."

LaRoche cursed softly—then grinned. "I must be crazy, but all right, Max. There are other ways to work off some of that mean you're feeling."

Max looked up at him. "How?"

The sudden punch dropped him to his knees.

"Let's dance a bit, you and me. Nothing fancy. And nothing fatal. Just man to man. For fun."

The music had stopped. Curious and intrigued, the others began to circle to watch.

Max licked the blood from the corner of his mouth, darkly amused. "There's no challenge there. You can't beat me."

"Maybe. Maybe not. On your hind legs, Savoie. Like men, nothing more. Afraid I'll embarrass you?"

He grinned ferociously. "No."

"Make it a wager," someone called.

"See? Our friends are anxious to earn a little fast cash off our sweat and blood. What do you say, Max? Ready to let me knock some of the arrogance out of you? I can get in a few good licks before you pulverize me."

Max straightened slowly. "Name the stakes."

"Me."

They both turned toward the strong voice, where Charlotte glared down from the porch, taking a savage satisfaction in the abrupt slackening of Max's expression.

"I'll go home with the winner. Whichever one of you can still walk, come get me."

And with that monumental claim of indifference, she turned her back and went inside.

"Thanks, Charlotte," LaRoche muttered. "You sure know how to suck the fun outta things."

Then the impact of Max's fist exploded his consciousness into a halo of bright lights. He shook it off to see the younger man fling out of his coat as he said, "Consider me highly motivated."

THE SOUND OF his footsteps sped up her heartbeat. Max's steps were usually light, barely making a noise. These footfalls were heavy, almost reluctant, and for one awful moment, she thought it might be Jacques LaRoche coming to claim her.

Then what would she do?

Go with him, of course. What choice had Max left her? Had her own fierce pride left her? Not that she planned to *do* anything with him, and if he thought different, she'd prove him wrong in a quick minute. But she'd go. That, or let Max put his foot down firmly on the back of her neck for the rest of their relationship.

Would that be so bad?

That seditious whisper shocked her.

To have him, would it be so bad to just give up all the struggling, all the battling, all the barriers? To admit that she wanted him, under any circumstances?

Yes—it would be bad for both of them. No matter how difficult, that tentative balance they'd struck had to be maintained. Which was why, when she saw him fill the door frame, no delighted relief showed in her steady stare.

"Disappointed?" he drawled in a chilly voice.

"In several things lately."

He looked so temptingly hot with his black hair mussed, his face flushed with temper and exertion, his eyes dazzling jewel-like. Though he showed no physical effects of his tussle with LaRoche, his expensive clothes were ripped, grass- and blood-stained, and beyond the resuscitation of the best dry cleaner. He was breathing light and fast through clenched teeth. The effort of restraint pounded off him like heat from a summer pavement. He was furious—and he was also afraid. She could see it flickering behind his posturing rage.

"Sorry you didn't get the chance to prove your point?" His words were like jagged glass.

"And that point would be?"

"That you would toss me away on a whim of chance."

She'd never believed LaRoche could beat him, but her sense of injury wouldn't allow her to mention that. "It wouldn't have been personal, Max. No big deal, right? It wouldn't have meant anything. Just brush it off. Isn't that what you were expecting me to do?"

He began to prowl the room, careful to keep away from her. His hands worked in frustrated fists at his side.

She held her ground, watching him, wanting him, unwilling to make the first move.

"I didn't want to hurt you."

"Really? And watching you fall into a fornicating free-for-all with those bitches in heat wouldn't hurt me? Knowing you were putting your hands on someone else, putting yourself *into* someone else, wasn't going to hurt me how? Thanks for being so considerate of my feelings."

He wheeled about, circling up against her, bumping her with his hard, lean form, his cheek against her hair, his hands trembling over the bruises he'd left on her arms. "It wasn't your feelings I was afraid of hurting." His words ground up from the sharp-edged terror weighing cold and heavy in his gut. "I would walk away from you forever before I'd have you look at me like—" He went still.

"Max? Like what?"

She put her hand over his and he leapt away as if scalded. "Don't," he growled. "Not now. Not when I'm like this."

"Like what, Max?" she pressed.

He brushed by her, reeling slightly as he stepped out onto the balcony. Below, the mood had shifted back to party mode. The music rose full of energy and spice while unidentifiable shapes danced beneath the moon. Max watched them for a moment, bombarded by the mingling of scent and sound that itched over his nerves.

"Like what, baby? Talk to me, Max."

She moved up beside him in the heavy shadows, and he sidled away with a gruff, "Don't touch me."

"I won't. Just talk to me."

For a moment there was just the rasp of his breathing, a harsh counterpoint to the good-time tune rising from the lawn. Then it came pouring out of him, pumping in an arterial gush, unstoppable.

"I came back for you and Mary Kate."

The instant she took his reference, a cold, familiar terror churned up her insides. Immediately, she was back in the awful warehouse, surrounded by unimaginable horror. Unimaginable to a girl of seventeen—not to the woman she was now, who had seen too many horrible things to be surprised by the ugliness humans could summon up from the darkness inside. Though she wanted to tell him to stop, she whispered, "Go on."

"After I'd killed them—those men, those animals—I bent down to see if you were still . . . if you were all right. They'd left you on the floor, tossed away like something used up and broken. I thought . . . I was afraid I was too late. When I touched you, you opened your eyes, those fierce, brave eyes, and they were empty. There was no soul in them. I thought they'd crushed that spirit that so amazed me."

"But they didn't, Max. Because you came back. Because you came back and saved us."

"I came back and saved myself." He shuddered as the memory of what he'd seen that night overwhelmed him. That night when he defied everything he understood, everything he believed, because of what he'd seen in the rebellious glare of an unknown girl's eyes: strength. Courage. Freedom.

"I've done terrible things, Charlotte. Things I

will never, ever share with you. Nothing I did made any impression on me. There was nothing inside me that could feel for those I killed.

"And then you touched my face, my other face, the face of the beast, and you looked at me as if you saw something beautiful. I was never the same after that."

He turned to her, eyes glittering in the darkness. "I put that look of helplessness and terror into the eyes of every man I killed, because I was like them—those men who raped and tortured you and Mary Kate. Jimmy never told me I could be more than that. He never told me that there was more to me than the monster. I'd forgotten what it was like to feel . . . until you, Charlotte."

"You weren't like them, Max," she told him softly. "You were never like them."

If he heard her, he didn't believe what she was saying. "You were my chance, Charlotte—my chance to do something good, something right. My chance to remember where I'd hidden away my soul when I was just a child. I swore that day that I would never do anything to put that look back in your eyes; that you would never, ever have reason to fear me.

"I don't know what I was saying down there. I didn't mean any of it. If I've hurt your feelings, I'm sorry. Better to break your heart than your bones." A glum caricature of a smile.

"I'm not afraid of you, Max. I've always known I was safe with you."

He grabbed her wrists so suddenly, she gasped. His grip was tight, too tight to be comfortable. "You're not safe now, Charlotte. *I'm* not safe. I've always been able to control the other part of me, ever since that first time when I was a boy. But I can't now. There's something loose inside me, something without a heart, without a soul, and without a care for what happens to you. Listen to me, Charlotte. *Listen.*" He shook her once roughly, then realizing what he'd done, he quickly released her. He shoved his hands deeply into his pockets, his breathing harsh with agitation. "I can't trust myself to touch you. I'm afraid of what I might do."

So she touched him, just a light brush of her knuckles along his taut cheek.

"Don't." His eyes were on her, wide and wild with objection.

"I trust you." And she stretched up to take his mouth, lightly at first, then slowly sinking into passion. He made a soft sound in his throat, a moan of helpless surrender, of desperate longing. His lips parted to let her in, and he was lost.

She flooded every part of him, becoming the beat in his blood. Wanting her pushed against all the weak spots in his levee of restraint, the small cracks becoming large fissures, finally leading to violent collapse.

He had her by the arms, swinging her around, thrusting her against the abrasive white stucco wall. Her head hit hard and for a moment her focus swam. His mouth ground against hers, shifting brutally until she tasted blood. When she tried to turn to one side to catch her breath, his hand clamped like a vise on either side of her jaw, making deep indentations in her flesh as he anchored her in place.

Through the red haze, he heard her muffled squeak of protest. He wanted to gentle his hold on her; he tried to ease back, to show her tenderness, but couldn't. Because the pounding in his head chanted *Take her. Take her now. Have to have her.*

His muscles coiled tight, vibrating with tension, ready to spring, to snap, to attack. There was no backing down, no controlling the animal inside or the hunger razoring across his consciousness. And then, through the primitive pulse driving him, he heard her voice.

"Max, stop."

He staggered back, his world spinning, bent over double as he panted hard into the swells of violent impulse.

"Max."

He held up his hands to keep her away as he stumbled backward into the porch rail. His eyes squeezed shut, blocking the image of his fingerprints marring her soft skin, of the fear and pain surely twisting in her expression. She'd run now. She'd run and she'd be safe, someplace far away from him.

The feel of her palm on his face was a cool slide of sanity over the madness consuming him.

"It's all right, baby. We'll get through this."

"Charlotte, stay *away* from me. Please, don't let me touch you. I could *kill* you. Don't you understand?"

"I understand that you might want to on more than one occasion. You piss me off enough for me to want to cheerfully choke the life out of you sometimes, too. But not tonight. Not just this minute."

She continued to stroke his fevered cheek, his brow, and he leaned into her touch. He clung to the quiet calm of her voice, focusing on it, centering on it.

"Do you trust me, Max? Can you trust me?"

He nodded, even as he fought back the blackness trying to crack through his chest. He kept his eyes closed, narrowing down the sensory bombardment so it was a bit more manageable. She lifted his hands carefully and fit them over the wrought-iron rail behind him, curling his fingers around the metal.

"You hold on and don't let go. Don't let go."

Curiosity nudged through the dark whips of madness. "What are you going to do?"

"Just taking a little pressure off the top."

"What? How are you going to—"

She slid down his zipper and opened his pants. "Just don't let go."

"Charlotte—"

The first soft sweep of her mouth buckled his knees. Then he was hanging on with frantic desperation as she took him in with a slow, velvety slide. His mind blanked, his breathing spilled out in short, shallow bursts as she began to work him. Gently at first, to snare his attention and channel his aggressive energy into a very specific focus. Then the light scrape of her teeth. His legs started shaking. Hot, immediate sensation pushed everything else away as she cupped him, caressed him with her mouth.

Her voice reached through the pounding in his head.

"Let go, Max. Let go."

She wasn't talking about the rail. And she wasn't going to let him resist, though he was struggling to do just that. She suddenly remembered that first time she'd coaxed him to lose himself to her—his amazement and surprise, the dizzying sense of power she'd felt from making his will collapse.

"I love you, Max. Let me have you."

He unloaded with the force of cannon fire.

She rode him down as his knees gave out and he sank to the porch boards in a shuddering heap.

After a long moment, his raw, hitching breaths eased and his world balanced. Carefully, very carefully, he slipped his arms about the precious woman resting against his laboring chest. Good, she felt so good.

"Better now?"

Because he hadn't quite mastered speech, he simply nodded. Cautiously, he put his hand on her head and gingerly combed his fingers through her hair. His movements were ridiculously weak and shaky but under his control. Testing the theory a bit more bravely, he rubbed his cheek over the mess he'd made of her hairdo, and everything inside him settled on a quiet sigh.

She'd stayed with him. He couldn't quite grasp the magnitude of her courage.

She reluctantly straightened to look into his eyes. Cool, beautiful green.

"Welcome back, Savoie."

"Glad to be here. Thank you, *sha*."

A smile. "Sometimes I love my job."

A smile back. "Maybe you wouldn't mind coming with me to work. I could tuck you under my desk in case of emergency."

"I *do* love you, Max."

Her kiss was soft and sweet, tempting emotions he thought better kept guarded for now. Her smile was tender as she traced his cheekbones with her fingertips.

"We should go down and take care of your company."

He caught her hand and pressed her knuckles to his lips. "The only company I want is yours."

"Then let's go chase them out of here, so we can go to bed."

Seven

MAX LET CEE CEE help him up, surprised at how much he had to rely on her strength. He was kitten-weak now that the adrenaline-pumped aggression had quieted. It still whispered about, prowling in the back of his consciousness, murmuring darkly even though his body was slack with well-satisfied relief. So as much as he longed to linger in Charlotte's arms, he didn't dare.

She fingered the blood-stained lapel of his jacket, her eyebrows winging up. "Yours?"

"Could be."

"We should clean up a bit, or our guests will think we beat the hell out of each other."

His thumb rubbed over her darkening bruises, his expression closed down tight. "Would they be wrong?"

She didn't know what to say, so she leaned in to hug him and felt the sharp stab of something in his pocket. She drew out her single shoe, then patted him down.

"Just one?"

"I'm afraid the other didn't survive the encounter."

"Geez, Savoie, those cost me half a paycheck."

A flash of guilt crossed his eyes. "I'll buy you another pair. I'll buy you a closetful."

Frightened by his intensity, she gripped his chin, holding him so he couldn't look away when she told him, "It's not about the shoes. I don't care about the shoes."

To prove her point, she gave the lone survivor a careless toss over the balcony rail—then hoped it didn't impale someone.

"I don't want to argue with you," she told him in exasperation. "Let's not do this, Max."

"Maybe you should just go home."

The flat words felt like a slap.

"Is that what you want?"

He didn't give an answer, and she couldn't find one in his impassive features.

"I thought I *was* home." Aggravated and more upset than she'd let him see, she went inside to rummage through their shared dresser to pull out a change of clothing.

"Are you leaving?"

She hadn't heard him come up behind her, and jumped at his quiet words. She whirled, then caught back a tart reply because he looked so miserable. She took a slow breath and asked with all the calm she could manage, "What do you want me to do, Max? Tell me what you want me to do."

He was still and somber for so long, she'd started to turn away when he said softly, "Stay."

"Okay." She picked up her clothes and carried them into the bathroom, where the bright light illuminated the damage done to her face and arms. She shook off her shock with a low curse and reached for a miracle in her makeup bag. As she was dotting cover-up over the ugly smudges, she saw Max standing in the doorway watching her without a flicker of emotion. She continued to resurface, gloss, and fluff. She shrugged out of the dress she knew she would never wear again, and covered the bruising on her body with jeans and a cotton pullover. Then she stared at her reflection. "I look like hell."

"You're beautiful," Max corrected tonelessly.

She met his opaque stare in the mirror and beckoned him to her. He stepped up behind her to rest his head on her shoulder, his eyes closing as she rumpled his hair.

"Change your clothes," she said softly. "I'll wait for you."

SHE SAW THE wisdom in presenting a united front when they came down the stairs together and relief lit the faces of the household staff lingering uneasily in the foyer.

"Are our guests behaving?" she asked Helen, acting as if there were no reason for the woman to have been fretting for her safety.

"They're loud and energetic, but they've kept their manners."

"Good." She glanced up at Max. "Let's go make sure some of them are sober enough to drive the rest home."

She reached out and curled his fingertips lightly into her palm, and they walked into the whirlwind of music, drink, and dance.

Aware of the speculative glances when they appeared together, a sedate and newly clothed couple, Cee Cee relaxed in her role of hostess where she couldn't before. When she pressed Philo Tibideaux's hand between hers, he responded sincerely to her condolences and thanked her for her part in bringing his brother to be buried. When Max attempted to do the same, the grieving redhead staggered back, muttering something that sounded like, "No thanks to you."

Seeing the question in Cee Cee's eyes, Max took her hand and urged, "Dance with me, *cher*."

The tune was a rollicking Cajun two-step, with Jo-El Sonnier's Acadian accordian pumping out "Evangeline Special." Max held her lightly, snapping her to and fro as she backpedaled in her bare feet. Usually when they danced together it involved lots of contact and some not-always-discreet groping. The fast, peppery rhythm kept them moving, circling and spinning, until they were both breathless. When the music slid into Ben Harper's tangy "Gold to Me," Max reeled her in a bit closer but they still didn't really touch. Cee Cee was surprised to find that rather nice, because then she could watch him move and there were very few things she found as appealing.

She doubted that Jimmy Legere had signed him up for dance classes, and she'd be surprised if he'd ever taken a turn about a floor before their first unconventional date. But Max Savoie was a fast study. Light on his feet, with a powerful grace, he picked up the sassy rhythms and had her stepping to a hip-and-shoulder-rolling cha-cha that was sexy as hell. And fun. She'd missed that—the snap and crackle of their banter, the unpressured tease of his sly smile, the way his eyes would smolder like a long-stoked fire. The way they did now. Their relationship had flared so hot and fast and all-consuming, they hadn't had much of a chance to simply enjoy one another. Like now.

She smiled at him, and his smile flashed back with answering warmth. The tempo slowed, slipping into John Hiatt's bluesy "Feels Like Rain." Coaxed into closer proximity by the sultry guitar licks and pulsing drumbeat, they swayed at a cautious distance for a moment, then leaned familiarly into each other, her face nestled up against his throat. In that comfortable embrace an easy desire simmered like a slow-thickening roux, and when the song ended they simply stood, wrapped up in the quiet passion.

"Sometimes I forget how much I like just being with you," she sighed, listening to his heartbeat and riding the rhythm of his breathing.

His lips moved against her hair. "Like on a date? You want to start dating? Should I court you and woo you again? Can we still date when we're sharing dresser drawers?"

"Why not?"

"Why not, indeed? If I'm going to pick you up for dates, I should probably learn how to drive a car."

"I can pick you up."

"How forward of you, detective. I prefer a genteel woman," he teased.

"No, you don't," she scoffed.

"I prefer you, Charlotte, above all things."

"You have remarkably good taste, Savoie."

His tongue traced along the curve of her ear. "And you taste remarkably good."

She smiled. "Time for our guests to go home."

It intruded stealthily, that gradual stiffening and withdrawal from the tender warmth of the moment. She wanted to hang on tight, to not let him retreat but found herself easing out of his arms, letting her palms slide reluctantly down the sleeves of his fresh white cotton shirt.

"I'll stopper the booze while you steer them to their cars."

When she started to step away he caught her hand, pulling her back. Then his mouth settled over hers, brief and devastating, before he walked quickly away.

She watched him, worried. He was avoiding her,

staying purposefully out of reach while his hot gaze rarely left her.

The last thing she wanted to do was leave him. But unless she could find some other answer, one that she could convince him to try, she might have to. She understood his fear, his concern, and loved him fiercely for it.

She didn't underestimate the danger. He humored her into thinking herself a match for his strength, but she knew the truth. If she miscalculated and he harmed her, killed her, how would he ever recover from that? With so much horror already weighing on his heart, how could he survive it?

It would be unfair to put him into that position, where the possibility could slip so quickly and fatally into probability. She couldn't control him— and now, he couldn't even control himself.

The lawn was mostly empty but for the leftovers of a good time. Bottles and cans, cigarette butts, discarded plastic cups and plates. She started picking up, needing to keep busy while she waited for Max to return. He was talking with LaRoche, Philo, and a few others, and something was wrong. LaRoche was trying to steer Philo toward their car, but he was determined to finish whatever he was saying to Max. His voice rose, wavering drunkenly and undercut with pain.

"Don't tell me how sorry you are. You brought this on us—they're here for you. They killed my brother because he wouldn't give you up. He's dead

because you dragged us all into your ugly business."

LaRoche interceded with forceful patience.
"That's enough, Philo. It's the drink talking, Max.
He'll be sorry for it in the morning."

"I'm not sorry," Philo bellowed. "You think
we're scared of you, Savoie? You're not invincible.
We don't need you. Your daddy's not the only one
who could be tempted to turn you in for a profit."

Max went very still.

As she approached, Cee Cee began to burn. Max
was somehow connected to the boy's death, so why
hadn't anyone said anything to her? LaRoche had
condescendingly claimed that she could do nothing,
but he was wrong. If not through their channels,
then through her own.

LaRoche dropped the drunken man with a tap
on the chin, then draped Philo over his shoulder
with ease. "Thanks for the hospitality, Max, and
for the dance." He grinned, rubbing his ribs. "Good
night, Charlotte."

She could feel Max's tension through her hand
on his back. He glanced at her quickly, and it was
apparent that she was in the way.

"Charlotte, you go on up. I've got to take care of
some things. I won't be long."

She wondered which situation had him more
worried: the one with Tibideaux or the one with her.

"Go ahead." She gave him a light push. "Take
care of your business." *And your secrets.* When

she strode back to the house, Helen met her on the porch. Her expression masked, she nodded toward the remaining stragglers veering toward their cars.

"What are those people?"

What, not who. Cee Cee chose to misunderstand. "They're Max's friends. They work the docks."

"He's never had a friend in his life, and now so many . . . and so strange. Mr. Legere would not have approved."

Cee Cee watched Max help load the limp Philo into the backseat of LaRoche's ancient Caddy. Then Max climbed into the front seat and they drove away.

"No, I don't suppose he would have. But they're powerful friends and Max needs them."

"Not as much as he needs you." Helen touched her arm. "Go to bed, child. Leave the cleanup to us."

Cee Cee dragged herself up the stairs and into a hot shower to ease her body aches. When she saw the bruises discoloring her grim face in the mirror, she snapped off the light, wishing she could switch off her worries as easily.

How deadly were the secrets Max kept from her?

SHE BOLTED UPRIGHT, bathed in sweat, shaking from the violence of her dreams. Dreams that seemed so close, so real, because of the pain that had followed her into wakefulness.

Only when she recognized where she was could she let go of the terror and let it recede.

She was alone in the big bed.

"Max?"

The need to have him wrap her up tight in his strength and warmth overwhelmed her. But there was no sign that he'd been here, though the bedside clock read four a.m.

She lay back down and closed her eyes, but the violent images were still there from the nightmare that was really a memory. Staring up at the high ceiling, listening to her panicky breath, she cursed herself for her weakness, just as she had then. And she longed for rescue now, just as she had then.

Too churned up to relax, she finally got out of bed, pulled Max's heavy leather coat out of the closet, and slipped it on, letting its weight and his scent embrace her. Then she crawled back into bed, hugging it close as she wished she were holding him. And surrounded by his presence, she sank back into a dreamless sleep.

WHEN SHE WOKE again nearly an hour later, it was to a strange clicking sound. She listened for a moment, trying to place the rhythmic tapping on the hardwood floor. Then dark ears appeared at the far edge of the bed, followed by a long muzzle. Baleful green eyes regarded her unblinkingly. She almost smiled.

"Figured you were in the doghouse, huh? You were right. Go away." She rolled over to put her back to him.

Silence, then the click of toenails on wood, circling the foot of the bed to come over to her side. A low, plaintive whining sounded until she couldn't stand it.

"Oh, all right." She patted the mattress. "Come up."

He bounded up onto the bed, huge and more than a little intimidating in his pure animal form. A cold, wet nose rooted under the covers, nudging beneath her hand for affection.

She shoved at him. "Stop it. Lie down."

He circled once, twice, then sank down to simply watch her through those uncanny eyes, nose on paws.

A small whimper.

With a snort of resignation, she reached down to rub his snout and was immediately drenched by an enthusiastic hand licking.

"Oh, hell. Come here, baby. You know I can't resist a big, dumb animal."

He edged up in a belly crawl, dropped his heavy head on her shoulder, and heaved a huge, weary sigh. His eyes closed.

Quarter to five. Where had he been?

Cee Cee stroked her hand absently over his head, between the stiff ears and along the surprisingly soft ruff. He gave a low animal moan of contentment as he flopped onto his side and pushed back against her. Smiling, she nuzzled her face into his thick black fur. With her arms around him, she drifted off until

the slow, silky touch of his tongue on her lips startled her awake.

Ready to shove him away, her objections melted
when her hands encountered smooth, strong shoulders. Murmuring his name softly, she shifted onto
her back, encouraging Max to slide up over her,
parting her lips to welcome his kisses.

Her hands tunneled into his short hair as their
mouths mated sweetly. A low sound escaped her
as her neck arched, his mouth trailing along it. His
hands pushed his coat open, his long fingers caress-
ing her breasts, making her heart flutter beneath his
cherishing touch. Her back bowed as she tugged his
head down, and the wet drag of his tongue was followed by exquisite suction. She was trembling when
he rested his head on her belly and anticipation
tightened through her as his hand rubbed along her
hip. His fingertips skimmed up her inner thigh and
paused there.

"I'm sorry I was rough with you."

"I'm tough, Savoie. I can take it." She parted her
knees to urge him to continue. "At the moment, I'll
take you anyway I can get you. Now, please."

She felt him smile, and then there was nothing
beyond the slow glide of his fingers up inside her.
She closed her eyes and let it build, let the glorious splinters of sensation roll over her in a splendid
wave of tension and relief.

She opened for his kiss, drawing him in, drugging

herself with the taste of him, losing herself to the feel of him.

He waited until her eyes drifted open to ask, "I want you desperately. Can I have you?"

"Now, please."

"Thank you, *sha*."

He tried to go slow, but that's not what she had in mind. The feel of him, so hard and strong above her, within her, didn't allow for gentle and easy. Her hands cupped his rear; her body rocked to his rhythm until her breath was ragged, and passion bloomed lush and wild as they lost themselves to one another.

He thanked her again when he finally rolled onto his back and sank into unconsciousness.

Cee Cee leaned up on her elbow to study him. With his features softened and the harsh angles gentled, he looked younger. And thoroughly and completely exhausted. But not just from the great sex. Fatigue settled over him like a blanketing weight, heavy and smothering. Concern nudged aside her glow of pleasure. He hadn't told her where he'd been until the blush of dawn.

She whispered, "What's going on, Max? What are you doing? Why won't you tell me so I can help you?"

There was something about Tito Tibideaux's death that he had to hide from her. Something he didn't feel he could trust her with? She hoped not.

Because he'd been right: She *didn't* have anyone

else to go to. She'd buried all of her family. Her dearest friend was in a hospital in California with little hope of recovery. Her work and Max were all she had.

And so, she would protect what was hers. The only way she knew how.

Eight

CEE CEE WAS LOOKING forward to the gathering of her fellow cops, even with Max in tow, because it would alleviate the awkward tension building between them and help her work out her frustration over her dead-end case.

Dovion was raising holy hell about the body mix-up. When he'd asked her if she knew anything about it, she'd regarded him with a steady stare and told him no, she didn't. She promised to follow up and see what she could find out with her investigation into the John Doe's death that, as LaRoche had predicted, was going nowhere.

She'd returned to the apartment the next day to find it professionally swept clean of belongings and blood. The window had been replaced. None of the neighbors had seen or heard anything, or knew anything about Tito except his habit of playing the horn at all hours. He had no written lease and paid his bills in cash or money orders.

When the dark-haired girl didn't show up for her bar shift, her boss had shrugged and given the hours to another. Her type came and went without notice all the time, he told Cee Cee.

How did one find a ghost, a shadow existing on the wind of indifference? How hard could she push for a truth that no one wanted revealed? She was down to pursuing leads as thin as cobwebs, waiting for the ax to fall on her case.

And for the past three days, she'd been walking on eggshells with Max. She didn't know what to do, how to act. He was a distracted, restless, short-fused stranger who treated her with polite caution—when he was around. He stayed in the city later each night. When he arrived at the house he prowled, unable to settle down. The staff avoided him as obviously as he avoided her.

They didn't share any meals; he was gone before she awoke. They almost didn't share a bed. He'd lie on his side until she drifted off to sleep, then he was gone. She didn't ask where; he didn't offer an explanation. He'd slip back into the room close to dawn, shower, and slide in beside her, exhausted. Only then would he turn to her, cradling her in his arms, his face buried in her hair. The absences and showers suggested another woman, but she couldn't quite believe that. Because he loved her so, and because the tension came home with him. But he was too fatigued to find release with her.

She was considering staying at her apartment.

Just for a while.

She'd almost convince herself that it would be best for both of them, when she'd glance up and catch Max staring at her. And before he could shove his impassive mask back in place, she'd see the puppyish adoration softening his gaze and the small, hungry curve of his sly-dog smile. And she'd remember his heroic rescue of her in a dirty alley, with the low, seismic rumble of his voice claiming, "I came back because I smelled your perfume." And his quiet vow of "You're my every dream" that turned her impenetrable warrior's heart into mush.

Then there were those damned flowers wilting on the nightstand, because tears came to her eyes every time she tried to throw them away. She even saved the petals that fell.

And if she were gone, who would have his back?

"You make me crazy, Savoie," she grumbled now.

"What?"

He had his head in his huge closet, anxiously going through his *GQ* wardrobe before the cookout at the Babineau's. He leaned back to regard her with lifted brows.

"The navy Prada pinstripe, I think. That should make them all feel inadequate as men and providers."

He stared at her for a long moment. "You're not helping, Charlotte. I've never been to something like this before. Is there a theme?"

She looked blank. "A theme?" A huge laugh. "A theme! Geez, Savoie, did you spend all your afternoons watching the Lifetime channel?" When his eyelids drooped dangerously, she shrugged. "Beer, cigars, sweat, and softball."

"Ah. Debauchery. Nice theme."

"We like it."

As he bent over to rummage through his bottom dresser drawer, she eyed his bottom, clad in snug knit briefs. She hooked a finger beneath the waistband to snap the elastic.

"This is a nice look."

He glowered at her over his shoulder. "I'm sure the spouses and significant others would enjoy it."

"Hmmm. Maybe too much. You're one dish I don't care to share."

He snorted and grabbed loose khaki cargo pants to tug up over his long legs and very nice butt. "Let's not tempt the unwise then, shall we?"

"Too late," she murmured. She couldn't help herself. Her palms skimmed up his ribs and she leaned in closer. He'd just gotten out of the shower. Moisture curled his black hair against the back of his neck and beaded on his skin. She caught a droplet with her tongue and chased it up to its place of origin near his shoulder. He froze.

"Detective, we're running late." His tone was steady, even if his breathing was not.

"They'll wait. I'm bringing the beer. That's always my job since I can't cook worth a damn."

"You can't cook?" He slid quickly away and pulled on a black and gold Saints muscle shirt.

"Have you ever seen me indulge in any domesticity?"

He stared for a minute. "No."

"There you go. I consider it a civic duty to help support my neighborhood take-out establishments." She tapped his chest. "The Saints are a football team."

"Oh." He looked bewildered. "Should I change it?"

She patted him, chuckling. "Max, have you ever seen a baseball game?"

"No. I ran a search on the Internet yesterday to read up on it, so I wouldn't embarrass myself. Just in case someone asks me a question. Fellas are supposed to know about sports, right?"

She traced the fleur-de-lis on his chest, because she liked the feel of him beneath the cotton. "Relax. After a few, the guys won't remember what they're playing anyway."

He smiled faintly but still looked nervous. Then his gaze swept over her. She was wearing tight baseball pants that ended just below the knee and a sports bra. A dangerous expanse of toned tawny skin was left bare between. The ball cap perched jauntily on her head pictured a crawfish and the slogan "Shuck Me, Suck Me, Eat Me Raw."

Max lifted an eyebrow. "Is that what you're wearing? Do any of the spouses or significant others not want to run you over with their minivans, detective?"

"What?" She gripped the bill of her hat defensively. "I won this in a departmental shucking contest. I'm proud of it."

"Dare I ask what you were shucking?"

She made a face. "You can ask."

His smile burst sudden and wide, and before she could react he pulled her up for a long, wet kiss. Somehow in the middle of their tongue tangling, he managed to ease the hat from her head and toss it into his closet. When she finally rocked down from her toes, she kept her fingers locked behind his head.

"What was that for?" she panted.

"Thanks for letting me come with you."

"You can come with me anytime. Actually, I prefer it when you do."

He grinned. "And I let you kiss me with that mouth?"

"You let me do more than *that* with it."

She snagged an oversized tee shirt out of her side of the drawer, and Max was pleased to see that it covered the way the snug pants cupped her butt. He didn't want anyone in his dish, either. And it covered the bruises on her arms.

"Let's go." she said. "You're buying the beer. And you owe me a new hat."

THE BABINEAU FAMILY bought into a quiet neighborhood on a cul-de-sac with an easy commute to the city. A small house, a small lawn with a swing set, and a big mortgage. The detective had lots of plans for it and for his little family, including a garage and a family-room extension for a big-screen TV and ESPN. Modest dreams for a modest man. His pretty young wife, Tina, loved it because her son's school was right across the street.

A huge gas grill had been dragged into the driveway, surrounded by a motley assortment of lawn chairs. The men loitered out on the concrete, while the women stayed in the shade of the carport.

Their hostess hurried down the sloped drive to meet them. "Cee Cee. Max, I'm glad you could make it." Because she was intimidated by her husband's bristly partner, she took Max's arm and hustled him up to where conversation had stopped. "Have y'all met Cee Cee's boyfriend, Max?"

Cold, sniper-scope stares fixed on him.

"Yeah, we know him," Junior Hammond muttered.

Feeling about as welcome as a communicable disease, Max said, "I'll get the beer." Maybe if he was bearing gifts, they wouldn't be so apt to lynch him under the basketball hoop.

When he set the cases down next to an ice-filled garbage can lined with plastic, Babineau gave a whistle.

"Imported. Are you trying to raise our standards, Ceece?"

She shrugged. "Max grabbed them for me."

Again the cool glares.

The wrong shirt, and now the wrong beer. The day was going to hell fast.

Their dislike of him didn't extend so far as to decline his offering, though. Even though it was only 10:30 a.m., the first case was quickly pillaged. When Cee Cee was drawn into an admiration society of a younger detective's new Sig Sauer, Max hung back. He didn't like guns. All he knew about them was that they were ruthlessly efficient in killing those he'd loved.

Then he spotted a familiar face: Devlin Dovion was basting ribs on the triburner grill. He was invited to all the departmental outings because no one made a better sauce, but he left the athletics to the younger men. A hit-and-run while he was tending a crime scene left him with rebuilt parts that worked better on some days than others. On the good days, he preferred not to push his luck. He looked strangely normal in his shorts, despite the scars crisscrossing his knees. His grillmeister shirt proclaimed "If you can't stand the heat, get me another beer."

Taking that as good advice, Max popped a cap with his teeth and carried it over to investigate the thick slabs of meat and bone.

"Anyone I know?"

Dovion grinned at him. "I leave my work at the office." He took the beer and nodded at the label. "Nice. Better than we deserve. Thanks."

Max lingered awkwardly, then finally asked, "Anything I can do?"

"You can chop up those vegetables for the sauce." Dovion passed him a wicked chef's knife, then watched in bemusement as Max sliced and diced his way through the peppers, onions, and tomatoes with rapid staccato that would have done K-Paul proud. "You learn that watching the Food Channel?"

The blade paused. Max frowned slightly. "I'm not sure we had a television. I don't recall ever watching one."

"No great loss there."

"I used to help my mama in the kitchen when I was a boy." Again he paused, surprised he'd volunteered the information.

"How old were you when she passed, Max?"

"Four, maybe five. I didn't have a lot of time to gather up memories, so I hang on to the ones I have as tight as I can." He scraped the veggies into the butter and spices Dovion had sizzling, and gave them a stir.

"At least you won't starve to death waiting for Charlotte to cook you something. I'm not convinced she knows how to turn a stove on."

Max didn't look up from the sautéeing vegetables. "Good thing for me she's got other talents."

"I wouldn't have thought compromise was one of 'em." When Max glanced at him, he added, "You being who you are, and she being what she is."

"It's what makes life interesting."

"Did you get your friend taken care of?"

Max stopped stirring. His expression was carefully neutral. " 'Cuse me?"

Dovion regarded him with annoyance. "Charlotte doesn't bend rules for anyone—except you. And I can't think of any other reason why she might tell me a lie right to my face. That's not going to become a bad habit, is it?"

"No."

"Good. I'd hate to see a fine career diminished. Don't draw her into what you're involved in, Max. And I'm not talking about Legere's business."

"What, then?"

"It must be something, or you wouldn't look like I was about to baste you over this flame."

Max said nothing. His silence spoke louder.

"I'm not stupid, Savoie. I know there's something . . . different about you and your new associates. As a scientist, I've been curious long before your handiwork started showing up on my tables, with that strange DNA and bite radius that can't be classified. Someday soon I'm going to want those explanations."

"I don't know that I'll have any for you."

"Don't force me to get them from Charlotte. Officially." Dovion flipped the ribs, then gave Max a long, somber look. "I'll let her know if any more unexplained cases come through. I'll let her decide whether or not you need to know. Unless you want to talk to me now." He waited a bit. "Didn't think so."

Max smiled faintly and moved away from the only person he might have enjoyed having a conversation with. He faded back, blending as he'd been taught until almost invisible. He observed how relaxed and comfortable Cee Cee was with her coworkers as they laughed over some joke. Pride in her warmed through him like the Tabasco Dovion was adding liberally to his sauce.

The last thing he wanted to do was pull her out of that packlike circle of camaraderie. And the last thing they were going to do was include him in it. Even Cee Cee was shutting him out, maybe or maybe not on purpose.

He couldn't blame her for seeking out more congenial company. His had been far from pleasant lately. As he watched her interact with her friends, he understood how important that was to her, this chance to unwind and bond with those who had her back any day or night of the week.

He glanced at the resigned cluster of women relegated to the shade and saw their acceptance of it, too. He chuckled softly. He'd just joined the ranks of spouses or significant others.

When he stepped into their territory, they looked at him in alarm. If they hadn't had anything in common before, they did in their immediate objection to him.

"Ladies, can I get you anything?" he asked with a polite smile.

Some murmured no-thank-yous. Some glared.

One had the temerity to spit, "You can get the hell out of here."

"Becky," another warned in a whisper.

As if the woman's angry words were going to send him on a rampage right in Alain Babineau's carport? What kind of monster did they think Charlotte had brought into their midst?

He had his answer as Becky said fiercely, "We know who you are and who you worked for. Maybe you were there when Jimmy Legere had my brother killed. Maybe you were the one who saw to it personally."

Very quietly, very respectfully, he told them, "I'm sorry. Please forgive me for upsetting you. That wasn't my intention." He backed out holding the woman's furious stare with the sincerity of his own.

Charlotte had been right to try to keep her affair with him separate from her daily life. To push his way in would only hurt her and frustrate him. He'd been wrong to cross that line, to ask her to do the same.

Dovion's words haunted him. He should never have involved her in that business with Tito. He should have found another way, and would have if he'd been thinking clearly. That was the problem: It was a struggle to consider, to focus, to evaluate with this churn of raw emotions throwing everything out of proper proportion.

Things were fracturing between him and Charlotte. He didn't know what to do, how to fix it, how to hold on. How to let go.

More weary than he'd ever been in his life, Max sat on one of the swing set's plastic seats and rocked slowly to and fro with the flex of his knees. Where no one could see him, he let his shoulders slump and his head hang low as the familiar headache began to pound behind his closed eyes.

"It's hard, isn't it?"

The sound of Tina Babineau's voice almost made him jump out of his sneakers. He hadn't heard her approach. He glanced to where she sat on the next swing, facing the opposite direction.

"What is?"

"Being the outsider."

He didn't respond. What would this pretty little detective's wife know about that?

She smiled wryly, as if she could hear his cynical thought. "My dad was career military. We moved every couple of years. New town, new school, new house, new everything. Just when you'd start feeling like you fit in, you'd be hauling the packing boxes out again. I'm the new face in this group, and I don't know how to get them to like me."

She could probably start by not sitting next to him.

"Is that so important? Them liking you?"

"It is to Alain."

"Isn't it enough for you just to be his wife?"

She smiled. "Now you sound like him."

"God forbid," he muttered. He looked at her lovely face, warm expression, and soft eyes. "What's not to like about you?"

"They're a tough group to break into. They trust each other with their fears and their pain. I don't think they believe I can cut it."

"I think you'll surprise them."

"*You* surprised them by showing up here." Those quiet, dark eyes shifted away. "Inviting you was a bit of selfishness on my part."

"So you'd have someone to play with on the swings?"

"It's because of Cee Cee," she admitted in a sudden burst.

"What is?"

"Alain denies it, but I didn't believe him at first." Max went cold inside. "What?"

"That they are . . . were having an affair."

"Were they?" Then softer, "Are they?"

She smiled at him. "No, it was just me being insecure. And now that I see you with her, I know he was telling me the truth."

"There you are."

The sound of Cee Cee's voice had Max's head snapping about before he had control of his expression.

She stopped with a jerk, startled by whatever she saw in his face. Her gaze shifted, seeing Tina Babineau's hand resting familiarly on his thigh, and her tone cooled.

"I've been looking for you."

"You must not have been looking very hard, unless you thought I was inside stealing the silverware."

She didn't smile. "Tina, Dovion is looking for something to serve his ribs up in."

The conscientious hostess, Tina was instantly up. Her hand touched lightly on Max's shoulder. "It was nice talking to you, Max."

He returned her smile guardedly. "Yes."

After she'd gone, Cee Cee was instantly on him with a silky, "And what were the two of you so cozy about?"

"Just discussing spouse and significant-other things." His bland tone suggested nothing more would be forthcoming.

She moved behind him, setting her hands on the tense line of his shoulders. She kneaded gently, then firmly, until he couldn't help but moan at the pleasure.

"I didn't mean to ignore you," came her quiet apology as her clever fingers massaged the base of his skull.

His eyes closed. "Were you?"

"Once Benny starts telling a story, it's hard to get away. It's seems like you've found a friend, though."

He made a soft sound of agreement, because words would have interrupted the soothing ripples made by her magic touch.

"What were you and Dev talking about?

"Cooking."

She was silent for a moment, just working his tight muscles. Then came a surprisingly genuine offer. "We don't have to stay. We can go, if you like."

As tempting as that sounded, it wasn't quite as compelling as the restorative enjoyment in her laugh as she hung out with her peers. "Then who would cheer you on in your athletic endeavors?"

"Unlike the rest of them, I don't need an athletic supporter."

He tipped back his head to catch her smile. The sight of it made his heart do a funny little flip-flop, and he was poignantly aware of how rarely he'd seen her actually happy with all barriers down. "We can stay."

She came down for a slow, sweet taste of his mouth. "They'll warm up to you, baby."

"Sure. With torches, while Dovion turns me over a fire."

As she chuckled and stepped back, he suddenly felt a prickle riding lightly along the surface of his skin, like a mild electric shock.

"Come on, Savoie. Lunch is ready."

"I'll be right there."

She hesitated, studying his expression. "Everything okay?"

"Hey, Ceece," Babineau hollered from the side yard. "Any more beer?"

"I'm fine," Max told her. "There's another two cases in the trunk. Want me to get them?"

"I've got it. I love you, baby."

She said that easily now, without thought or effort. And he smiled.

He waited until she was gone. Then he closed his eyes, let himself empty of exterior distraction, and reached out with a very light mental touch.

His eyes flashed open, and quickly scanned the small hedged-in backyard. He got off the swing and moved slowly, casually toward the far corner of the house. There, he crouched down slightly to peer under the raised deck.

"Heya."

A boy regarded him from where he was seated in the shadows. He was young, maybe ten, eleven.

"I'm Max. And you are?"

"Oscar."

"Oscar." He smiled. "Babineau?"

"He's my mother's husband. Now that's my name, too."

That may have been his name—but that was hardly all he was.

Nine

MAX SAT ON the steps leading up to the deck, waiting for the gangly boy to crawl out of his burrow to regard him with cautious, curious eyes.

"Not much for parties?"

The boy stared at him solemnly.

"Not much fun when there's no one like you, who understands you."

With a heartbreaking simplicity, the boy told him, "There's no one like me."

Max smiled slowly. "I am. I'm like you."

He looked uncertain, suspicious. "Are you crazy, too?"

"No." He hung on very carefully to his anger. "I'm different, Oscar. And there's nothing wrong with that. Nothing."

He watched the boy process that information, mulling it over, struggling between what he'd been told and what he wanted to believe.

"Let me have your hand, Oscar."

He took the small, fragile hand in his, holding it lightly so the boy could pull away if he chose. Holding the tentative gaze with his, Max bent to quickly snuffle up his scent. Though the boy seemed alarmed at first, he didn't jerk away. And after a long moment, he leaned hesitantly to sniff at Max's palm.

"There," Max concluded. "Now we will always recognize one another, even before we're in sight."

"Max?"

He turned toward the sound of Cee Cee's voice, and when he looked back the boy had disappeared.

"Hey, come on. If you turn your back on this lot for more than five seconds, all you'll have left is a platter of bones."

Funny, he mused; that's probably the same way they viewed him.

Wonderfully spicy smells emanated from Dovion's stack of ribs beside a table groaning with food. The departmental clique broke up as officers went to sit with their wives and girlfriends. Cee Cee stuck Max with balancing their plates as she piled on everything the heavy cardboard could hold. A potluck pro, she'd tucked their napkin-wrapped utensils down the cleavage of her sports bra to leave her hands free.

As Max stepped around the corner of the table, Junior Hammond was suddenly in his path.

It could have been an accident.

Somehow Junior managed to knock up against the bottom of both plates, sending them flying. But before the surly detective could have his laugh, Max had caught the plates with enough speed and agility to have every last morsel, from pea salad to potato chips, right back where it started.

Junior stared at the plates, mouth ajar.

" 'Cuse me," Max murmured, executing a sharp turn that brought his elbow in contact with Junior's beer, leaving the disgruntled bully wiping off his shirt.

Cee Cee steered them to the concrete front-porch steps, where they sat close to but separated from the loud group gathered in the drive.

He knew she was watching him, puzzled, unbearably curious, worried by whatever she'd seen in his expression. But he couldn't talk to her about it. Not here. Not yet.

He ate what was in front of him, quickly, efficiently, because it was there, because he'd been hungry once before. And while he did, he studied Cee Cee's friends and associates with a complicated covetousness of what was missing from his life.

He saw camaraderie, trust, family; simple things that rang huge and unattainable in the cavern of his soul. Things he thought of, dreamed of, knew nothing about. But wanted—desperately.

These weren't his unnatural clansmen, who'd gathered on his lawn with their feral cycs and carnivorous females. These were men and women, amazing to him because they were so ordinary in the way they went from day to day. Happy, belonging, decent, admired. Their enviable state was out of his reach because of who he was, because of what he was. Charlotte could thrust him into the middle of that all-American setting all she wanted, but he'd never fit, he'd never be included. And that knowledge cut deep and keen to the heart of him.

"You've got some sauce on you."

"What?" His attention came back to Cee Cee. He reached for his face, but she stilled his hand.

"I'll get it."

The feel of her tongue flicking across the corner of his mouth shocked him into immobility, a fact she cleverly took advantage of.

"Oops, missed a spot."

Her lips fit to his, providing a sizzle of heat equal to Dovion's sauce. Then she laid her cheek on his shoulder with a quiet sigh. The cheek carefully dabbed with cosmetics to cover the fading bruise.

"Thank you for being here with me. I figured I'd always be the only one who came to these things alone. And now I have you."

Because her tone was so poignant, he made his reply light and teasing. "And I'm such a prize."

Her hands rubbed up and down his back and arm. "Yes, you are. Those clucking hens must be squirmingly jealous of my hot boyfriend. I'll bet they're dying to know what it's like to go to bed with someone so sexy and powerful and rich and dangerous."

"Would you like me to do them all, to relieve their curiosity? I will, if that's a sacrifice our relationship demands of me."

She chuckled and squeezed him tight. "No, I

don't think so. Let them wonder. You're my dish. I plan to take you home to enjoy all by myself, down to the very last drop." She made a smacking sound with her lips that created an uncomfortable tightness at the crotch of his pants.

Though he was smiling, he murmured, "If you wanted to fit in with them, you should have chosen a boyfriend who was a bit more . . . conservative."

She leaned back, keeping her hands on him. "Are you disagreeing with my choice?"

"Not at all, detective. You know I defer to your wisdom on all things."

"Oh, bullshit. Since when?" Smiling, she added, "Besides, there's nothing I like better than the way you fit me."

That's exactly what he needed to hear to make all the tension melt away. Until Alain Babineau approached them.

"Hey, Ceece, grab your glove. We need to warm up before the vice team gets here, so maybe they won't kick our asses so badly this time." He moved on to load up the cooler with the rest of the beer and join the migration across the street to the school's baseball diamond.

Tina met them as they reached the road. She touched Max's arm lightly. "I'm sorry for what Becky said to you."

Cee Cee's head snapped around. "What did she say? Max? What did she say to you?"

"It's not important."

Tina's grip tightened. "I just wanted to let you know that not everyone feels that way."

Max smiled thinly. "Yes, they do. You don't have to apologize for them."

"I think she should apologize to you. I don't appreciate rudeness in my home."

"*What?* What's going on?" Cee Cee's gaze flew between Tina's surprisingly tough expression and Max's look of dismay.

"No," he said quickly. "Please let it go. She had every right to say what she did. It's okay."

Tina sighed in aggravation. "It isn't, but I'll let it go. This time."

Gaping after her, Cee Cee then rounded on Max. "What did that bitch say to you? Don't make me have to go knock it out of her."

He gripped her shoulders, hard. "No. You'll do no such thing. Not when she was only speaking the truth."

He watched realization dawn on her face with unpleasant clarity. "Becky's brother." She hesitated, but had to ask. "Have you killed cops for Jimmy Legere?"

He saw her horror, her sudden panic, and he wanted badly to lie to erase that ugly suspicion. But he couldn't.

"I don't know, Charlotte. When I was younger, I never asked any questions." Not until her. "I'm sorry I don't have a better answer."

She took a step back, whirled, and ran to join her teammates.

He followed more slowly. Why had he insisted on coming here? What had he thought to prove? He should have heeded Cee Cee's warning. But he'd wanted so desperately to participate with her in something normal, something not life or death or weighted with moral consequences.

And what had he brought to the party along with the imported beer? Suspicion and remembered pain. And Charlotte was looking at him the same way. As an outsider.

The spouses and significant others sat in a tight cluster halfway up the bleachers. Figuring they wouldn't care to have him next to them, or worse, behind them, he sat on the front row. When he saw Tina start to get up, he lifted a subtle staying hand.

Sitting alone, he took a solemn joy in watching Charlotte. Tall, strong, and the athletic equal of any of the men on the field, she moved with unhesitating confidence at her position as shortstop. She dove in fearlessly to field ground balls, whipping them powerfully to the appropriate base, clapping and calling encouragement to her teammates. A warm curl of lustful appreciation wound through him, and a slight smile curved his lips.

Awareness of someone beside him was a startling surprise. He glanced down to see Oscar Babineau seated on his left, but was careful not to show any sign of reaction.

"Heya. You like baseball?"

"This is softball. A baseball is smaller and harder."

"Oh." Who knew?

"Do you belong to Detective Caissie?"

He canted a look at the boy, who appeared to be watching the warm-up. "That's an odd way to put it, but yes, I do. We belong to each other." He started feeling better, having said that out loud. "Do you know Detective Caissie?"

"She comes over sometimes. She's pretty."

"I think so, too."

They watched the team work for a while, then Oscar asked, "Did you mean what you said? About us being the same?"

"I always mean what I say." He touched him with a light mental glimmer, just a gentle whisper to see if the boy was ready for it.

The return push struck the breath from him. Strong, direct, and unschooled. The same way his had been when he was young.

"I'm sorry. I didn't mean to hurt you." Oscar shrank back, his eyes round with alarm and regret.

Max managed a smile as he struggled to steady his senses. "It's all right. Not so hard next time. Don't force it."

The boy's amazement didn't dull. "I could feel you—here, on the inside."

Max glanced up at Tina who was watching her husband with an adoring gaze. "Do your mother and father know what you can do?"

"They don't want me to be different. I have to take pills that make me want to sleep all the time. Sometimes I throw them away. Please don't tell my mama. It would make her cry, and him mad."

"I won't. You have my promise. And I want you to promise something, too. Don't let anyone see what you can do. Keep it quiet, hidden. Can you do that?"

He nodded, then looked up as Cee Cee jogged over to them.

"Hey, Ozzy."

"Hey, Detective Caissie."

"I didn't know you two knew each other." She glanced from the boy to Max.

"We met a little while ago and are getting better acquainted."

"You've got my sunglasses." Her tone was brusque, her gaze avoiding his as he fished in his shirt pocket for his Ray-Bans—which, like many other of his belongings, had somehow become hers. The way he had become hers.

Passing them to her, his fingertips slid over the back of her hand. She didn't pull away. And slowly, her wounded stare met his.

He held her gaze and said quietly, "I can't change what I am or what I've done."

Slowly, she reached out to touch his cheek. "I know. But I'm going to need some time to get on top of this. Okay?"

"Sure."

And as she straightened, her stare lifted to meet Becky Rossiter's with a .40-caliber intensity.

Max watched her rejoin the other players, his mood heavy.

"Does she know you're different?"

Max glanced at the boy and smiled. Ozzy had Tina's delicate build, brown hair, and large dark eyes. "Yes, she knows what I am. And she loves me in spite of it. Or because of it. A little of both, I guess. If you're in trouble, if you're afraid, you can go to her. You can trust her. You can tell her anything. Okay?"

The boy nodded.

The opposing team arrived, a rough and motley-looking bunch of undercover operatives who remembered Max from a botched sting to get weapons Jimmy was allegedly moving south of the border. Their pride still hadn't recovered from the slick way Legere had wiggled out from under their meticulous months of surveillance and setup. And they knew that was because Max Savoie had somehow, uncannily, managed to I.D. their inside man. Who had then disappeared.

The fact that Charlotte Caissie was banging Savoie wasn't news. Not when it had been all over the news. That she'd drop him right in their laps to rub their noses in it was something else altogether. And as they began to play, his presence amped up the rivalry between the two units, with the unfriendly focus centering on Detective Caissie.

She snatched up a low ground ball and was whirling to rifle it to second base. It could have been unintentional, the way a train runs over someone unwisely on the tracks. Only trains don't jump the rail to ensure impact.

The collision between her and the baserunner almost knocked Cee Cee out of her shoes. She saw a great deal of spinning sky, then the hard-packed ground knocked the wind out of her. It took her a long, panicked moment to suck oxygen back in, and by then the faces of her teammates swam above her.

"Don't move," was Babineau's advice. Since she couldn't, she took it.

"While you're up, could you get me a beer?" she wheezed with a strained smile. Because she was beginning to realize that more than her wind had been crippled.

"You took one helluva knock," he said.

"Yeah, someone forgot to tell Showboat this isn't a full contact sport." She flipped up a finger at the big vice detective who was stupidly smirking as Max came to kneel down beside her. He reached without hesitation for her left ankle and was almost kicked in the face as pain spasmed up her leg. "Geez, Savoie, stop your prodding!"

Because he was touching her with extreme care, and knew a growl of bravado when he heard it, Max paid no attention as he unlaced her shoe and peeled off her sock.

"Maybe you shoulda told him that a few months back, Caissie," Stan Schoenbaum drawled.

Max's gaze lifted slowly, his eyes hard chips of pale jade. "What did you say?"

Schoenbaum was already turning away, chuckling over his remark with his buddies.

Seeing his body coil, Cee Cee grabbed his arm. "Max, he's just an asshole. Ignore him. That's what we all do. Help me up. Max."

He shifted his attention back to her, but she could feel the tension building even as he curled her arm around his shoulder and stood with her. The instant she tried touching her foot to the ground, huge waves of pain threatened to take her under. She couldn't even protest when Max lifted her gently into his arms to carry her to the bleachers, where Dovion was waiting with improvised ice packs from the beer tub. She sucked air and gripped Max's shoulder while Dovion examined her ankle, then, pronouncing it a probable sprain, wrapped it tight and put her on ice.

"Looks like you're one run down and a couple men short," Schoenbaum taunted from midfield. "I say that because Caissie is probably twice the man as most of you."

When Cee Cee started up, Babineau pressed her back down with a firm hand. "He's not worth it, Ceece. We'll get 'em next time." His tone dropped to a fierce rumble. "But I would love to shove those words right down that bastard's throat."

"I'll play."

Cee Cee and Babineau looked to Max in surprise.

"I'll finish the game for her. Is that allowed?"

Babineau saw the blood in his eyes and smiled thinly. He called to the other team, "Savoie wants to know if he can take the field. Whaddaya think?"

Max Savoie within reach, where accidents could happen . . .

"Let him play," Schoenbaum yelled back with a cunning smile.

"Okay," Max said, setting Cee Cee's NOPD hat on his head and reclaiming his sunglasses. "What do I do?"

While Cee Cee hesitated, Babineau nodded to the field. "Get the ball to the base before the runner. Catch it before it hits the ground if you can. Three outs, we're up."

"I can do that."

"Max?" Cee Cee gripped his arm, her concern telegraphed in the pinch of her fingers. "Don't hurt anybody."

Her few words spoke volumes. For the past week he'd been on the edge of restraint, sizzling like the delayed fuse on an explosive. If he let go here, in front of her team, in front of an audience not of his kind, the blast would have consequences beyond her ability to do damage control.

"Just a friendly game, right?" He smiled in a not-so-friendly fashion before following Babineau out to the field.

The first hit was a short pop-up. Max timed it out and went back to get under it, readying for an easy catch when, out of the corner of his eye, he caught movement. Junior Hammond rushed in from covering second base and rammed him like a linebacker. As Max staggered, Hammond gave him a hard elbow to the face under the pretext of reaching for the ball. The ball dropped to the grass between them and the runner held at first.

"Pay attention," Hammond growled. "If you don't know how the game's played, get off the field."

Max wiped the blood from the corner of his mouth and smiled wolfishly. "I'm getting a pretty good idea of how to play. I think I'll like this game."

The next hit took a high bounce just beyond the reach of the pitcher's glove. Max leapt high to bring it down, then ran it to second just for the sheer joy of shoving Hammond out of the way as he stepped on the bag, then fired the ball to first for a double play. Then Max put down his hand to help Junior off his butt. He wasn't terribly surprised when the man spat in his palm. Max wiped his hand on the back of Hammond's shirt under the guise of a no-hard-feelings pat.

A bouncing ball to the pitcher, a quick throw, and the top of the inning was over. As they changed positions, every member of the vice team went out of his way to slam into Max in passing. By the time he rejoined Cee Cee on the bench, she was fuming.

As excited as a first-time Little Leaguer, Max was

too pumped to notice her fury. "Did you see my throw? I got two outs."

"Those *bastards*."

"All we need are two runs and we win. Think I'll be able to hit the ball?" Then his expression went flat. "What? Did I do something wrong?"

We. She choked on the word. There was no *we*. There was them versus Max, her guys included.

She squeezed the hand he slipped over hers. "You did just fine. *Very* hot. I want you now."

He grinned wide. "Do I have to ice down more than just your ankle?"

She didn't think there were enough cubes in the beer tub to cool down her temper. She was watching Stan "Showboat" Schoenbaum stir up an ugly mood. Stan, who never got over being steamed when she wouldn't give him a tumble, despite the fact that he was married. Time for him to get fricking over it. But not at Max's expense.

Max was studying the first batter, measuring his stance, the angle of his shoulders, the arc of his swing as if his ability to mimic what he saw was the most important thing he'd ever do.

Cee Cee watched the pitcher deliberately throw outside the strike zone, walking the first batter, then the second, followed by two quick outs. Then she understood: They wanted Max to take the final pitch of the game. They were setting him up for a fall, and she didn't like it.

"Max." She put her hand on his arm, needing to

put an end to things before there was trouble. So far it was just an exchange of male aggression, physical but not dangerous. Max's adrenaline seemed safely channeled by the rough-and-tumble competition, but the way he was lately, that could end in an instant.

"Savoie, you're up."

When her grip tightened, he glanced at her impatiently. "How far do I have to hit the ball to get both runners in?"

Shit.

"Drop it in over by the teeter-totters. That should do it."

"When I win the game, I'm going to expect you to plant a big, wet one right here." He tapped his mouth with two fingers.

She didn't smile. "Be careful."

His brow furrowed. "This is softball, not roller derby."

"Today it is. Watch yourself. Knock it a mile, then let them bring it in. You don't have to run the bases."

He stared at her. "But this is the only chance I'll ever get to do it."

Her anxious heart melted. "Then bring it home, baby. I'll be waiting right here with that kiss."

"Be back in a minute."

He loped over to home plate, squaring up the way he'd seen the other players do.

"Where do you want it, Savoie?" the pitcher

called with the pleasant malice of an executioner asking head or heart.

Max took a practice swing. "Right about here. Be gentle with me. I'm a virgin."

"That's more than some of us can say," Schoenbaum hollared from centerfield.

When Max straightened in offense, the ball went whizzing by.

"Strike."

Feeling foolish for letting them pull him off, Max concentrated, measuring the distance to the teeter-totters. The runners were taking cautious leads from their bases. He was conscious of Cee Cee's attention, and he wanted to claim that kiss just a little bit more than he wanted to cram the bat down Schoenbaum's throat.

The ball came in like a bullet, almost taking out a kidney as he took a fast hop forward to avoid being hit.

"Come on, Streeter," Cee Cee shouted from the bench. "Don't make me limp out there and beat the crap out of you."

Max calmly changed sides at the plate, taking a checked swing as a southpaw. "Is this better for you?" he called to the clearly startled pitcher. He measured the distance to the playground one more time, almost tasting that kiss.

He saw the perfect pitch coming. He waited for it . . . swung . . . and connected with an explosion of sound. As the runners tore madly around the bases, he simply watched the ball sail unerringly to hit the high end of the teeter-totter, dropping that side to the ground. Then, with a satisfied smirk, he started around bases at an unhurried trot, the sound of loud whistles and cheers at his back. Not for him, of course, but for the runners rounding third and heading home. And that was okay.

The outfielder finally came up with the ball, and threw with all his might for a relay that would never be in time. The tying run crossed the plate as Max started away from second. Schoenbaum whipped around and rifled the ball right at the back of Max's head.

He heard it coming and turned into it, his hand going up to catch the ball inches from his face. He gave it a slight toss to the dirt and glanced at Schoenbaum with a icy disdain. "Not very sportsmanlike."

"And how sporting was the way you took out Freddie Peyton? Where did you dump his body after you tore out his heart, Savoie? I'm going to put yours right next to it."

Ten

MAX WAITED FOR his charge, and caught Schoenbaum's fist the same way he'd stopped the ball. He
squeezed hard, until pain flickered behind the rage
in the other's face. Then Max put his face up close
and personal.

"You got a problem with me, you come to me.
You don't blindside Detective Caissie like a sneaky
little coward."

"That's your doing, Savoie. No one trusts her.
No one's going to cover her back."

Max's hand went to Schoenbaum's jaw, lifting him up onto his toes. He could feel his blood
heating, beginning that fierce, savage rhythm, and
should have just let it go. But he couldn't. "If anything happens to her out there on the streets where
you're supposed to protect her, they'll be wondering
where *you're* buried."

"Are you threatening me?"

"No."

Because he'd promised Charlotte he wouldn't
hurt anyone, he shoved hard, sending Schoenbaum
reeling backward as he turned away.

"Who's the coward?" Schoenbaum taunted. "Me, for doing my job, or you for hiding behind that tough guy wannabe in a skirt who traded her respect to spread her legs for the likes of you?"

Max came around fast, ducking his punch, driving in low to smack his elbow into the other man's ribs. When Schoenbaum doubled over, he brought his knee up into his face, then danced lightly back on the balls of his feet in fierce amusement.

"Are you sure you want me to embarrass you like this in front of all your friends? I thought a stun gun and someone half your size was more your style."

He'd recognized Schoenbaum by scent, the minute he'd gotten up close to him. He'd been a year or two younger than Oscar Babineau when Schoenbaum, then just a beat cop, and two of his pals grabbed him up as he was leaving St. Louis No. 1 cemetery, where he'd been sitting with his mama while Jimmy attended the burial of a business associate. It was a rare occasion for him to be caught alone.

They smelled of liquor and violence. Jimmy had always told him never to fight back against the police or give them any reason for trouble. He hadn't been afraid; he hadn't been doing anything. But apparently they didn't need a reason to zap him with enough volts to have him jerking, drooling, and compliant. They'd tossed him into the back of their squad car, drove him way the hell out in the middle of nowhere, and took turns beating him as a substitute for the hated Jimmy Legere. They'd laughed as he crawled away, throwing their empty beer and liquor bottles at him. Considering how drunk they were, they'd been surprisingly accurate with their aim. And then they'd driven off.

The Taser had scrambled his nervous system; he hadn't been able to shift or heal himself. So he'd hidden in the darkness and slowly made his way home, managing to creep up onto the porch at daybreak. In shock, disoriented, he wouldn't let anyone come near him. He'd wedged himself under the porch glider until Jimmy came racing back from the city, where he'd been frantically combing the streets in search of him. He'd been coaxed from hiding to wind himself about Jimmy's feet.

Jimmy never said a word, carrying him inside, cleaning him up, keeping him quiet until he finally managed to throw off the brutal damage done. When Max had asked why they had done such awful things, Jimmy responded, because they could. And they would, if they thought they could get away with it. It had been Max's introduction to the police.

Max had thought Jimmy had forgotten about the incident, until he'd taken the scent of the undercover Freddie Peyton and told Jimmy that he was not who he pretended to be. Jimmy had used the broken end of a whiskey bottle to carve up the officer like a Thanksgiving turkey. Not because he'd infiltrated Jimmy's organization, but because he'd made a broken and bleeding child cower under a glider, waiting for him to come home.

And now it was time for Max to take care of his own business.

The rest of the vice team gathered in a loose circle around them. On his belly in the grass, Schoenbaum nodded to his unit.

Cee Cee came off the bench as the bat cracked against the back of Max's head, then between his shoulders. A cry tore from her as he went down hard. She stepped forward, and nearly swooned as her weight came down on her ankle.

"Dammit, don't let this happen," she told Babineau as the vice team took advantage of that first stunning blow to land as many more as possible. "Do something. *Do* something!"

Babineau's expression was hard; so was his tone. "He murdered one of theirs, Ceece. We'd like to think you'd do the same if it were one of us."

Glaring at her friends who hung back, she saw their grim satisfaction as they watched. She glanced toward the bleachers. Tina was scrambling down them, but the other women's expressions were even more bloodthirsty than their men's. She understood their rage and grief, and shared it enough to have hesitated when, for the first time, she wondered in agony if her colleagues, her friends, might have died by Max's hand at Jimmy's direction. She had felt the unexpected shock of anger when he'd answered, "I don't know."

But that didn't matter. Because it wasn't who Max Savoie was anymore.

Finally shaking off that first cowardly blow, Max rolled up to his feet and took a semicrouched position. The fools crowded in, not knowing what they provoked.

"Max!"

Bloodied, but not even breathing heavily, he met Cee Cee's glittery stare and heard her cautioning whisper.

"Don't bruise them up *too* badly, baby."

Her slow, fierce smile of support settled the rage tumbling wildly inside him.

Max straightened, his posture relaxed and ready. He grinned at his assailants, a quick, bold gleam of white. "All right, I'm done being obliging. If you want to continue this, I suggest you call in backup."

Apparently they needed convincing.

In less than two minutes, eight of them were on the ground moaning, and Max had Schoenbaum by the throat.

Schoenbaum squirmed until the fingers compressing his windpipe loosened. He whispered hoarsely, "So Caissie holds your chain now instead of Legere. If she said kill me, you'd tear out my throat, wouldn't you?" Though he'd swear later that it must have been the lack of oxygen, he thought he saw Savoie's eyes go blood red, and his ruthless smile become sharp.

A growl vibrated from his deadly foe. "Without

blinking an eye. So you'd be smart not to piss her off. She holds a grudge a lot longer than I do."

With a brusque shove from Max, Schoenbaum stumbled free.

Nodding to those still on the grass, Max called, "Thanks for the game. I enjoyed it."

He walked the baseline across third, then home plate, before striding toward the bench, aware of how the others scattered. They'd only heard whispers of how powerful he was, and now they'd seen for themselves.

They were impressed. And more than a little afraid.

Cee Cee met his steady gaze as he gestured around the bases.

"My kiss, detective."

"Right here, Savoie."

Her uplifted arms went about his neck as his mouth came down on hers for a brief, hard press that was more possessive than passionate.

"Time to go," he announced, slipping an arm beneath her knees to hoist her up to his chest. She didn't protest, which surprised him. "Is there anything we need to take with us?"

"I have everything I need," was her soft reply. She smiled. "Leave the beer. They'll need it to soothe their injured pride. Let's go home, Savoie."

As he carried her easily off the field, Cee Cee regarded the other spouses and significant others, seeing the awe and just a hint of envy in their expressions. And she tightened her arms about her man.

Dovion hoisted a bottle to them. "Well played, Max."

"Your support was what sustained me," he replied cynically.

"It wasn't my support you needed, Savoie. Good to see you again. I'm looking forward to that talk."

Max moved on without breaking his stride.

Tina and Oscar Babineau fell in beside him, with Alain trailing at a cautious distance. "Don't think too badly of us, Max," Tina said.

"Why would I?" Max seemed genuinely surprised. "I had a great time."

"Right up until vice decided to use you as a piñata," came Cee Cee's surly remark.

Max shrugged. "What did you expect? I'm a serpent in the middle of their family fun. I think I got off lightly." He grinned. "And so did they."

When they reached the curb, Max regarded Cee Cee's car with a frown. Catching his uncertainty, she said, "I can manage the clutch as far as my place."

"I can drive you over," Babineau offered.

"No," Max snapped. "We'll be fine."

Oscar said, "See you later, detective, Max."

Cee Cee smiled down at him, a bit bemused. The kid had never said more than a mumbled hello to her before. "Bye, Ozzy."

He and Max exchanged slight smiles as Max projected a gentle mental nudge.

Tina Babineau looked between them with a jolt of quickly hidden alarm. Then she simply stared at Max as her arms wrapped tightly about her son's shoulders.

BY THE TIME Max settled Cee Cee on the sofa, pain was ripping up from her ankle in hot, angry bites. Obediently, she swallowed the four pain-reliever tablets he brought her, then leaned back against the cushions, eyes closed, listening to him move about her apartment with an easy familiarity. She wasn't sure why that bothered her, except that she hurt and felt quarrelsome. By the time he'd finished pounding a tray of ice cubes into slivers to fill her cold pack, her head was pounding, too.

He approached cautiously because of her frown and sat at the far end of the sofa. With a pillow plumped over his lap, he settled her foot on it and carefully packed her in ice. He was so gentle, so solicitous, she wanted to kick him just from illogical bad temper. So she closed her eyes and tried to shut out her strange moodiness.

Finally, he broke the silence. "I'm sorry I ruined your party."

"It wasn't my party."

"I made you regret bringing me. Why did you say I could come, if you knew what was going to happen?"

"Because I didn't think you'd actually go. I was stupid to think—" A heavy sigh, then a wicked chuckle. "I did like watching you knock Stan

Schoenbaum on his butt. Arrogant bastard. That got your female audience all worked up."

"And you?"

"If I could have stood up, I'd have taken you right there on third base." Her heel nudged his crotch. "You're hot stuff, Savoie."

"Did you think Alain Babineau was hot stuff while you were having an affair with him?"

He asked so casually, she almost missed the enormity of his question. "What? *What* did you say?"

"Are you having an affair with—"

"I heard you! Why would you ask me such a thing? Why would you *think* such a thing?"

"I don't know."

"You don't *know*?" Her temper blew up. "I suppose that neurotic little twit told you I was banging her husband. And you believed her?" Silence. "And when would I have time for this torrid affair, when I spend my every free second tending to you?"

"Forgive me for being so needy. If you want to bang other men, just let me know and I'll make sure you have the time available. How inconsiderate of me to monopolize your dating calendar."

She kicked him, and the jolt of agony that shot through her ankle was worth it. "Stupid man. Why would I even think to look at someone else when I have you?"

"Add that to the many things I just don't know," he replied as he slid carefully out from under her injured foot.

Now he was angry, too. Standing at the balcony doors with his back to her, his posture was straight and still.

"Max, I'm not sleeping with my partner. One, because I'd never do that to you, and two, he's a married man. Do you believe me?"

"Yes." A pause. "Were you involved with him before me?"

She made an exasperated sound. "Before you was before you. It doesn't matter."

"You're not going to tell me?"

"It doesn't concern you. You, of all people, are well aware that I was no dewey-eyed virgin the first time we got together. I'm not bugging you to tell me your history." But now that she thought of it, a curious shaft of jealous discomfort jabbed through her.

"I don't have a history. There's just you."

"What?"

"When would I have time for any torrid affairs, detective, when I spent every free second murdering cops and little old ladies and kittens?"

His sarcasm blew right by her. "Just me?"

"Before I met you, I never thought about it." His voice lowered to a husky rumble. "After, I never thought of anything else but you." His shoulders moved in a heavy sigh. She could almost see the energy draining from him as he said, "I should go. Is there anything you need before I leave?"

"I need you to come here." He didn't respond.

"Max, please come over here to me. Don't make me have to get up."

He came reluctantly, his features erased of any emotion. At the couch he sank down onto his knees, avoiding eye contact with her.

The instant he was within reach, her arms were about his neck, pulling his dark head down to her breast. She held him quietly, her cheek pressed against his hair. And finally all her compressed feelings came loose.

"I'm sorry, Max. So sorry."

"About what?" he murmured. "That I didn't have sex before I met you? I've been trying to make up for it ever since, and you've been very obliging."

"I didn't do anything," she confessed miserably. "I didn't do anything to stop them."

He sat up and turned to face her. His eyes, those beautiful eyes, were clear and wide and remarkably free of any blame. "Is that what has you so upset? Charlotte, *sha*, I don't expect you to swallow what I've been, what I've done, without a bitter taste. I know my past is a terrible burden to you. And there's never a day goes by that I'm not grateful that you're strong enough to bear it. Don't ever apologize to me. Not ever."

He leaned forward and her lips parted, hoping for his kiss. Instead, his mouth touched lightly to her brow.

"Take me to bed, Savoie. Sleep the rest of the day away next to me. Be with me. Just stay with me, Max."

He scooped her up and whisked her down the hall, freeing one hand long enough to rip back the covers on her bed.

"Clothes on or off?" he asked gruffly.

"Off. Yours, too."

"I thought you wanted to rest."

"We will. Eventually."

"Shower first or later?"

"After. I want you all hot and sweaty and naked and mine."

He sat her down on the edge of the bed, where they took turns stripping off each other's shirts. As Cee Cee was nibbling down his chest, he stopped her.

"You didn't sleep with Schoenbaum or Junior Hammond, did you?"

Her expression registered her distaste. "God, no."

"Okay. Continue, please."

She was already at his zipper.

"Let me get my shoes first, *cher*."

But she'd already pushed his clothing down and was running her tongue along his hipbone. Her hands skimmed down his back, palming the hard curve of his flanks.

"Geez, Savoie, is there any part of you that isn't perfect?"

"Well, I don't know how to drive a car, and I thought the Saints were a baseball team." Then he lost his ability to speak as she caressed him.

"I want you so much, you've got me jumping inside like frog legs on a skillet."

He made a gaaking sound. "That isn't a particularly appealing image."

"Crawfish, then. Since we've finished the shucking, let's move on."

Her mouth slid down him, strong and hot, and he nearly lost himself right then. Within a minute, his breathing was labored and she had him trembling uncontrollably.

"Let go, baby. Let go," she coaxed.

There was no way he could not comply.

The instant she released him, he flopped onto his stomach with a groan. She tapped the back of his thigh.

"Feet."

He bent his knees so she could unlace his Converses and strip him down the rest of the way. When his legs dangled limply off the edge of the bed, she gave his tight butt a light smack.

"Scoot over."

He collapsed on the opposite side without opening his eyes and murmured softly as she kissed his shoulder.

"Get some sleep. I'm going to expect you to service me enthusiastically later."

He smiled, eyes still shut. "I love my job."

She soothed her palm up the sleek length of his back. "And I love you."

But he was already gone.

A SHARP TWINGE from her ankle woke Cee Cee from a heavy slumber. Her digital clock read 6:30. The last of the day's heat was just creeping across the sill in filtered beams of sunlight. And the bed beside her was empty.

She tried to sit up, and the pain tore a curse from her.

"Hey, what are you doing? Don't get up."

In her doorway, Max was all sleek and freshly showered, wearing sweat bottoms that she'd borrowed once and never remembered to return. He looked and smelled amazing.

"I thought you'd left."

"And pass up on the chance to smother you with annoyingly good intentions while you're incapacitated?" He grinned. "Not a chance. I was just getting you something to eat."

Her brows shot up. "In *my* kitchen?"

He made a rude noise. "Only if you wanted me to stir-fry some of your rodent food. I took a tour of your take-out joints." He came to lift her shoulders up and tuck the extra pillow behind her.

"You're fixing me dinner?"

"I can't exactly take you to a restaurant dressed like this, now can I?" His head ducked down for a quick taste of her bare breast before heading back to the hall.

"Max?" Her pulse had jumped into a hurried gallop.

He looked back over his shoulder. "Yeah?"

Her heart gave a funny little quiver. "Nothing."

He returned carrying a tray. "I got you some sesame noodles, a couple of egg rolls, and a cup of hot and sour soup."

"Where's my fortune cookie?"

"Sorry, I ate it. I'm going to be lucky in love."

"Then that's good fortune for both of us."

He smiled and sat cross-legged on the bed facing her, the tray balanced in his lap. He fished in the noodles with a pair of chopsticks. "Open."

"I only sprained my ankle, Max. I can feed myself."

"Where's the fun in that? Let me spoil you a little, detective. It's not often you'll give me the chance, and I enjoy it."

She enjoyed it, too. Too much. She sighed and made like a baby bird. He poked in the noodles.

"Aren't you having anything?"

His gaze slid away in subtle evasion. "I've already eaten."

She didn't need him to explain. Calling on his inner beast to repair the battering he'd undergone required red meat. Red and raw. And though it didn't bother her, it made him uncomfortable, so she let it go.

"Split an egg roll with me."

He did so, chewing thoughtfully as he watched her.

"What?" she demanded.

"Hmmm?"

"What? Is there something else?"

"No." He was smiling. "Have some soup. Careful, it's hot."

She slurped it up, watching him over the rim of the cup. His stare was intense and unblinking. She handed him the empty cup and insisted, "What? And don't tell me nothing."

"You are so beautiful, I can't look away."

He reached out to rub his knuckles beneath her jaw, then cradled the side of her face, drawing her forward to meet the soft touch of his lips.

"Tray," she whispered, leaning back slightly so he could slide it onto the nightstand. She melted beneath his kiss, letting him lean into her until the feel and scent of him surrounded her. She sank her fingers into his hair as he began to nip and lick his way down the arch of her neck to the thrust of her breasts. Her eyes closed as she moaned a low sound of encouragement.

And then her cell phone rang.

Max paused, his head resting between her breasts, while she flipped open her phone.

"Caissie. Babs, what's wrong? No, that's all right. Oh, geez. I'm so sorry. Sure. Sure, no problem. Okay. No. Don't worry about it."

Max eased back, alerted by the tone of her voice, by the twist of anguish in her expression. "Charlotte?"

"Tina's parents have been killed," Cee Cee told

him quietly. "They just got the call. They have to go to Fort Worth and don't have any place for Ozzy. Alain asked if he could stay here, and I said okay. It's okay, isn't it?"

"Of course."

"They're on their way over."

He was instantly off the bed, pulling clothing out of the dresser for Cee Cee. He was suddenly very afraid that nothing was okay, and the Babineaus were bringing an unexpected and terrible danger right to the door.

Eleven

I APPRECIATE THIS," Alain said as his wife and stepson entered Cee Cee's apartment. Tina was pale, red-eyed, and worn looking.

"Don't give it another thought," Cee Cee said.

"Mama, look. Guinea pigs."

While Oscar pulled Tina over to the cage, Cee Cee asked Alain softly, "What happened?"

"I don't know yet. They didn't tell us much. Some kind of home invasion. Pretty ugly, I'm guessing, from what they didn't say. I'll give you a call tomorrow and let you know the particulars. Thanks for stepping in."

"I never thought I'd be a first choice for babysitter."

"Actually," Babineau said uncomfortably, "it was Savoie he was asking for."

"Max? Max didn't even know he existed until today."

"Well, apparently he made an impression. A lot more of one than I've ever been able to."

Cee Cee pressed his arm. "Don't do that, Alain. Just be there for Tina. She's going to need you."

"Right." His stare fixed on Max, who'd just entered the room. "Savoie, that little guy means everything to us."

"Understood." He looked to the boy and smiled. "Heya, sport. Gonna spend some time with us?"

"Mama said it was okay."

Max and Tina exchanged a long look, then she nodded. "It should only be for a day or two at most. I've packed everything he needs. He's a really good boy."

Max put out his hand and Oscar slid under it easily. "We'll be fine. Don't worry about anything. We'll keep him safe."

"Tina, we should get on the road."

She glanced at her husband and nodded, then her arms wrapped about her son. "Be good. Do what you're told. Take your medication." She turned to Cee Cee. "Make sure he takes his pills. Just remind him." Tears began to gather in her eyes.

Awkward with a show of sympathy, Cee Cee embraced her rather stiffly and was startled at the other woman's demonstrative hug.

"Don't worry. Ozzy will be fine. Take all the time you need. This is something you can't hurry. Okay?"

Tina nodded against her shoulder and then stepped away. "Thank you. Thank you both." She rushed out and Babineau followed.

Shutting the door, Cee Cee turned back to the boy. What the hell did one do with a ten-year-old? For the moment, he seemed intrigued with Porky and Baco. Max glanced up and smiled when he caught her anxious look. He came to join her where she was hanging on to the doorknob, balancing on one leg like a graceless flamingo.

"Detective, sit down before you fall down." He picked her up before she could protest and deposited her on the couch. Then he reached for the phone.

"Who are you calling?'

"I'm going to have a car pick us up and take us out to the house."

"Why?"

"Helen knows about kids. And it'll be safer. There's security there."

Safer. That's the second time he'd spoken about it as if it should be a primary concern. And she was wondering why he thought so.

"Can I take the pigs out?" Oscar wanted to know.

"One at a time. Be careful of them. They're fast."

The boy opened the cage, which started the fat, little hairballs skittering. He watched them patiently, then grabbed, his hand moving so fast, Cee Cee just stared as the boy cradled the frozen rodent to his chest. The only hand she'd ever seen move that fast belonged to Max Savoie.

"Be gentle with him, Ozzy."

"I will." He began a careful stroking that soon had the small creature chutting and purring.

She glanced up at Max, who was at the sliding glass door. He was staring outside, so still that the hair prickled on her arms. Something was going on. Something Max wasn't sharing that had him on edge and on high alert.

After fifteen more minutes passed, he announced quietly, "Let's go. Oscar, we're going to go stay at my house. There's a lot more room there."

"Can I take the guinea pigs?"

"I don't have a place for them there," Cee Cee told him. "But you can come back over here tomorrow with me to feed them. Okay?"

He gave the fluffy animal one last pat and returned it to its cage. "Okay."

Max secured the sliding doors, saying crisply, "Oscar, get your bag. Straight out to the car." He snatched Cee Cee off the couch as if she were another piece of baggage.

"Max, what the—?"

"Later."

The driver opened the door to the big black town car, expressing no curiosity over the boy or why his boss was carrying his police detective girlfriend. He'd worked for Jimmy Legere too long to ever have questions.

"Thank you, Pete. Home. The scenic route."

Pete nodded, knowing he should look for a possible tail.

Sitting between the two of them in the wide backseat, Oscar Babineau's lower lip began to shiver.

"My grandpa and grandma are dead," he announced in a frail little voice. "They didn't tell me, but I heard Mama and Alain talking. I hear them when they don't think I do."

Cee Cee exchanged a look with Max; his was carefully veiled.

"Are you going to find out who killed them, Detective Caissie?"

Though it was totally out of her jurisdiction, she heard herself say, "Yes. Your dad and I will find out and make sure they're punished."

Oscar nodded, accepting her word without question. He didn't cry as he leaned against her, nor did he refuse her clumsy embrace. But his slight form trembled until Cee Cee thought her heart would break.

With the resilience of youth, Oscar was all attentive interest as the gates to Legere's estate parted. His wide eyes took in everything as he followed Max out of the car at the sprawling plantation home.

"Wow. Is this where you live, Max?"

"I grew up here."

"Wow. Look at all the room to play."

Max glanced about, surprised. "Yes, I suppose there is." Though he never had.

Helen and Giles were on the porch, awaiting their arrival.

Max placed his hands comfortingly on the boy's shoulders as he introduced them. "Helen, could you take Oscar's things up to the room next to mine? Giles, why don't you show Ozzy around while I talk a minute with Detective Caissie."

"Sure." The big man came down the steps, smiling to calm the separation alarm in the boy's face. "You like cars, bub? We got some honeys. Only thing the boss man there is afraid of." He grinned at Max, and the boy relaxed enough to trot off with him.

Cee Cee was struggling to get out of her side of the car when Max came around for her. Resigned to her fate, she lifted her arms to him and let him hoist her up.

There was no escaping the intensity of her dark, probing cop's eyes. "How is it possible, Max?"

He was wondering the same thing. "You answer my questions, then I'll answer yours. Deal?"

She regarded him suspiciously, then nodded.

They settled on the side porch, where they had a good view of the yard. Max had Cee Cee's foot in his lap and was gently rubbing her badly swollen ankle. He bent to kiss her big toe, then was all business.

"Tell me everything you know about them."

She sighed. "Not much. Father Furness introduced them. It was puppy love at first sight."

The corner of Max's mouth lifted. "What a jaded romantic you are, detective."

"Yeah, well." She shrugged. "She was one of the father's projects—you know, putting together the broken pieces. Like with me."

He understood: a rape victim. He eased his hands higher up her leg, massaging her calf with a light, soothing pressure. "She's Oscar's natural mother?"

"As far as I know, yes."

"And his father?"

Cee Cee shrugged. "No idea. She never talked about it to Alain. He said it didn't bother him, but I know it drove him crazy. Knowing someone had hurt her and not being able to do anything about it."

"Yes." He understood the helplessness and fury. At least he'd been able to deal personally with Charlotte's attackers.

She reached down to hold his hands. "Oscar's one of you."

"Yes."

"Tina, too."

"Yes."

"Alain doesn't know."

"I'm not sure Tina really knows."

"How could she not know what she is?"

The same way he hadn't known: because there had been no one to show him. No one to teach him. Forcing him to grow up surrounded by fear, separated by the difference he didn't understand.

The sound of Oscar's laughter drew his attention to the yard, and he saw Giles swing the boy up onto his shoulders and gallop about the grass with surprising animation.

Bittersweet regret swelled inside him. He couldn't

remember ever having such a moment, such joyful innocence. Not ever. The intense longing for what he'd missed twisted fiercely in his soul.

The truth would rob Oscar of those simple pleasures. What right did he have to strip away the things he himself had so desired and been denied?

His poignant feelings were swept away by one cruel fact. To make sure Oscar survived, he had every right. Because somehow, some way, the boy was more than just one of Max's kind.

Oscar was part of him.

"DETECTIVE CAISSIE?"

The anxious whisper woke Cee Cee. For a moment she wondered wildly what a child was doing in her room, then she remembered.

"Ozzy? Are you okay?"

She could see the boy's lanky silhouette at the foot of the bed she shared with Max, and was hugely relieved that she'd put on a tee shirt before falling asleep. She struggled to sit up, thinking the boy had probably had a bad dream.

"Something's wrong with Max."

Her gaze darted to the empty sheets beside her. Panicked, she scrambled to the end of the bed to seize the boy's arms. He was shaking, which made her alarm shoot higher.

"What happened to Max? What's wrong with him? Ozzy, tell me!"

The boy was pale as a ghost, his dark eyes huge and swimming with tears, and uncertainty. "He said I could come to you. He said I could trust you."

Cee Cee took a breath, then a deeper one to overcome the terrible fright quivering through her. All she could think of were those cold beasts in their suits, crouched and ready to lunge.

She made her voice calm, firm, and comforting. "You can. Ozzy, you can. Talk to me. How do you know something's happened to Max? Did you see something? Hear something?"

He shook his head, causing his tears to splash onto her hands.

"Ozzy, did you *feel* something was wrong?"

Relief crumpled the last of his hesitation. "It just woke me up, like someone was shaking me. He's hurt. Real bad." The child's features convulsed, as if even now he was sharing that pain.

"Where is he, Ozzy? Do you know where he is?"

"Someplace close."

She rubbed his bare arms and quieted her tone. "Take a breath, Oscar. Slow. Slow. Close your eyes. Reach out for him. Real easy. Real quiet. Can you find him?"

Oscar's head came up, his eyes came open, bright and glowing as he looked straight out the open balcony doors. "He's out there."

Biting back a curse, Cee Cee eased off the bed and

hopped to her dresser. Just pulling on loose workout pants broke a sweat on her fear-chilled skin. She left her feet bare.

"Gimme a shoulder, kid," she urged as she tucked her Smith & Wesson carrying silver loads into the elastic waistband. "Let's go find him."

The stairs took a teeth-grinding forever. Then Oscar was leading her out across the dark yard, the grass wet and cool under her feet. A faint light flickered through a grove of oaks and down a long slant of rough-cut lawn. She hadn't been to this part of the property before, but recognized the utility of the stone-lined cave cut into the opposing hillside. Its semicircular opening was caged by wrought iron. Before the turn of the twentieth century, landowners had used the coolness of the crude underground Quonsets to house their food supplies and their dead until roads were passable in the spring. The bars kept marauding creatures away.

She saw Giles St. Clair in the bright glow of his cigarette, and as she drew closer she realized the bars were now being used to keep a creature inside.

"Ozzy, you stay here. *Right* here. Okay?"

"But Max—"

"If Giles is here, I'm sure Max is fine. Let me go check. Wait."

A jerky nod.

There was no way to manage a stealthy approach.

She slid and swore her way down the embankment.

When Giles caught sight of her, his features froze in surprise and dread. And then relief as he jogged over to help her the rest of the way.

"Detective, you shouldn't be out here."

"Tell me quick what the hell is going on."

The big man looked uncomfortable. "His orders. To keep everyone safe."

"From what?"

"Him."

"Let me see."

Giles lifted a heavy-duty flashlight that illuminated the area. She stepped closer to the heavy grill and saw Max locked inside. He was on his back on the brick floor, one foot shackled by a short chain to the wall. She could hear the harsh rasp of his breathing and the low rumble that growled beneath it.

"Open it."

Giles stared at her as if she'd gone mad. "No, ma'am. No way. You and the boy go on back up to the house. He'll be fine soon. He comes around quicker every night."

"Comes around from *what*? How long has this been going on? Giles, don't look to him, talk to *me*. Why have you locked him in there?"

Giles looked very wary. "I didn't, detective. He did that himself. I'm just looking out for him, to make sure he don't hurt himself."

Her momentary pang of gratitude hardened as

she watched Max writhing on the cold stone and heard the low, awful sounds he was making. "What do you call that?"

The big guy's face pinched tight with uneasiness. "Better than it was. Charlotte, please go back up. He don't want you down here."

"I don't much care *what* he wants. Open it."

"He's not himself."

"I know what he is."

"If any harm comes to you by his hand—"

"He won't hurt me, Giles. I have to see for myself that he's all right. Please. I can't see him like that and just walk away. Please."

Muttering softly, he undid the padlock holding the gate closed.

"The key for his ankle."

He passed it to her. And the admiration in his gaze went a long way toward shoring up her courage.

Because Max was not himself.

She gave Giles her gun; she didn't want to think that she might need it. "Take Oscar back up to his room. Tell him Max is sick, that I'm going to stay with him. He doesn't need to see this. Go on—I'll be fine. You take care of the boy. Don't let him be afraid. I'll take care of Max."

Reluctantly, Giles lumbered up the hill to where Oscar stood frozen.

She listened for his low assurances, and waited until they started to move away. Then she entered the cavern with caution, approaching Max carefully, the way she would any sick or injured wild thing. She kept the beam of the flashlight low and indirect so as not to alarm him.

"Max, it's Charlotte."

At the sound of her voice, he scrambled up to his hands and knees, regarding her with unblinking eyes shot through with blood red and molten gold. His features were taut, all sharp bones and sunken hollows. Misshapen. His hair stuck up in haphazard angles, glazed stiff by sweat. Shaking so hard he could barely maintain his balance, he edged back farther into the shadows.

"Go away. I don't want you here." She almost didn't recognize the hoarse whisper as his voice.

"Max, what is it? What are you doing?"

"Get out. You can't be here."

She reached out a tentative hand, and he shrank back with a low moan.

"Charlotte, please. Please go."

She'd seen the ravaging effects of silver before. Once from a bullet, once from a treacherously offered drink, once from a bite. And once from her own hand. Silver was somehow streaking through his system, its toxic hold poisoning him. What she didn't know was why. Seeing him suffer so shook her badly, and made her mad as hell.

"I'm not leaving. I'm not afraid of you. It's all right. Come here to me."

Gritting her teeth, she knelt down and waited, her hand outstretched and steady. He kept to the shadows, panting unevenly, his eyes burning with that unnatural fire. Alarmed and afraid for him, she coaxed gently, "It's all right, baby. Come here. I'll stay with you. Let me help you."

She waited until his palm crossed hers, then pulled him toward her.

Max collapsed across her knees, giving himself over to the chills and fever that wracked him, entrusting himself to her care while he was helpless. Just the feel of her arms around him was better than any balm, soothing the raw rips of pain twisting through him. Her hand was on his sticky hair, her lips against his ear, her scent filling him, calming him.

It's better if you don't fight it, his father had told him. Easy to say; hard to do when agony was gnawing at every nerve ending. A low, plaintive sound escaped him, and instantly he was surrounded by the fierce tenderness he'd come to depend upon.

"I've got you, Max. You rest. I've got you."

"I love you, Charlotte."

Her kiss touched to his damp brow. "I'll try to remember that later, when I'm kicking your ass."

A smile trembled across his lips as his eyes closed and his body sagged.

Safe.

PAIN FROM HER ankle woke Cee Cee to a bright morning. Sun pooled across the hardwood floor, bringing the promise of warmth.

She pulled the sheet over her head, cursing irritably. Her hand strayed to the other side of the bed, which was unoccupied.

Finding Max gone didn't improve her mood. The one thing she looked forward to on weekends was waking up with him. Waking up just before he did, to watch him sleep. Having him wake her with the softest of kisses, followed by slow, smoldering passion.

Hard to do that when he wasn't there.

The scent of rich chicory coffee coaxed her out of the covers, but it was the sight of the table set up at her bedside that nudged her from her grumpiness. Coffee in a carafe, waffles warming in a chafing dish, strawberries mashed and sweetened. And a single red rose atop a folded note.

"Dammit, Savoie. You make it hard for a girl to stay pissed off."

She rubbed the soft petals of the rose against her lips as she read the short message printed with neat precision.

"You looked too beautiful to waken."

She made a rude noise. "Coward."

"I couldn't let you try to kick my butt on an empty stomach. Back in a couple of hours. Will tend to your rodents for you. You are my every dream."

She scowled as her heart went noodle soft. "Think you're pretty smart, don't you, Savoie?" There was no real annoyance in her tone, and she was smiling as she cut into the first waffle.

As she was finishing the last of the coffee, Helen knocked softly and peered in.

"You're awake."

"Awake and fed."

"Can I get you anything else?"

"I'm fine, thanks. Is Oscar up yet?"

"He left with Mr. Savoie about an hour ago."

"Really?" Where could the two of them be going without saying a word to her? She kept her tone nonchalant. "Did Max happen to mention where they were off to?"

"Something about going to Mass."

Twelve

MAX ENJOYED CHURCH. Though not particularly religious, he liked the discipline of ritual and pageantry. He understood the necessity of guidelines in one's life. And he never got tired of listening to Father Furness tending to heart and soul.

Not only a man of God but also one of strength and compassion, the priest had Max's eternal gratitude for housing Cee Cee when she was a child, taking her in while her undercover-cop dad was out on the streets in places she couldn't go. St. Bart's was a humble bastion of hope and comfort and, much like the burly father, wasn't much for pretense. The frightened, the wounded in body and spirit, the confused, and the lost were all welcomed within its doors.

Doors recently reopened after a devastating fire failed in its attempt to close them. A fire ordered by Jimmy Legere to conceal the attempted murder of Charlotte Caissie's best friend, Mary Kate. An order Max hadn't been able to follow, on a night that ultimately led to Legere's death. An ironic fated circle, if one believed in those things. Today, Max did.

"Max, come to see if your money was well spent?"

"Oh, I have no doubt about that, Father."

"And who's this? Hello, young man. Yours is a familiar face." He looked up at Max for an explanation.

"This is Oscar. Charlotte's partner, Alain Babineau, married his mother last year."

"Yes. Of course." But that's not what he saw when he looked in the boy's eyes, and Max knew it.

Long ago Father Furness had taken in Benjamin Spratt, who, like Max, had been confused and frightened by what he was. He'd housed Dolores Gautreaux and her baby until they were able to return to their clan. He took in more than the lost, Max had recently discovered from Jacques LaRoche. He also took in those like himself—those who were not human. Max wasn't sure what to make of that yet; a lifetime of cautious habits was hard to break.

"We need to talk, Father."

"Yes. I can see that we do."

They went to the small park across the street to watch Oscar Babineau on the old playground equipment.

"You know I can't betray a confidence, Max."

"I need you to tell me enough to keep him safe. Tina's parents were killed."

"How?"

"I don't know yet. Who is his father?"

Father Furness was silent a moment. "She

brought the child to me, a beautiful baby girl, and asked me to find a safe place for her. Someplace she would never be found."

"A baby girl? Tina?"

"Christina." He smiled wistfully as he watched Oscar on the jungle gym. "I didn't ask any questions. I assumed she was illegitimate, that the circumstances of her conception were less than ideal, so I agreed. I found a good, solid couple who'd just lost their own baby girl. They paid extremely well to have some paperwork altered. He was in the military, always moving, about to go overseas for four years. Far enough for whomever was searching to lose the trail."

"But they just found it again, didn't they?" It *wasn't* him they were after. It was Oscar.

"When Christina came to me heavy with child, just a child herself, I couldn't turn her away. After the boy was born and old enough to travel, Mary Kate—Sister Catherine—convinced me to have St. Bart's sponsor them on a mission assignment. They lived in South America until the boy was six, then returned when our funds got too low to sustain them there. That's when Mary Kate introduced her to Alain Babineau."

"Someone else who could keep Tina and the boy safe."

"And close to you, should you ever discover who they were."

Max took a quick step back, his features going stiff. "What do you know about me?"

The priest smiled. "Probably a lot more than you'd be comfortable with me knowing. I wasn't always a servant of the church, Max. A long time ago, I had a different master. Someday, when you decide you can trust me, we'll talk about it. But now, you were right to be concerned." He looked toward Oscar, watching him through worried eyes. His voice lowered. "Keep the boy safe at all costs, Max. You're the only one who can. And you must be prepared to lose everything that's dear to you. You might be their leader—but the boy may well be their future."

CEE CEE WAS just finishing up a phone call when she saw Max in the hall. He started to fade back when he saw her, but she pointed to him, then to the leather couch along the wall. He obediently came into the study where Jimmy Legere had once conducted his nefarious business, but instead of sitting tamely to wait for her, he went to stand at the doors opening onto the shaded porch.

Distracted by his presence, by his solitary stance, Cee Cee wrapped up her call to Babineau with assurances that Oscar was fine and that he missed them and he would be in good hands with them until Tina brought her parents home to be buried the next afternoon.

Then she said, "Talk to me, Max."

"About what, Charlotte?"

Because his back was to her, the effect of her narrowed glare was lost. "Let's start with why you've been poisoning yourself. Yes, let's start there."

He spoke matter-of-factly, as if what he was doing was no big deal. "You know silver is deadly to us. It's the surest way to kill us. It keeps us from shifting, from healing."

"And you're pouring it into yourself every night, why?"

"I'm building up a tolerance to it. It takes time, but eventually it won't be able to bring me down."

She suppressed a shiver, thinking of those creatures in Tito's room, the way they just shook off the effects of her bullets. Could they have done that if the bullets had been silver? "And is this, this self-torture a common practice?"

"No."

"Has anyone survived it that you're aware of?" The panic in her heart was disguised by the anger in her tone.

"Just one." A pause. "My father."

"Rollo told you." If she could have reached him, she would have smacked him upside the head. "Rollo the wise and reliable. Did it ever occur to you that he was lying? That maybe he wanted you sick and weak and possibly dying, so he could take everything that was yours?"

His words were calm. "Yes, it occurred to me. I decided it was worth the risk."

"*You* decided? You decided that you'd just trust your life to a lying, cheating con man who sold you out not once, but twice, so he could make a buck? Come over here so I can hit you for being so stupid."

"No, I don't think I will."

"Then come over here and hold me—because I'm really scared for you right now."

The unplanned tremor in her voice brought him to kneel by her. The whack of her hand against the side of his head didn't surprise him, but her silent tears as she hugged him close did.

"It's so dangerous, Max."

Needing her to understand, he said simply, "Not as dangerous as standing out there in the open unprotected. I can't be vulnerable, Charlotte—not if I want to keep those I care about safe. I can't have any weaknesses. Too many things depend on me now."

"Things more important than me?"

Months ago, his answer would have come without hesitation. Even a week ago, he would have said no, nothing could matter as much as her.

But he was silent—and Cee Cee realized that something huge had happened to unseat her from that treasured first place she'd stolen from Jimmy Legere.

She'd taken it for granted. She'd assumed she was the priority in his life, because he'd told her so, again and again. And she'd liked it, liked knowing that someone held her in such tremendous esteem and devotion.

She'd never been considered first by anyone

before. Not by her mother, who'd chosen the bottle; not by her father, who'd chosen his badge; not by her best friend, who'd valued her revenge.

But Max—Max had made her the focal point of his existence for twelve years. He'd placed her above his loyalty to Jimmy Legere, ahead of his newly discovered clan; he gave more importance to her than to his own life. He made her feel special, adored . . . loved.

And now, he'd suddenly pushed her off that pedestal with his silence, with his lack of reassurance. The startling abruptness of her fall slapped the breath from her.

She let him go gradually, relaxing her grip, forcing her anguished heartbeat to slow, determined not to make the same mistake that Jimmy had. Jimmy hadn't known when to let go.

She kissed his brow, stroked his hair, making both gestures light, surface comforts. Then she gently pushed him away.

He rocked back on his heels, his hands still resting at her waist, his gaze worriedly searching hers. She couldn't let him know he'd just torn the heart and soul from her.

"No more of this nonsense," she scolded firmly. "I'm not going to let you go through this alone. I'm going to be here for you, right *here*—not out there, like some animal in a cage. No arguments."

He seized her face in his palms, his mouth over hers. She gave herself up to the sweet drugging pleasure of his kiss for a poignant moment, then pushed him back again. When he told her fiercely, "You are everything to me," she just smiled. Because she knew that was no longer true. And because that was far too hurtful to deal with, she focused on the professional.

"I was just talking to Alain. He had more information about Tina's parents."

Max settled cross-legged on the floor beside her chair. "Her adoptive parents," he corrected. "What do they claim happened?"

"A home invasion. Quite brutal. They believe her father put up a struggle before they were both shot."

"Shot," he mused.

"So the story goes."

He glanced up. "But you don't believe that, either?"

"There were no defensive wounds on his hands. I think they were both bound and beaten. The shooting, the robbery—that was just smoke." She was remembering the tortured body of Tito's girlfriend on his bed, and she guessed the scenario. The couple bound, he tortured, but neither talking. She threatened; he refusing to give in. A military man, he wouldn't take to threats easily. Then they shot his wife, and he'd give them nothing after that, so he no longer had value. How long would it take them to link Christina, the daughter her parents had protected, to Tina Babineau?

Max was remembering the battered face of Tito

Tibideaux and said, "I thought they were looking for me, but I'm not so sure now. I think it's Oscar."

"Why? What's so important about him?"

Max shook his head. "I can't explain it. Charlotte, he's my—" He broke off and glanced over his shoulder toward the door. A moment later, Oscar appeared.

"Hey, Ozzy. I was just talking to your dad. They're going to be home tomorrow. Your mom's going to call you just before suppertime to see how you're doing." She had until then to decide what she should tell her partner.

Oscar stood silent, then dampness welled up in his eyes. Before Cee Cee could think of what to do, Max crossed to him. He crouched down so they were eye to eye, and said something quiet to him that brought the boy's arms in a quick hug about his neck. Cee Cee expected Max to recoil, but he pulled Oscar into an easy embrace and just held him, his eyes closed, his expression intense.

When Cee Cee recognized the look on his face, she thought with greater sympathy of Jimmy Legere, and how he must have felt as she intruded on the loyalty and love Max had for him.

Max stood to let Oscar dash upstairs, watching the boy with a complexity of emotions flitting across his usually impassive features. Then he turned to Cee Cee and his expression became guarded, shutting her out. "I've got to take care of some business this afternoon."

"Fine. You don't have to entertain me. I've got to speak to Father Furness about arrangements anyway."

Then Oscar was clattering down the steps. He had a ball and glove in one hand and grabbed Max's with the other. Smiling slightly, Max let himself be drawn outside to the yard.

"That's something I never thought I'd see," Helen said.

Cee Cee glanced up at the housekeeper, who regarded the man and boy with bemusement. "What's that?"

Helen only smiled, but Cee Cee understood. Max enjoying an ordinary moment, just having fun.

Then the older woman, who'd cared for Max as much as he'd allow while he was growing up, looked more closely. "Must be déjà vu."

"What?"

"For a moment there, I thought I was looking at Max as a child."

Cee Cee didn't answer. For just then, Oscar caught a bouncing ground ball and his face lit with a rare, wide grin.

And she saw Max Savoie in that smile.

MAX WAS BEHIND closed doors for most of the afternoon. Jacques LaRoche arrived with four men she recognized from the encounter when Rollo was killed. Dangerous and dedicated individuals, they served one deadly purpose.

From the distant parlor sofa, she watched Max's gathering of professionals. The hard-eyed foursome from LaRoche, Giles, Teddy, and a half dozen of Legere's most trusted muscle men. She wondered about the wisdom of combining the two forces, and worried over the circumstance that would cause him to unite the so very different groups. And her heart ached from the exclusion. An hour later, Giles led the lot of them down the hall to the nerve center of the estate's security, leaving Max and LaRoche to private council.

The two of them emerged from Jimmy's study, still in intense conversation. When LaRoche glanced up and saw her foot propped up on pillows invalid style, he grinned knowingly.

"I'll bet infirmity is hard for a warrior like you to take."

She scowled. "I can still take you. You'd have to come over here within reach, though."

He chuckled. "I'm borrowing Max for a while."

"You don't have to clear it through me." Her cool gaze slipped to where Max stood silently in his shadow. "Max is a big boy. He does pretty much whatever he wants, with or without my permission."

"I'll bring him back no worse for wear."

Just bring him back, she thought as she waved them away.

Max started off with LaRoche, then suddenly wheeled about into the parlor to drop down on one knee beside the sofa where they'd once lounged naked and replete after mind-blowing sex. Where he'd let down his defenses to share secrets from his past. Where he'd told her the sofa could be hers if she wanted it to be, and she'd been frantic wondering if he was proposing more than cohabitation. Making her wonder what she really wanted from him, and for how long.

Max surprised her with an open-mouthed kiss that stole her breath. And her heart.

"I won't be long." Then he was gone.

And she knew what she wanted from him.

Forever.

TRYING TO FIND a way for them to survive the coming hours, Max stared up at the dented roof of LaRoche's Caddy and breathed in the scent of Charlotte. Anger bubbled beneath his surface calm as he turned to La Roche and asked, "Isn't it about time you told me the truth?"

And just like that, Jacques spilled everything. When he was done, a long silence settled.

Then Max's low growl. "You took her there into danger?"

"No one takes her anywhere. She was going, with or without me. I figured she might be safer if I was watching her back."

"Tell her that to her face."

"Tell that to the Trackers she emptied her gun into." He shook his head in admiration. "They never expected such fight in a female, Shifter or

Upright. You should have seen her, Max. Damned shame she's not one of us."

Max scrubbed his hands over his face. "Why can't she stay out of things?" he said to himself as his fear and frustration swamped over. "I don't want her in the middle where she could be hurt or killed. This doesn't involve her. We aren't her people; this isn't some case she's on. Why can't she just let it alone?"

LaRoche glanced at him. "You don't know?"

"No!" he shouted. "I don't know! Why don't I *ever* know anything that's important? My head's full of useless stuff. I can rebuild the engine of this car and I don't know how to drive it. I can speak seven languages and I've never been out of these parishes. I run a multimillion-dollar enterprise, but I don't know how to write a check. I can have all the females I want without saying a word, yet I can't manage a simple conversation with the only one I want.

"How am I going to keep her safe, Jacques, when I'm a bigger danger to her than anything she faces on these streets? What am I supposed to do when she won't listen to me, when she throws herself in harm's way without even thinking about how I'd go on even a day without her? She's alone on the streets because of me. How can I protect her when she won't let me, when she won't stay away?"

"Stop trying to keep her away. Invite her in and keep her close. Let us help you take care of her, the same way your Upright people do."

"How? She can never be one of us."

"But that doesn't mean she can't be part of you."

Jacques's words knocked him back in the seat like a punch. Dread and uncertainty held him there. *Mate with her. Bond with her. Join with her. Forever.*

Simple yet potentially deadly solutions that brought a whole new level of torment to his mind.

And set the animal within him on fire.

MAX HAD FINALLY fallen into a deep, exhausted sleep.

Volunteering to see him through his self-induced agony had been easy to commit to, but so very hard to endure. Yet Charlotte could see Giles was right. The effects of the silver were hideously painful, but not as severe as when she'd nursed him through it before. Weary, she slipped out onto the balcony for some fresh air. As she leaned on the rail, suppressed weeping struggled for escape. But that wouldn't help him or her.

What was she going to do? How was she going to keep him safe? How was she going to keep his and Oscar's secret when it kept getting more dangerous and out of control? And what could she tell Alain without telling him all? He was already suspicious of the circumstances around the two deaths. He was on guard and alert, but he had no idea what he was up against. And he'd stand no chance against those preternatural killers.

What the hell did they want from Oscar? From Max?

The night was thick and there was no breeze bringing comfort, so she turned to go back inside. A shift in the shadows had her reaching for her non-existent gun.

A figure stood just outside Oscar's door, its eyes glowing hot and gold. One of the men LaRoche had brought in that afternoon. He made no move toward her, no sound to acknowledge her, but seeing him there made the terror lessen a bit. With a curt nod, she stepped across the threshold into her bedroom. And right into Max.

Technically, it was Max.

He caught her by the upper arms, not with his fingers but within the curl of his massive claws. She didn't move, fearing he might inadvertently harm her. Moonlight glinted off his eyes, reflecting ruby-like flashes. His features were concealed by darkness, but she knew she wouldn't be looking into his familiar face.

"Max, I thought you were sleeping."

He leaned in close and she heard him take in her scent in quick snuffles. A low, throaty vibration rattled through him, and she knew a sudden spike of fear. What if he didn't recognize her?

"Max, it's Charlotte. Are you okay?"

She held very still, eyes closed, as his breath stroked light and fast against the side of her throat. Then the slow, wet rasp of his tongue. Over her ear, up her cheek, across her mouth. Tasting.

He crowded against her, big, strong, dominant;

pushing her backward, making her stumble until her injured ankle refused to hold. With a soft gasp, she fell back against the wall, pinned there by the press of his bulk.

"Max?"

His breathing grew harsh, blending with the rumbling growls that increasingly alarmed her. She didn't react as he continued to sniff and lick her, his manner more and more aggressive. Bumping her back against the wall, rubbing his coarse cheek into hers.

This was what she'd wanted—this part of him, the beast that Rollo had warned would tear into her mercilessly and make them one. Then she'd never have to worry about losing him again.

If she survived.

His teeth scraped along her jaw and she shuddered helplessly, crushed between two equally unyielding planes. She levered her hands up, palms flat upon his hot, brutally hard furred chest. His heart hammered beneath her resisting push, the fierce, savage beat of a conquering army rushing a weaker foe.

And she panicked.

Because this wasn't Max. There was no sign of him in the creature trapping her with its overwhelming size and strength. The hot pant of his breath on her face, faster and faster; the threatening snarls. The feel of him, so foreign. Not Max's powerful sleekness, but something altogether different in texture, in tone, in scent, in behavior.

He still wore the sweatpants he'd been sleeping in, but the fabric was stretched to the limit to contain the sudden bulk of his thighs, the thickening of his waist, and the frightening increase in his sex to something he could hit a home run with. That part of him pounded with a life of its own against her belly, hard, insistent, like the weapon used in the slaying of the two women Rollo had attacked and murdered.

She could see their faces on Dovion's table, could feel the fear and agony they'd endured, because that same terror lived inside her. The memory of it screamed through her and she fell into it, floundering wildly. Because Max wasn't there to pull her safely out.

She hit him, striking his altered face with mindless desperation, thinking only of escape now, of escape from the nightmare of her past.

The instant she went from passive to offensive, he responded with primitive instinct to hold on to what was his. He grabbed for her just as she shoved and dropped. She managed to duck under his arm but her ankle buckled, sending her to the floor with a cry of pain. Before she could scramble forward, he was on her, his weight smashing her against the hardwood.

Then light from the hallway swept into the room, and Oscar Babineau stood staring at them in silent distress.

Seeing his fright snapped Cee Cee back to her

senses. Wincing, she got her knees under her so she could rise in front of Max, blocking him from the boy's view.

"I'm sorry, Ozzy. Did we wake you up?" She smiled. "I shouldn't be so stubborn, trying to get around on my own. I took a fall and Max was helping me up. I guess I'm going to have to get some crutches tomorrow. Give me a hand, will you?"

Oscar cautiously came into the room, letting Cee Cee grip his shoulder while she struggled to wobble up on one leg. There was no question she was hurting, and he began to relax.

And then Max was there, solicitously cupping her elbows, his head bent close to hers as he murmured, "Let me help you."

She was lifted up with one arm tucked under her knees and deposited atop the bed covers. Then he was gone, slipping out onto the balcony to mingle with the shadows.

"Are you sure you're okay?" Oscar asked with surprising maturity, still pale but determined not to leave her without making certain.

"I'm fine now. I'll stay put for the night. Thanks for checking on me."

"I thought . . . I thought you were fighting." She could see his confusion at the signals he must have picked up from Max.

"No. We disagree sometimes, but we don't fight." Smiling, Cee Cee didn't think she could feel lower as the boy nodded and returned to his room. She spent the rest of the night alone and awake, afraid to close her eyes lest the nightmare return. The dream, she told herself shakily. It was the dream she feared, not the man she loved—who was also a monster.

FRANCIS PETITJOHN LEANED over the desktop to snap on the small light.

"Holy Mother!"

As Petitjohn leapt back in shock, Max lifted his head off the blotter where he'd been sleeping fitfully. He rubbed his gritty eyes and blinked up at Jimmy's cousin. "T-John, what are you doing here at this hour?"

Petitjohn took a rough breath and pressed a hand over his galloping heart. "I could ask you the same thing. You about scared me out of clean shorts. I've got a meeting with Cummings in a couple of hours and forgot one of the spec sheets. I didn't know anyone was even in the building."

"I wasn't planning to doze off. I was just going over some things."

Francis glanced at the empty desktop. "I'll just get those figures and get out of your way."

Max rolled back in his chair to give Petitjohn access to his file drawer. A twist of guilt got hold of him; he'd been paying little attention lately to the legacy Jimmy had placed in his care.

"How are things going with that?"

T-John glanced up at him. "Fine. We—you should make a small fortune off it."

"Just what I need, another fortune."

T-John gave him an odd look. "Yeah, right, Max. Anyway, I need to get some copies made."

"Is this something I should sit in on?"

Francis's smile was easy and slick. "Naw, just follow-up stuff. Same materials you went over on those estimates."

Estimates? He vaguely recalled the paperwork, but not whether he'd actually reviewed it. He sighed wearily and pinched the bridge of his nose as if that could stop the cannon firing off through his brain. "I appreciate you handling this, Johnny."

T-John's smooth smile thinned like ice over treacherous waters. Only Jimmy had called him that when he was in a rare fond mood, and he clearly didn't like hearing it from Max. "Nothing I like better than making a killing, Max."

"Let me know how things go."

"You'll be the first to hear."

When the door closed, Max turned out the light. The darkness suited his mood and was gentler on his raw eyes. He rested his head atop his folded arms, hoping the pain would ebb enough for him to rest. But the driving pulse kept hammering inside his skull, restless, chaotic, unsettling. He longed to go home, to let Charlotte cradle him close and soothe his feverish thoughts. It was the only place he could find comfort.

But he didn't dare go to her. Not after what had almost happened. How could he keep her safe, if she wasn't safe with him?

He was trying to do too much for too many, and was failing them all. Jimmy, LaRoche, Charlotte, and now Oscar. How could he choose which to concentrate on and which to let go? Those who could make do without him were the ones he held most dear. And he heard Father Furness's warning whisper through him. *You must be prepared to lose everything.*

He found himself on the phone.

"Caissie," came her husky voice.

"I didn't mean to wake you."

A pause. "I wasn't asleep."

"I'm sorry."

"Max? Where are you, baby? Please come home."

He squeezed his eyes shut with the same viselike tension that crushed his heart. "Charlotte, it's better this way."

Silence, then the gentle caress of words that could almost heal every sorrow. "I love you, Max. I need you here with me."

He hung up, because nothing was further from the truth.

The *last* thing she needed was the danger and possibly fatal heartache he represented.

Thirteen

HE DIDN'T COME home.

He wasn't there by the time she joined Oscar in the back of the town car for Pete to drive him to school. She rode along, bewildered by her sudden protective attitude toward a child who was not her own.

Once Oscar was safely behind his desk, Cee Cee decided the best place for her was behind her own. As she limped through the station, Joey Boucher called out, "Nice ride, detective. I need to get me a sugar daddy."

"Then you'd better get yourself a pretty face, Boucher."

Laughing, he fell in step beside her, not offering assistance because she would have stuffed his sympathy down his throat. "He's really something, that fella of yours. Never seen moves like that before."

"Yeah, he's something. Is there something you were wanting, Joey?"

He cleared his throat awkwardly. "I just felt bad about the whole thing, about what was done and how he was treated. If you care for him, he must be an okay guy, right?"

"Right. He's a peach. I'll let him know you apologized for enjoying the show while he was getting the crap kicked out of him. Maybe he'll take you off his list of those to dump into Lake Pontchartrain."

When the young officer stopped in his tracks, paling, Cee Cee sighed in exasperation. "Come on, Joey, don't start making out your will. He doesn't carry a grudge, even though I might. He's strange that way."

"Oh. Good." Looking considerably relieved, he continued to dog her to the elevators.

"Was there something else, Joseph?"

"You asked me to keep you up to speed on that floater."

"And?" She tried to keep from betraying any undue interest.

"Well, it seems we got a description on two of the possibles. Owner of some rib place remembers the kid talking to a couple of real slick customers. From up north, by their accents. Clean-cut, buttoned up tight. He thought they might be Feds." He raised his brows at Cee Cee's look of surprise. "Yeah, that's what I thought, too. Info cost sixty bucks."

Cee Cee smiled at that. "Rib business must be good."

"Same two characters were ID'd on the docks, along with three other men, all suits, chasing the kid. The piece they took off the vic—standard Fed issue."

"What the hell's going on, Joey?"

"Got me. Chief has a call out to some pals at the Bureau, to see if they're sniffing around anything in particular down here."

"When aren't they?" she muttered, bristling with territorial defensiveness. She patted his arm. "Thanks, Boucher. Keep me posted."

"When's Babs going to be back? Heard about his missus's folks. Bad business."

"He should be in this afternoon. Let anyone who's interested know the viewing's tomorrow from five to nine at St. Bart's and the funeral's on Tuesday."

"I'll do that. And don't forget to tell Savoie what I said."

"Relax, Joey. He's not going to tear your heart out over a game of softball." Then she relented. "All right. I'll tell him when I see him."

But Max didn't show up at the house that evening. She waited on dinner until the meal grew cold, and her hopes colder. With Oscar back at his home and Max missing, the big rooms echoed with loneliness. As the hour grew late and her mood grew low, she made a call, but only got his voice mail. There were so many things she longed to say to him but she stuck to business, relaying what she'd learned from Boucher. She concluded the call with a rather brusque, "Let me know what I can do."

As she stood out on the balcony, staring blindly into the night, she mulled over the circumstances surrounding Tito Tibideaux's death. She didn't buy into the Bureau being behind the torture and bizarre killing of a local kid. It didn't smack of their by-the-book self-righteousness. If they were after something in her district, they would have had the courtesy to knock first, despite the egos involved.

But the whisper of government interest opened up a whole new shadowed complexity. And a whole new world of danger to Max and his clan. Whoever was down here, willing to do murder to find answers, was just getting started. No way Tito's death wasn't related to the two bodies awaiting burial. That suggested some very professional, very scary, and very deadly forces were in play; badass boys who considered themselves above the rules.

What did they want with Max? Or Oscar?

And how was she going to help protect him if he continued to keep her in the dark?

THE VIEWING FOR Tina's parents was a mix of NOPD, retired military, and parishioners of the church. While Cee Cee stood off to one side with her gloomy partner, Tina and a somber-faced Oscar greeted visitors and friends. For a boy dealing with such a tragedy, Oscar, in his new clothes and shiny shoes, was all restrained manners—until sudden relief burst over his face like the sun from behind clouds. Cee Cee followed his gaze and felt her own

features brighten as Max Savoie entered the sub-
dued gathering.

Wearing an expensive suit, dark glasses, and a
two-day stubble, Max gave her a quick acknowledg-
ing glance on his way to pay his respects. Cee Cee
felt Babineau stiffen beside her as his wife accepted
his quiet words and offered embrace.

A scowl darkened the detective's countenance as
the hug lingered a bit too long. Tina hadn't lost control with any of the other guests, but she clung to
Savoie with white-knuckled hands, her face buried
in his silk shirt as Oscar reached up to take hold of
his arm. Almost as if they were family.

Cee Cee rocked back from the notion in uncomfortable alarm, which deepened when Tina was
coaxed from her vigil to join Max on one of the velvety sofas. She welcomed the curl of his arm about
her shaking shoulders as if they were dearest friends,
instead of practically strangers. Oscar sat on the
other side of him.

Cee Cee and Alain weren't the only ones noticing. The NOPD wives and significant others had
their heads together to tsk-tsk the impropriety, and
Cee Cee could have cheerfully jammed the funeral
lilies down their throats.

She was bothered by it, too. *She* should have
been the one to claim his attention—the one to muss
up his fancy shirt and reap the comfort of his strong
arms. All she'd gotten, after two days, was a quick,

impersonal glance. Ordinarily she would have strode over, plunked herself down on the sofa, and made herself unavoidable. But two things undercut her courage: the sound of her question, "More important than me?" going unanswered. And the boy having Max's smile.

GILES WAS OUT in the parking lot, leaning against the car. He straightened when he saw Cee Cee hobbling toward him, then frowned at the sight of her woebegone features.

"Gimme a cigarette, Giles."

He drew out his pack and flicked out a smoke, lighting it for her and waiting while she blew a chain of rings toward a disinterested moon.

It didn't help. She got the feeling nothing was going to. Cursing softly, she ground the filter tip out beneath her heel after one last long drag.

"Take me home."

"Do you want me to see if Max is ready to go?"

"No, that's all right. To my home, my apartment."

Giles shook his head. "You're supposed to stay out at the house."

"Says who?"

Giles didn't answer, fearing he'd already said too much.

Instead of tearing into him with the expected interrogation, Cee Cee sighed wearily. "Max doesn't want or need me crowding him right now. He's got a lot on his mind and so do I. Just take me home. You don't need to worry about me. I'm not anyone someone's gonna want to mess with tonight."

Without comment, he opened the car door and helped her in.

"I'M SORRY," TINA Babineau murmured as she wiped her eyes. "I thought I was all cried out. I didn't mean to get you all soggy."

"It's no big deal." Max smiled, meaning it.

"I really appreciate you and Cee Cee taking care of Oscar. I didn't know where else to leave him, and I didn't want him to go with us to . . ."

"He was no trouble."

"Did he remember to take his medication?"

Max's smile was filled with reassurance. "He didn't forget anything."

She straightened her sedately tailored suit with fluttery hands, suddenly uncomfortable with this man she hardly knew. Her husband hinted that he was a bad and dangerous customer, but that's not the impression she'd gotten. He'd seemed very direct with his feelings for Alain's partner, and for some reason her son had established a tight bond with him—the kind Alain had yet to manage. Perhaps that was behind much of her husband's dislike and distrust of the quietly powerful Max Savoie. She didn't want to think it had to do with his protectiveness of Charlotte Caissie.

She glanced up with timid gratitude. "Still, it

was very kind. Oscar's gotten quite attached to you. That's not like him; he's usually shy with new people." As was she. What was it about this hard-featured man that inspired such confidence?

"He's a special boy."

There were layers to that simple statement, the same kind of complex and mysterious layers contained behind the impassive front of the man who spoke it. Tina stared at him for a long moment, then said, "Yes, he is."

"And we're going to have to talk about that sometime soon, you and I."

She didn't speak or even move.

"Tina, the Slaters are leaving," her husband interrupted quietly.

"I'd better say good-bye." She smiled rather stiffly at Max. "Thank you again. Come along, Oscar."

Alain waited until she left before letting his politeness slide a notch.

But Max wasn't paying attention. He was scanning the room.

"Where's Charlotte?"

"She left. Said something about propping her foot up and doing some paperwork. She has to go up against Judge Carbone in the morning on a case we finally got to trial. Nothing that concerns you."

"Oh." Disappointment took a sharp bite out of his mood. He knew he'd hurt her with his avoidance, and had wanted to soothe her with gentle words and an even gentler touch. But he was so weak where she was concerned; if he wavered even for a moment, he'd be lost. Just a word, just a touch wouldn't be enough—and for the moment, he couldn't give her any more. He didn't dare. He needed to keep the hungry beast inside him at bay, and he couldn't do that when the scent of her alone could push him into a madness growing out of his control. He needed to focus, and he couldn't think when she was near him. She quickened that hard, primitive beat within his heart, within his groin, within his mind that overpowered reason or restraint. And he was afraid what it might take to satisfy it.

So, he would hurt her with his distance and he'd hold his desires in tenuous check until he could figure out a way to deal with both. At least he had the consolation of knowing she was tucked away safely at Jimmy's, freeing him to take care of other matters.

"Savoie, I don't give Cee Cee advice on how to live her life or with whom," Babineau began in a tough, no-nonsense tone. "She wouldn't listen to me anyway. But when it comes to my family, my word is the bottom line."

"Okay," Max agreed, having a fairly good idea where he was going.

"Don't take this personally, but I don't want someone like you hanging around them."

A wry smile. "I'm afraid I don't know any other way to take it."

"You'll get over it. Just stay away from them. You're a smart guy. I shouldn't have to spell it out for you."

"No. You don't. I know how to spell." Max put his dark glasses on, even though it was black outside, then he stood, noting that Babineau didn't take a step back, the way most men did. "You have a nice family. Keep them safe."

"That's my priority." With a curt nod, he went to join his wife, standing in staunch support at her side until the last of the guests said good night.

After exchanging a few words with Father Furness, Tina leaned into him with a fragile, "Let's go home."

"Where's Oscar?"

"He went out to the car already."

Alain's vague stir of uneasiness took a nasty turn when they left and he saw another shape sitting beside his stepson in the backseat. He jerked open the rear door to find himself staring at a huge black dog.

"Oscar, where did this animal come from?"

"Max told me I could have him stay with me tonight to keep me company. His name is Baby. Detective Caissie will tell you he's really very smart and very loyal and that he'll take care of me."

Babineau scowled. "Detective Caissie, huh? Where's Savoie?"

"He already left." The boy's arms looped around

the big animal's neck. "Please say he can. Just for tonight. I'll take care of him. He won't be any trouble. Please?"

"It's just one night," Tina urged from the front seat.

Babineau looked at the beast suspiciously, remembering their first encounter at Cee Cee's stairs. He had no great fondness for dogs after a neighbor's pet sent him to the ER as a child to get eight stitches. This animal had no collar, no tags, but it appeared well kept and mannerly. "Baby? What kind of name is that for a dog?"

The animal seemed to grin at him.

"All right but just for tonight, Ozzy. Don't get too attached to him."

As the car started forward, Babineau glanced in the rearview mirror to see the big animal lie down with its big head on the boy's lap. Its eyes met his in the mirror.

They were strangely bright green.

CEE CEE WENT right from the courthouse to the graveyard.

A respectably sized group gathered out in the drizzle to put the two souls to rest. Father Furness had just begun the service. She could see the Babineaus in the front row, her partner's arm curled protectively about his wife's shoulders, Oscar sitting between them. She approached quietly to stand behind the filled rows of seats, her hair wilting in the mist as she observed that image of family from afar.

Then a large umbrella opened above her head.

"You're all wet, detective."

She didn't glance up at him, but her insides began a tight quivering. She was afraid to reach out to him, afraid she'd clutch too tight and wouldn't be able to let go. She wasn't sure what to say.

Then he said it for her. "I've missed you. Things aren't right when you're not with me."

His hand laced with hers and her world steadied. They stood together, hands linked, beneath the dark sky.

As the attendees filed into the church for a meal laid out in the new multipurpose room built with Jimmy Legere's money, Max hung back, oblivious to everything but the woman at his side.

"Don't you want to go in?" she asked, smiling faintly. "There's probably sandwiches and green Jell-O salad and dry cake."

"I want you."

His soft reply made her heart leap into overdrive. Her smile grew nervous. "Right here in front of God and everyone?"

"I can't think of a better place than here."

"Out of the rain would be good."

He took her arm carefully and led her to the parking lot, moving slowly to accommodate her awkward gait. He opened the rear door to the town car and told Giles gruffly, "Go in and get something to eat."

Giles gave Cee Cee a quick look, waiting for her almost imperceptible nod. "Sure thing, boss man."

As their driver slid out, Cee Cee slid in—all the way to the opposite side of the big backseat, Max noted with some chagrin. He sat down on his own neutral side and shut the door. She didn't look at him, seeming to be very interested in the backs of her hands.

"Giles tells me you refused to go back to the house with him last night."

He watched her jaw tighten. "Giles talks too much."

"Is that because you didn't want to be there with me?"

"No. I didn't want to be there without you."

"You weren't at your apartment. I called. You didn't answer your phone. Or your cell."

"I couldn't sleep, so I went into work to put in some computer time. I turned off my phone because I didn't want to be disturbed."

"By anyone, or just me?"

"Don't be childish, Max."

"Is that what I'm being, detective? I apologize. I know you've no patience for childish behavior."

"Oh, for fuck's sake," she growled. "I'm not the one who had someone else's wife crawling all over him." He just stared at her until she took an anguished breath. "Oh, God, what a thing to say.

What a terrible thing to say. I'm sorry." She turned her head to hide the tears welling up in her eyes. This wasn't the right time for this, the right place. But there was no reining in her runaway fears.

"Is he yours?" she blurted out suddenly.

"Who?"

"Oscar." Her voice choked with suppressed emotion. "Is he your son?"

Shock set him back in his seat. "What? *No*." Then his tone gentled. "Is that what you thought, Charlotte?"

"I'm not the only one thinking it."

"I don't care what anyone else thinks. Just you." His brows drew in close. "Why would you ask me that?"

She rubbed her eyes with an unsteady hand. "I don't know what I'm thinking. I'm too tired to put two thoughts together."

He reached for her, his hand lightly rubbing her shoulder. "How long has it been since you've slept?"

She looked at him, her eyes dulled with weariness and hurt. "Since the last time you were next to me." She took a shaky breath then asked, "Could you just hold me, Max?"

He opened his arm wide and patted his chest. "Right here, *sha*."

She scooted across the seat to slip her arms around him, to burrow her face into the damp lapel of his coat and tuck her knees up tight. Encircled by his warmth, his familiar scent, by his all-encompassing care, she closed her eyes and finally let the tension ease from her body and mind.

He brushed his fingers over her in light, soothing gestures.

"I'm so sorry, *cher*."

She made a soft sound and tried to get her mind to resurface. "What? About what?"

He laid his cheek atop her head. "I've hurt you. I've frightened you. I've made you ill and unhappy. This isn't good, what's going on between us. It's not what either of us wants."

"Are you . . . are you breaking up with me, Max?" Her voice was soft in the storm of his own confusion. "Is that what you want? If it is, I'll just go now."

His embrace ratcheted up like handcuffs, holding her fast against him. *Don't leave me. Don't leave me. Don't leave me.*

Then he heard Stan Schoenbaum's vile claim that none of them would watch her back. Because of him.

"It would be best for now, don't you think? Until things get sorted through."

She was very still. In a quiet, reasonable tone, she asked, "Is that what you think? That it would be better for both of us to be apart?"

"Yes. That's what I think." But he couldn't get his body language to support his words. His breath came in quick, desperate snatches. He was kneading her hip and shoulder possessively, rocking slightly as he rubbed his face over her hair.

"Then I'll go." Even as his heart quaked, she added, "As soon as you tell me that you don't love me enough, that you don't need me or want me enough to get through this together. If you don't want me with you, I'll go. But you have to say it, and you have to make me believe it. Then I'll stay away until you ask me to come back."

She lifted her head and leveled a stare with those gun barrel-direct eyes.

He'd spent a lifetime denying what he felt, what he needed, what he wanted in his soul. He could turn those things off like a switch—and be in darkness again.

He took a breath, a diver going under where waters were cold and unforgiving, but at least familiar. His gaze went cool and opaque, his expression smoothly blank. All he had to do was repeat the words.

She waited to hear them, her stare daring him, doubting him even when he began in a low, firm voice.

"I don't want you with me. I don't need you with me."

There was no change in her expression. Not the slightest flicker, so he kept on.

"I don't love you enough—"

He choked.

He tried to take a breath and couldn't. He tried to hold her stare, but suddenly couldn't see at all.

"I'm sorry. I can't. I'm such a coward." He closed his eyes, letting his forehead rest on her shoulder. "I can't get through a day without knowing you're there for me. But I don't know how else to keep you safe. I don't know what to do. You must despise me."

She kissed the top of his head, then buried her fingers in his hair. "You are so dense sometimes. But you're mine—and I absolutely cannot let you go. Haven't you figured it out yet, Max? Our strength is in each other. You know I'm right, don't you?"

A pause. A slight nod. "Yes. Okay. Yes."

"Then you can thank me for coming to that conclusion. Right here, Savoie. Thank me."

He slid a glance up to where she tapped her mouth with two fingers, and almost smiled.

"A kiss? Is that what you want?"

"Well, world peace would be nice. But right now, I want the kiss."

Obligingly, he skimmed his lips over hers. Lightly, like the first delicate spring shower on parched ground. And with a welcoming moan she opened for him, letting him drink deeply from her well of sweet longing. He eased back with a few quick nibbles, then guided her head down to his shoulder. She rode his huge sigh with intense satisfaction.

"We'll talk," he promised, "but first you'll sleep."

"We both will."

Holding her close, he shut his eyes. "Yes." Knowing he'd be able to, at last.

Giles returned to the car and blinked at the sight of them curled up together. As he hesitated, Max murmured, "Just drive for a couple of hours or so. It doesn't matter where."

Shrugging, Giles started the car and eased out of the crowded lot. He had a sudden taste for hot sauce over in Lafayette.

In the backseat, Cee Cee rubbed her cheek against the Max's shirt and was seduced by the thunder of his heartbeat beneath her ear.

"I love you, baby," she whispered, drifting off again.

"Back atcha, *cher*." A long silence. Then, before he knew she was asleep, he whispered, "Charlotte, I think he's my brother."

Fourteen

RESTED FROM THEIR sleep, it was time to talk.

It was too early for *Cheveux du Chien* to have many customers. At Max's back table, they were undisturbed as Cee Cee began to drag the whole truth from him. Or at least as much of it as he was willing to give her.

She was still wearing her court suit, and her ankle was screaming abuse because of her dress shoes. Max had her foot in his lap, and was doing marvelous things with his hands as he quietly told her about Schoenbaum's threats and his fear of her being out on the streets without backup.

"That pig. That jerk. That . . . Argh! I'd like to pinch him like a fat tick."

"Would you like me to do that for you, *cher*?" Max asked mildly. His gaze lifted from his study of her toes to regard her with a cool elevation of his brows. Waiting.

She wasn't sure if he was kidding or not. "No. But thank you for the offer."

He shrugged. "Let me know if you change your mind."

She caught the faint trace of his smile and was relieved. "Max, no one is going to leave me hanging out to dry on the streets. That's not how things work. These guys have had my back, and I've had theirs for a decade. Okay? Schoenbaum only told you that to rile you up and scare you."

"He did a good job," Max admitted.

That got her temper percolating—thinking of the worry the arrogant vice detective had caused him. She'd have a talk with Stan, and because she wasn't a fool, she'd watch her back more carefully.

"I know how important your job is to you," he continued. "The fact that Jimmy used to curse you over his morning coffee practically every day is a testimonial to how good you are at it."

She shared his slight smile and waited for him to go on, her gut tensing because she didn't like where he was heading, any more than he liked going there.

"I don't want to take any of that from you, Charlotte. I don't want you to be less than you are, to compromise yourself because of me."

"You let me worry about walking that line."

He cupped the back of her head in his hand. "I do worry, because I can see how difficult I've made things for you. And I'm so proud of who you are."

"We're sharing drawer space, Savoie. I don't take that lightly. And that's worth a little heat from the department now and then. I'm not going to fold just because things get difficult."

"The things I've done, the things I haven't told you about—"

She cut him off. "Are done. We can't change them; we can only deal with them. Accept them." She smiled slightly. Father Furness would be glad to hear she'd finally gotten the message. "The things in our pasts are what make it possible for us to be together in spite of everything else."

A faint smile. "And you don't see the irony in that, detective?"

"Irony is my middle name." Then she asked, "These things you've done, you're not doing them anymore, right?"

"Only nine-to-five." Seeing her eyes widen in alarm, he said. "No, Detective Caissie. I have been behaving myself. I want . . ."

"What?"

He looked uncomfortable, then confessed, "I want you to be proud of me, too. I want to go places with you and have your friends see me as something more than Jimmy Legere's trained killer."

She touched his face. "To hell with them. I love you, Max. I want to be with *you*."

He rubbed his cheek into her palm. "But is that going to be enough, if it's all we can ever have? I want a life with you, Charlotte. I want a home, family, children, respect. I want to invite your friends over for beer and softball without them spitting on me. I want to play catch with our son."

She flinched away. Was it the thought of having a family with him?

She held his gaze and asked, "And what if you can never have those things with me?"

"Then I'll deal with it, Charlotte. Having you in my drawers is all I need. The first time you kissed me, you gave me everything I'd ever desired. The rest is optional."

His mood took a sultry turn as his hand eased up her smooth, nylon-clad leg.

"Am I enough for you, *sha*?"

"I don't know, Savoie. Let me think about it."

But she was leaning toward him, her lips parting. The taste of her was wild and hot and got his blood pounding in his chest. Her tongue touched his coyly, teasing him, then she sucked him in hungrily. He let himself be devoured.

His hand followed the sleek curve of her thigh under her skirt, drawn to the heat of her, which throbbed beneath his palm with a reckless, wanting beat of its own. The slow rub and circle of his thumb startled a voluptuous shudder from her and the quick, hard gasp of his name. Her scent was like a potent drug, filling his senses, dazing his mind, waking the beast in him.

As a low sound rumbled through him, she tensed and began to push away.

He wasn't inclined to let her move.

His free arm hooked about her waist and pulled until her chair butted up against his and her injured leg rode up his almost to his crotch. The more she resisted, the firmer he held on, so she relaxed, easing her hands across his shoulders, stroking her fingers through his hair.

"Easy, baby. Easy. Now's not the right time for this. I want you, too. But not here."

With a snarl he shoved back, rising in a taut, lethal move. Her heel dropped from his lap, hitting the floor with teeth-grinding pain.

"Not here. Not there. Not anywhere," Max growled, pacing tightly around the table. "There *is* no right time for us anymore. Just No and Stop and Don't." He pressed the heels of his hands to his temples, then crossed his arms behind his head, his body rocking.

Cee Cee watched him, feeling his pain and distress. It got worse every night, and she was afraid for him. Afraid *of* him. How long before he lost the ability to control what raged inside him?

"Max," she called softly, aware that others were looking their way. "Come sit with me. It's all right. Come here, baby."

He hesitated, then dropped back into his chair, bending forward so that his head rested on her knees. Gingerly, she stroked his dark hair as he moaned in a strange, rough voice, "I'm sorry. I'm sorry."

"It's okay, Max. Everything's going to be all right."

A low, anguished laugh. "No. No, it's not."

She wasn't sure what to do with him. Take him home where nothing, no one, could restrain him? But she had no idea how long he would listen to her voice. Stay here, where being among his own kind tempted his waning will?

He clutched at her legs. In a voice that sounded almost like his own, he whispered, "I don't know what I'm doing, Charlotte. Don't let me hurt anyone. Don't let me hurt you."

How was she supposed to prevent it?

He rubbed his cheek over the tops of her thighs, looking up at her through eyes hot and fever bright.

She touched his face gently. His skin burned beneath the slick of sweat. And she told him quietly, determinedly, "I'll keep you safe."

He sat up and reached for his water glass, his hands unsteady as he gulped it down. The jerky, twitchy motions reminded her of the countless addicts she'd seen stressing out for the lack of a fix. What would it take to fix him?

But it wasn't really a question—because she knew. She knew what he needed.

The club began to fill up with familiar faces. Max greeted them with restless energy, his smile a quick flash, his conversation flowing with reckless animation. And all the while, he clutched at her hand, fingers kneading hers in fierce spasms. His eyes stayed half shut. She knew if he looked up at her, there'd be no trace of their beautiful green color. He was slipping away from her.

Whenever one of the women drew near, a noticeable tension stretched through him. His gaze would slant toward them as he slowly drew in their scent. Then he'd catch himself and bring Charlotte's hand up for a hurried kiss, rubbing her palm against his flushed cheek so he could inhale her unique fragrance to regain an awkward balance. He wouldn't look up at her and she was glad, afraid of what she might see in his eyes. Torment, violence, perhaps even resentment.

"Let's go home," she suggested worriedly, hating the way his nature battled against his conscience.

His gaze flew up to hers briefly and the anguish in them ripped her heart in two.

"No. Let's stay here for a while. Until I feel better."

He didn't want to be alone with her. He was afraid to be alone with her. He preferred to suffer in company than risk seeking ease with her.

"Max, come home with me. Let *me* make it better."

He froze when she leaned toward him. As her lips grazed his, he moved his head sharply to the side. "No. There's nothing you can do for me. Just keep your distance. Just be with me. I can ride it out. Please don't make things more difficult for me."

She touched his shoulder lightly, feeling helpless and anxious. "I won't, baby. I won't." When she stood, his gaze jumped to her face in alarm. "Just a quick trip to the ladies' room. Will you be all right?"

"Sure. Sure."

He looked like hell.

Before she could consider what she was about to do, Cee Cee wove her way to the bar where Jacques LaRoche was chatting with several patrons. When he saw her, he came down to her end, smiling.

"Charlotte."

"I need you to do something for me. No questions."

LaRoche made it easy for her. He didn't look up from the glass he was polishing. "Anything. Ask."

"I'm going to go home and I want you to keep Max here. I want you to get him so drunk he can't think, so drunk he can't control what he is, or stop himself from what he needs to do."

"Which is what, exactly?"

Anguish and frustration flooded her face with hot color. "Dammit, Jacques, do I have to spell it out? Get him laid."

That brought his head up. He blinked. "Say what?"

She leveled a fierce stare. "You know what's going on with him. He won't let me take care of it, and I can't stand watching it tear him apart. We need to get past this before it tears *us* apart. You must know any number of your women who are willing to be with him. Don't you?"

"Yes."

She took a breath, her courage faltering before pride muscled in. "I don't want to know any details. I don't want to know who she is. But I want her to know one thing." Her gaze chilled. "It's just tonight. Just this once. He's mine and I will not share. If she ever comes near him again or thinks to make any demands, I will not be merciful."

"I believe you. And I'll make sure she does, too. Are you sure you want to do this? He loves you, and he's no fool. He'll know you're not okay with it."

"I hate it, dammit. But I love him. I love everything about him, everything he is. And this is a part of it. He won't let me help him through it, so I'll just have to deal with it. And I don't know any other way. Do you?"

"No. I'm sorry. Just the old-fashioned way."

She nodded grimly.

"Charlotte? If there's a child?"

The thought was a cold blade to her womb. But she didn't flinch as she said, "I will love any part of him."

"I'll see to him for you, and I'll send him back to you."

"Tomorrow. Not tonight. I'm not quite that brave."

"You sell yourself short, *cher*. I think you can stand anything you put your mind to."

"Anything but losing him. Good night, Jacques."

"You amaze me, Charlotte."

She didn't feel amazing or strong or noble as she approached their table. She slowed her step and forced the tension from her muscles so Max wouldn't sense something was wrong. She came up behind his chair to touch the back of his head. He leaned back into her palm, his eyes lifting.

Immediately, he frowned. "What is it?"

"I have to go. I just got a call."

"Something bad?"

"No, just time-consuming. I'll be out most of the night. Why don't you stay here and unwind, and I'll see you tomorrow after work." Her fingertips strayed behind his ear where the hair ended in a slight curl.

"Okay." He reached for her hand, just missing the tips of her fingers. "Charlotte?" She backed away, unable to give up the sight of him. As he started to stand, LaRoche elbowed his way through to place a shot and a beer on the table in front of him.

"Happy birthday."

His glance flickered to LaRoche. "It's not my birthday."

"How do you know? You said you didn't know when it was, so I'm making it today. Drinks are on the house."

"I don't want—" He looked over his shoulder, but she'd already turned away and was striding for the exit. "Charlotte?" The weight of LaRoche's hand kept him in his chair. Just before she reached the door, she glanced over her shoulder and touched two fingers to her lips, then was gone.

Two HOURS LATER he was nearly gone himself. His head pounded and whirled. The too-loud music seemed to play at the wrong speed. He wanted to go home, but every time he mentioned it, Jacques filled his hand with another drink. Thinking he should just throw up and get it over with, he let his eyes slip shut, closing out the blurred visuals that no longer made any sense to him. Maybe if he just nodded off for a moment . . .

Fingertips pressed lightly to his temples to begin a soothing massage. He made a low sound of liquid contentment. *Charlotte.* He took a deep breath, and beneath the thick haze of smoke and liquor was the seductive tease of *Voodoo Love.* Soft lips touched the side of his neck, sucking, licking. Heat shot through him in a cauterizing blaze. *Charlotte.*

Everything churned up inside him. Want. Need. Hunger. And that deep, primal pulse sent the blood hammering through his heart and to beat fiercely down below.

"Take me," she whispered against his ear.

Yes. It was time. Past time.

He let her half haul him up out of the chair. He was none too steady on his feet. His vision was skewed and doubled; his sharp senses lay dulled beneath the weight of drink.

As she pulled his arm about her shoulders, something nagged at the back of his mind. Something wasn't right. Not right at all. But he couldn't quite grasp what it was.

From behind the bar, Jacques LaRoche sighed as he watched Amber lead Max out the back door. And he hoped he hadn't misjudged Savoie's gutsy girlfriend's devotion.

CEE CEE PACED her crowded living room, trying to keep from watching the clock, trying to shut out the memory of Max dancing with one of their women, smiling at something she said while her fingers teased through his hair. *Stop. Stop!* She willed the taunting image away. *Don't think. Don't feel. Don't cry.* Still, the tears wobbled in her eyes until she dashed them away. She got a beer out of the fridge and dropped onto the couch, swallowing the cold brew down in a few quick gulps. She wanted oblivion. She wouldn't think of it as making love, not even sex. Just a simple biological cure for what ailed the man she loved.

Oh God, what if he didn't come back to her?

What if, as a smirking Rollo had suggested, once Max got a taste of what his own kind offered, he grew dissatisfied with what she could provide?

She didn't doubt that Max loved her, but she couldn't discount the pull of instinct. She'd watched that brutal tug-of-war within him for weeks. And she'd just pushed him away from her side.

All the bold words she'd tossed at LaRoche soured on her tongue. She'd said she didn't want details, that she didn't want to know who, but jealousy shredded those sentiments. With punishing desperation, she wanted to know everything. Did they kiss? Was there touching? Was he coaxing this other female up to the same heights of pleasure she believed her own? Or could it be just biology?

Dammit, Max. You're mine. You're mine. You are mine!

If she hadn't been so weak, he wouldn't be mining some other lover. She headed into the kitchen to set the empty bottle down next to the parade of its brothers on her counter. If she'd convinced him she was strong enough, tough enough, that she loved him enough, she'd be wearing his mark, she'd be surrounded by the smug certainty of belonging to him. Instead of quivering in her kitchen, wishing she could take it all back.

The sound of the empty bottle hitting the floor startled her. She bent quickly and began picking up the pieces, sweeping them up carelessly with her hands when she could no longer see through the tears. After she'd brushed the shards into the waste can under the sink, she straightened and saw him standing just inside her open balcony doors.

"What are you doing here?"

"Do you want me to go?"

She stared at him for a long moment. "No."

She couldn't see him clearly there in the shadows, and she needed to, desperately. She needed to see his expression: guilt, relief, regret?

He took a few steps forward and to her dismay, there was no trace of emotion on his face.

"You were crying." A flat observation.

She held up her hand. Blood beaded in bright dots on her fingertips. "I broke a bottle. I cut myself."

No flicker of concern. He made no move toward her. "I thought you were working."

"I—it was resolved by the time I got there. So I came home."

"Not back to me."

"No. I was . . . I was tired."

"Don't lie to me."

Her heart gave an anxious little leap. She didn't know what to say. He wouldn't betray a clue of what he was feeling, so she had nothing to react to. Cautiously, she asked, "What do you want me to say?"

"Why would you leave me there like that? To be rid of me? I don't believe that. I won't believe it unless I hear you say it."

Nothing he could have said could have surprised her more.

"Tell me, Charlotte."

"You think I was here bawling my eyes out because I wanted to get *rid* of you? That the idea of you banging some other woman was *okay* with me? I'd rather gouge my eyes out than see that in my mind!"

He said forcefully, "Tell me what that was all about, then."

"You needed something, so I arranged for it to be taken care of."

"Just like that. Without mentioning it to me."

"What would you have said?"

"I would have said the only woman I want to touch or taste or love is the one I'm looking at right now."

Anger burned away the hurt. "Don't you dare tell me I'm the only one you need! You selfish bastard— why can't you trust me? I'm every bit as tough and capable as any of those brainless pairs of boobs."

"I know you are. And I trust you without question."

"With your heart but not your mind. With who you are but not with *what* you are."

"I don't understand."

She came around the kitchen bar to stalk up to him. "Yes, you do. You don't give me the credit of understanding what you are, what you need."

"You're the one who shoved that pair of boobs in my face, detective. You're the one who told her—" He broke off.

"Told who, what?"

"That I was demanding something you didn't want to give. That the idea of mating with me was so repellent, you were looking for a way to back out without hurting me." It sounded weak and ridiculous when he said it out loud, but it had felt like a knife in the gut at the time.

"And you *believed* that? That I'd use you and I'd abandon you? How could you think that?"

His voice was quiet. "Because it's been true of everyone I've cared about."

Fifteen

FURIOUS, CHARLOTTE SEIZED him by the ears and shook him hard. "Not me. It's *not* true of me!"

When he only stared at her through those opaque eyes, she shoved away.

"Don't you hide behind that. You don't *want* to believe it—because then you'd have to let me in, to let me close, and you don't want to do that. You want to keep that part of you separate, like it's some exclusive private club I can't join. I've been on the outside of everything my entire life, and I'll be damned if you're going to shut me out now. What are you so afraid of? That I can't take it? That I'll fail you? That I'll bail on you? What I can't take is watching you struggling through this alone. What are you scared of, Max?"

"Me," he blurted, then rushed on before he could regret it. "I'm afraid of me, of these feelings I don't understand, that don't have anything to do with love or desire or even sex. They're violent and uncontrollable. They're like a fever that's consumed me. I'm afraid it's going to destroy everything we've found with one another."

"It won't." Her hand stroked down his taut cheek. "Let me take care of it. Let me take care of you."

He shook his head. "I won't take a chance on hurting you."

"You're hurting me when you push me away. You're hurting me when you don't trust me enough to let me share what you are. You're hurting me when I have to think about you going to someone else for what you won't take from me." Her voice plummeted to a low, despairing place. "Did you have sex with her, Max?"

"I'm sorry, *sha*."

Her heart imploded, crumpling with a pain she'd thought she was prepared for. She wanted to turn away from his woeful confession, to beg him not to answer, but he was already rushing on.

"She was wearing your coat. You must have left it on your chair. I could smell your scent. I wanted it to be you. I wanted it to *be* you, Charlotte. And I would have let it happen—until she tried to kiss me." That discovery had shocked him sober. "But there was nothing she could say that would convince me that it was all right. And there's nothing you can say that will make me believe that if I *had* gone through with it, things would ever be the same between us. You would have seen Amber every time you looked at me."

"I'm seeing her now, and I don't like it," she said fiercely, shuddering with relief.

He ventured a wan smile as his hands cupped her face between them. "You are everything to me, Charlotte."

"Prove it, Max."

He froze.

"Prove that you trust me. Prove that I'm the one you want beside you for the rest of your life."

"You are."

"Words don't cut it, Savoie. It ends right here, right now. And you won't say no. And you won't back away. And you will trust me not to say stop."

His breathing shivered. His eyes were wide and a bit wild, with fear, with desire, with respect. "God, I love you."

"Prove it," she dared.

His hands pressed tighter, anchoring her to accept his kiss, a hard, urgent kiss that spoke of passion and desire.

She jerked away. "Stop it, Max. We're not going to end up in bed. That's not what this is about. I don't want you to be careful with me. I don't need you to court me. There's more to you: that more you never let me see, because you think it will send me screaming away like a child afraid of a nightmare. I want what you are. *All* of you. Now."

His gaze was guarded as he took a step back. "I'm not an animal, Charlotte. I'm not going to just grab you and throw you on the floor."

"Why not? Don't you want to?" She moved in close, backing him against the closet door. Her hips bumped his, grinding into his as insistently as her words pursued him. "You know you do. You know you'd like nothing better than to have your brand on me, so you can show me off and swagger around and try to control me. That's what you want, isn't it? Isn't it?"

She stretched up to take his mouth in a wet, wicked tangle—and bit down viciously on his lower lip, startling him. Her hand moved down the buttons of his shirt while she continued to taunt him with her dark, flashing eyes.

"You know I want you. All you have to do is look at me and I'm ready for you." Her hands pushed up through the dark mat of his chest hair. She reached up to nip at his chin, his jaw, his earlobe. "I like that you're dangerous," she whispered there. "I like that you're powerful. It excites me to know that if someone tries to harm me, you would rip through them like an industrial shredder. The way you did those two men in the alley who tried to attack me. And the fact that you're strong enough to crush me, but will go out of your way to be so gentle. Do you know how hot that is? How hot that makes me?"

She licked up his cheek, up to the corner of his tightly closed eyes, then buried her nose in his hair to snuffle him up until he trembled.

He wheeled abruptly away from her, warning, "Be careful, detective. Be careful what you ask for."

"I don't want to be careful. And I don't want you to treat me like I'm going to break. I'm not fragile.

I like to play rough, and sometimes I can be mean. Sometimes I like to roll around and get dirty. I'm not afraid of a good fight."

She came close again, charting the harsh angles of his face with her fingertips, touching the seam of his lips with the tip of her tongue, letting him kiss her. Then she pulled away and said casually, "Alain Babineau and I were lovers."

"What?" That got his full attention.

"You want to know why he couldn't keep me? Because he couldn't control me. He wasn't stronger than I am. He wanted me to be less, so he could be more.

"I don't want a man who can't go toe-to-toe with me. I don't want a man who'll back down or back off, one I can lead on a leash. I once dared you to make me love you—and you did. You aren't afraid of who I am. You don't pull away because of what's been done to me. I can't intimidate you, and I can't make you run away."

She pushed him, sending him back a few quick stumbles. "Step up, Savoie. Take me if you want me. Take me if you can." She shoved him again, but this time his feet stayed planted. He had her wrists in his hands, but let go when she tugged. "Coward," she threw at him. "Come *on*."

She pushed again, and this time he dragged her up against his chest, holding her there with his superior strength, with the intensity of his gaze.

She smiled. "Come on, big, bad, mobster boy.

King of the Beasts." Her gaze was heavy lidded, her mouth pursed and ripe. "If you want to put your mark on me, you're going to work for it. You want to sniff at me and mate with me, I'm not going to make it easy. You're going to have to win that privilege. Are you man enough for that? Or have those expensive suits and power lunches tamed you into something I have to lead around on a leash like a lap dog?"

Her elbow hammered into his ribs, giving her just enough time to slip away and put the couch between them.

And just like that, he changed. Nothing obvious. She saw it because she knew him so well. His posture altered, becoming sleek and fluid. His gaze gleamed, centering on her with a focus that was preternatural in its stillness. Danger oozed from him in palpable waves.

This was what he was when she wasn't watching. This was the deadly predator whose name created fear in men who let nothing scare them. Quick. Terrifying. Brutal beyond belief.

And hers, if she had the courage to claim him.

"Your manners and elegance are slipping, Savoie. You're looking quite fierce."

"I am fierce. You have no idea what beats in the heart of me."

"I do. *I* beat there," she boldly claimed.

He didn't deny it. His teeth bared. "No one dares get in my way when there's something I want."

"I dare. I'm in your way, Savoie. Always right there in front of you, in your face. So what do you want?"

"You."

He was up and over the couch. Having anticipated his move, if not his speed, Cee Cee dodged into the small dining area. He stalked her around the square table, his unblinking eyes never leaving her face. In that lean, hungry look was the edge of darkness that had shadowed him for weeks. Stripped down to his primitive urges, he seethed with them, and Cee Cee began to tremble with alarm, with anticipation.

She feinted left, then dashed for the kitchen to streak through it to the more maneuverable living room. He caught her by the waistband of her jeans, jerking her off her feet, flinging her face down across the pass-through breakfast bar with a force that knocked the wind from her. She gasped like a landed carp until she got a sweet pull of oxygen. Then she was squirming, writhing like a slippery fish, but she couldn't shake him.

One hand clamped on the back of her neck while the other tore down her jeans. Because she'd vowed not to, she didn't make a sound, but she fought him in earnest. Pinned and helpless, the worst kind of memories tore into her.

The way he tore into her. Without warning, without care, lifting her right off her feet.

She clung to the far edge of the counter, her eyes squeezed shut as he pounded into her, huge, hot, and hard. She couldn't have found the breath to cry Stop if she wanted to.

She could hear the hoarse rasp of him panting against her ear, the sound unlike any she'd ever heard. Fierce, frightening. His nails, sharp as daggers, nicked the side of her throat as he gripped the neck of her shirt and ripped it halfway off her. Dark, ugly images swarmed up, reminders of pain and torture and . . . *Oh, please, God, let it be over.*

Then he said her name, snatching away her fright in an instant.

"Charlotte, take me. All of me."

And then the feel of his bite, sharp and swift, piercing the tender skin and taut muscle between her neck and shoulder. The shock of it stunned her with sensations so startlingly pure, yet strangely sweet and powerful. A galvanizing heat seared her, cauterizing the jagged edges as it exploded, sending an orgasm shaking through her with his next violent thrust. Washing over her, rolling over her to carry her into cool darkness.

MAX WAS ON fire, his body, brain, and blood all beating to the driving pulse of near madness. There was only sensation; nothing existed beyond the scorch of urgency. Unstoppable, uncontrollable, the tension finally burst in an explosive rush.

He saw colors everywhere, so bright they had depth and weight. Dazzling, beckoning as he reached to embrace them. He heard his father's voice whispering, *"This is what you are. It's beautiful."* He stretched out to gather more, trying to hold it, to capture it as it slipped away, leaving him strengthless as he slid to his knees on the kitchen tiles, toppling into a black velvet void.

When he blinked his eyes open, everything was wonderfully clear. The low-grade fever and constant throb in his head were gone. Not sure where he was, he got his elbows under him and levered up, dislodging a weight over him. Wha—

It was a limp Charlotte Caissie. He said her name groggily. Her head rolled to one side, and he saw all the blood.

For a moment, all he could do was stare. At her still features. At the savage wound. At the scratches marring her tawny skin. And the blood everywhere, staining what was left of her shirt, streaking her thighs.

"Charlotte?" No response. His hand trembled as he touched the side of her throat, where a thready pulse fluttered. "Charlotte!"

He gathered her up, clutching her close as paralyzing terror began to build. What had he done? The sound of his low, moaning howl woke him from that stupor.

Her cell phone was clipped to the waistband of the jeans tangled about her ankles. He dialed Stuart Curry's number, and a recording told him that Jimmy's doctor was unavailable. He punched in the first two digits of 9-1-1, then stopped. An ambulance, the hospital would mean questions.

He hated the cold reason that stilled his hand. But that fierce protective instinct held firm, forcing him to take another direction.

Dovion's sleepy voice answered the number on Cee Cee's speed dial. "Charlotte, it's one in the morning."

"She needs help. I don't know what to do."

"PUT HER OVER there." Dovion pointed to a steel table.

Max stood, crushing her close to the frantic thunder of his heart. He couldn't let her go, couldn't let her go. His breathing quickened until his head was light and spinning.

He barely remembered how he'd gotten there. Racing down the steps with her so boneless in his embrace, only to stare at her car with its intimidating stick shift. He didn't know how to drive. And it would take too long to bring a vehicle from his house to pick them up.

He'd pounded on the downstairs neighbor's door until a bleary-eyed young man answered. Max had thrust the contents of his pockets at him. Hundreds of dollars; it didn't matter. He didn't recognize his own voice as he begged for a ride. *Please. Please. There's been an accident. My girlfriend . . . from upstairs. She's a policewoman. I can't drive. I can't help her. I don't know what to do. Please.*

"Max."

The feel of Devlin Dovion's hand on his arm

snapped his thoughts back to the overly bright room and the man he'd called because Cee Cee trusted him.

"It's all right, Max. You can put her down."

The firm, quiet voice reached through his frenzied mind, and very gently, he let her go.

"Sit down. Put your head between your knees. I don't allow throwing up in here."

Max took a tight breath that tasted of acid and fear. He took another, one deeper and stronger. "I'm fine now."

Dovion gave him a critical look, then nodded. "Move aside."

Max stepped back. The effort of maintaining a calm facade automatically reined in the chaos of his emotions. He watched Dovion sum up the situation with a practiced eye, struggling with the same need to disassociate what he was seeing from the woman he cared about.

"What's happened? What am I looking at?" His gaze cut to Max. "Is this a sexual assault?"

"Yes . . . no." Then flatly, "No."

Dovion assessed the blood on his face, on his hands, on his clothes. His tone chilled. "Did you do this? Did you hurt her?"

"I would never hurt her. I love her. I would never—" He couldn't finish, so he simply stood, silent and still.

Dovion turned back to the tattered and pale Charlotte Caissie to examine the wound at her neck.

"Is this the same animal that was involved in the Cummings case?"

Animal.

"No."

"Where did you find her?"

"At her apartment."

"How long between the attack and when you found her?"

"I don't know." More softly, "I don't know."

He watched as Dovion cleaned her up, the same way he would one of the corpses on his table. He undressed her carefully, respectfully, cutting off the ripped remainder of her clothing, quickly washed away the blood, then did a thorough exam. The damage done to her pale, vulnerable flesh was glaringly apparent under the lights.

Afraid he was going to throw up after all, Max knelt at the end of the table, his hand curled about one bare foot, pressing his cheek into the delicate curve of her cool arch. His heart shuddered. What had he done?

He realized Dovion was collecting evidence of a crime, and said nothing to stop him. What could he say?

"Hey, Dev."

The sound of her voice, so weak and disoriented, nearly broke his control.

"Good morning, Charlotte."

"What are you doing here?"

"I work here."

"Am I naked?"

"I'm getting no prurient enjoyment from that fact. You have my word on it."

A pause as she took in her surroundings. "Am I dead?"

He chuckled. "Not that I'm aware of. Max brought you here. He was worried about you."

"Did I get hit by a truck?"

"You've been attacked, Charlotte. What do you remember?"

A long silence. "Max is here? Max?"

He took the hand she reached out to him, holding it carefully. The way she smiled at him brought balance back. And a terrible, terrible guilt.

"Detective, I do not enjoy watching another man looking at you naked."

"Why did you bring me here? I'm fine—" As she tried to move, a groan tore from her. "Geez, Savoie, what did you do? Run a streetcar up through me? For fuck's sake, find me something to put on."

Clutching the sheet given to her, she sat up with Max's assistance. She touched her shoulder, wincing slightly. Dovion had dressed it with gauze and tape and though it no longer bled, she felt as if the jaws of a steel trap had cut through to the bone. She shifted her attention to Max.

"Are you all right?"

Something flickered deep in his unblinking stare, a furtive shadow of unrecognizable emotion.

She squeezed his hand. "Why did you bring me here?"

His tone was flat. "You were unconscious and bleeding, and I didn't know what else to do."

Dovion interrupted. "Charlotte, you should check into the hospital. I don't have the facilities here to tell if there's any . . . internal damage."

She remembered his description of the injury done to the two attacked women. They'd been ripped apart inside. Fear and objection collided.

"I'm fine. I just want to go home."

"I haven't finished collecting evidence."

She stared at Dovion, not understanding. "Evidence of what?"

"A crime, Charlotte. You're in shock. I don't think you fully realize what's been done to you." He didn't look up at Max, who continued to stand at her side. "I need to finish."

"I'm not in shock, and no crime's been committed here except maybe an overenthusiastic crime of passion."

Dovion went rigid. His features tightened in outrage, in poorly contained fury as he reevaluated his first assumption—and hated his conclusion. "Don't treat me like an idiot, Charlotte. You don't need to protect him."

"Give me what you've collected, Dev."

"Charlotte—"

"*Now*, Dev. I'll be damned if photos of me are going to pop up on Junior Hammond's screen saver." She made a joke of it, but her stare was serious.

Protest narrowing his gaze, Dovion handed over the kit he'd begun to put together. "Charlotte, we need to discuss this."

"No, Dev, we don't."

She eased off the table, clutching Max's hard forearm while struggling not to drop the sheet. Dev Dovion had seen quite enough of her for one evening. Her body was one big screaming ache, but she displayed none of that distress, fearing she'd be whisked off to the ER regardless of her wishes. She bound the drape into an awkward toga and slipped her arm gingerly into the sleeve of the long coat Max held for her. Bundled up inside it, she cast a plaintive look at her longtime friend.

"Thanks, Dev."

"Let me take you home, Charlotte." Obviously he wasn't convinced that Max presented no threat, and she wouldn't allow that thinking. From either of them.

"I'll be fine, Dev. Really. Max, let's go." She tugged his arm, but his gaze was fixed with Dovion's.

The older man's glare cut through him like one of his bone saws. "I was wrong about you, Savoie." His look clearly said he wouldn't make that mistake again and that he couldn't hide behind Charlotte forever.

Instead of speaking in his own defense, he said quietly, "I appreciate what you've done."

"There's not much I wouldn't do for her." The implied threat was clear.

Max just nodded and curled a supportive, possessive arm behind Cee Cee, waiting for her to lean into him in a show of solidarity.

She didn't fail him.

Dovion stepped back and let him steer her out of the ME's domain.

As soon as they were alone in the hall, she turned on him and whispered fiercely, "What were you thinking, bringing me here?"

"Forgive me for worrying about you, detective. It seemed the right thing to do at the time."

"And if he decides to follow up on his suspicions?"

"I wasn't thinking about that." He'd thought that Dovion would be swayed into silence by his fondness for Charlotte. Even with her bleeding in his arms, he'd been thinking with the quick caution bred into him by his mother and Jimmy Legere.

Animal, Dovion had called him.

And that's exactly what he was.

Sixteen

*H*E WATCHED HER sleep.

Deeply, motionlessly, until the dreams began.

The clock read 4:15. Darkness hung heavily on the humid air. She lay beneath a sheet wearing the loose tee shirt he'd slipped on her when he'd brought her home. She'd been asleep before Pete arrived with the car and hadn't stirred since. He'd stretched out fully dressed atop the sheet beside her and waited, watching for any signs that she needed to be rushed to the hospital.

The first soft whimper alerted him. Her head tossed from side to side, her breath quickening, shivering.

"Shhh. Shhh. It's all right, *sha*. I won't let anyone hurt you." The words tasted bitter upon his tongue as he tried to calm her night terrors. It was too late for promises now. The promises he'd made to her back then had been broken.

Usually the sound of his voice quieted the demons of memory. But perhaps because he'd created new ones earlier that evening, she only grew more agitated. Her restless movements intensified, her knees beginning to work as if she were running from some faceless, formless threat. Afraid she'd reopen the wound Dovion had dressed, Max stroked his palm over her hair, repeating that empty vow. She knocked his hand aside and started to roll away on a sob. He pulled her carefully to his chest, holding her close for warmth and comfort as he murmured, "You're safe, Charlotte. I'll keep you safe. Quiet now. Quiet, *cher*."

Her palms pressed against his shoulders, pushing wildly for escape. Her cries were low and raw.

"No, please. Don't. Max."

He released her instantly.

The sound of her plaintive moans ripped at him, left him feeling helpless and drowning in shame. He couldn't see her pain and fear and do nothing. But what could he do if she rejected his embrace?

She flinched away from the first prod of his nose. But the slow, repetitive drag of his tongue along her cheek distracted her from the dark memories. She shoved at him, muttering, "Don't, baby. Stop it." But her hands began to stroke the thick, black furring about his neck. With a sleepy murmur, she buried her face in it and curled up against him with a sigh, slipping back into restful slumber.

Resting his muzzle on outstretched paws, his eyes glowing in the dark, Max lay awake. As daylight began to pinken the edges of his room, Cee Cee finally released him to roll onto her other side.

He thought a shower might make him feel better,

but it didn't. He decided to get breakfast and bring up coffee. She'd want that when she awoke, even if she might not want him.

Downstairs, Giles was holding the front door open for a weary Helen and her daughter, Jasmine. He'd sent them to Cee Cee's apartment to put it back in order, so she wouldn't have to face the evidence of their violent mating. When Helen saw him at the bottom of the staircase, she simply stared at him.

"Is everything taken care of?" His tone was a cool slick over the choppy emotions he submerged.

"Yes, Mr. Savoie. Like nothing happened." Her voice matched his for chill civility. Then she approached him purposefully. Her hand cracked against his face, snapping his head to one side from the force. Though her eyes flashed with fury, her words remained respectful. "Will that be all, sir?"

"Yes. Thank you."

As she hustled her daughter toward the back of the house, Max shifted his impassive gaze to Giles. His relationship with the burly bodyguard had been warily evolving into something resembling friendship, but that was gone now. He read it in the other man's expression, saw the loathing, the fear return. Torches and pitchforks.

"Do you need me for anything else, Mr. Savoie?" His rough voice was frigid.

"No. Thank you, Giles."

The big man turned away from him without another word, but his censure lingered.

Max went to Jimmy's study, shutting himself inside the room. He sat in his mentor's large leather chair and brought his feet up to hug his knees, resting his flaming cheek atop them.

Only one hand had ever dealt him a blow that shook him as badly. He'd been just three or four years old, but he could still hear the sound, still feel the sudden, startling impact of his mother's hand.

He'd been so shocked, so devastated, that the impression of the act remained upon his spirit the way the imprint of Helen's palm lay upon the pallor of his skin. He'd deserved it then, just as he deserved it now.

And in the quiet of early morning, he withdrew to the place he'd created within himself, where the pain and confusion couldn't reach him.

CEE CEE GLANCED at the clock, then bolted up out of bed. Holy geez, she was slated to continue testimony at nine! That gave her only fifteen minutes to be out the door if she was going to make it into the city on time. She was dashing for the bathroom, when she realized she wasn't limping. She stopped, surprised, and tested her ankle. Not even a twinge of pain. Pleased, she continued on. But as she tugged the tee shirt over her head, remembrance sucked the breath from her.

She stared for a long moment at the gauze pad Dovion had taped over her shoulder, covering Max's brutal mark. She carefully peeled off the bandage, wincing as the adhesive yanked at her skin. Then she gazed at the savage scoring made by his teeth, remembering the similar wounds on the bodies of his father's victims. Except . . . these were pink and puckering. Almost healed.

Perplexed, she stepped under the hot spray, scrubbed up, toweled off, then snuck up cautiously on the overwhelming fact.

She belonged to Max Savoie.

She'd never belonged anywhere before, nor to anyone. She'd worn her independence like armor to protect against the truth that she was so achingly alone.

Until Max. Until his lost soul had reached out to touch hers. Until his love had wrapped around her and made her whole.

And now they belonged to each other.

So . . . what did that mean?

She didn't have any court attire here, so she snagged one of his luxurious silk shirts and tucked the soft, slate-colored fabric into her snug black jeans. After running quick fingers through her hair, she jogged down the stairs to find Helen and Jasmine staring up at her in surprise.

"I'd love a cup of coffee, if one's ready. I'm late for court and have to gulp it on the run. Could you ask Pete to bring a car around?"

"Go ahead," Helen told her daughter softly.

"Where's Max? He hasn't left already, has he?"

Helen's features stiffened, matching her tone. "I believe he's in Mr. Legere's office."

Giving her a puzzled glance, Cee Cee started for the closed door, only to have Helen touch her arm. She paused.

"Are you all right?"

The prickly woman's concern surprised and touched her. "I'm fine. My ankle doesn't hurt at all. No excuse to play hooky anymore."

Looking uncomfortable, the older woman asked, "No other . . . ailments?"

What did she know? What had she seen?

Cee Cee covered her alarm with feigned embarrassment. "I drank a bit too much. I hope I didn't make a fool of myself last night. I don't remember how I got here."

"Max carried you—you in a hospital sheet and him wearing your blood."

"I cut my hand. I broke a bottle in my kitchen."

Helen glanced at her unmarked hands and made no comment. "I'll get you that coffee."

She didn't have time to soothe Helen's suspicions, nor was she sure how to approach Max. Max, who chose to seclude himself behind closed doors, instead of being with her when she awoke. The man to whom she was now bonded for life.

The study was cool and dark, the curtains drawn tightly across the windows. He was stretched out on the sofa, his eyes fixed on her as she moved toward him. Nervousness jittered through her. She felt no different. Wasn't she supposed to be experiencing some sort of telepathic stirring? Some supersensory tingling? Some new awareness of him? But no. Nothing. Why didn't he say something? She finally broke the silence with a quiet, "Good morning."

No reply. His expression was a careful blank, his stare cool and unblinking. She hadn't seen him so pulled back inside himself since he'd stood at Legere's back. What was going on?

Ordinarily she would have dropped down onto his lips for a kiss, but the lack of anything in his eyes made her cautious. She perched on the edge of the couch, nudging her hip against his waist. Her palm rested on his shirt front, riding his slow breaths, measuring the quiet beats of his heart. Everything about him was so quiet and controlled, after so many days of feverlike restlessness.

"How are you feeling, baby? Is the headache gone?" She brushed his brow with her fingertips.

He shifted slightly to evade her touch. "I'm fine. I feel the same way I've felt every morning for the majority of my life."

Not much of an answer. Or was it? What was he trying to tell her? That his desire for her had disappeared along with the urgent instinctual needs?

"And you?" he asked carefully. "How are you?"

"Fine." She paused, giving him the opportunity to say more, to tell her what was really going on.

But he said nothing, letting the silence stretch out. Everything or nothing could have changed in their relationship over the past hours. Wasn't he the least bit curious which it was?

She said, "I'm great, actually. My ankle doesn't hurt anymore. But I'm worried."

"What about, *sha*?"

"About why you haven't touched me or smiled at me. About what you're not saying. About what happened last night between us."

"I need some time, Charlotte. Now that my head is clear, I've got some things to sort through. Could you give me some time?"

She would never betray how that wounded her.

"Sure. Whatever you want. I've got court and I'm late. I guess I'll see you . . . later."

As she started to rise he caught her hand lightly, holding on to her. Then he let go without another word.

But she couldn't let him go that easily.

She heard his quick inhalation as her lips touched his, felt his heart jerk, his pulse leap. Yet his eyes never flickered; his mouth was pliant yet unresponsive. She forced herself to stand up. Her smile was small and wry, her tone tough.

"See you around, Savoie."

She walked away, her stride brisk with a confidence she didn't feel. She didn't see the way his expression buckled briefly, but Helen did as she waited with a travel mug.

Cee Cee took the coffee with a nod of thanks, then paused as the housekeeper said, "Here. For court."

Mystified, Cee Cee looked at the objects placed

in her palm. A simple gold necklace and small hoop earrings to relieve the severity of her appearance.

"Thanks." An unexpected knot of emotion rose in her throat. Swallowing hard, she said quietly, "Take care of him, Helen."

"I will, detective."

HER STINT ON the witness stand was brutal, but the hammering questions from the defense couldn't shake her or her testimony. Not even when the slick attorney casually slipped in the fact that she was romantically linked to high-profile criminal Max Savoie. Her stare cold as a double barrel, she asked the relevance of her personal life to the fact that his client had shot two young video store employees, both in retaliation for his own firing and for the one hundred seventeen dollars and thirty-nine cents in the cash register. The defense backed down, but the smudge was already on her credibility. It wasn't enough to outweigh the evidence she'd gathered, though, or the strength of Babineau's collaborative statements.

Then her news nemesis, Karen Crawford, was on the courthouse steps afterwards, thrusting her microphone at her like a knife.

"Could you tell me the connection between your lover, Max Savoie, and this case?"

"None, other than what you'd like to invent in your ratings-hungry little mind. Get out of my face unless you have any real questions."

When she and Babineau returned to the squad room to dig into paperwork, he said nothing due to her tense and angry mood. She couldn't wait to leave but had nothing to go home to, and that unhappiness added to her temper.

When her cell rang, she answered with a growl. "Caissie."

"I saw you on the news. You looked very sexy in my shirt."

The sound of his voice was an immediate balm to her emotions, but she refused to be placated. "Yes, that's the impression I was going for: the hot girlfriend of the city's crime lord."

Silence, then a low chuckle. "My, you're in a bit of a snit, aren't you, detective? I was going to invite you to join me for a drink, but perhaps there's some other activity you'd prefer."

"Are you offering to let me slap you around, Savoie?"

"If that's what you'd like to use me for, I'm all yours."

"Are you?"

"I'm not about to let anyone else take my place. I'll have that drink waiting for you."

She snapped her phone closed and stared at it for a long moment, at odds with the anticipation percolating through her. She was so easy, she concluded in disgust.

"Go ahead," Babineau urged. "I'll finish here while you go kiss and make up."

She looked at him, startled.

He snorted, irritated by her surprise.

"What? I *am* a detective. It's not that difficult to track your surly humor back to Savoie. You're getting to be as predictable as an old married couple."

As she was striding toward the door, Joey Boucher called to her. She waited for him to catch up, fingertips tapping impatiently on her thigh.

"Hey, Ceece. News from the chief on our missing John Doe."

"Yeah?"

"No records of any official Federal business. D'you think that means something unofficial? Something with some different initials? Maybe some black bag group snatched our vic to cover up whatever they were doing?"

"You tell me, Joseph. 'Cause they sure as hell aren't going to."

She stood in the shadows of the club, letting the music pound against her. She couldn't see him but she waited there, thinking about him, concentrating on him, reaching out for him with her thoughts, with her emotions.

Max, can you feel me? I can't find you.

Nothing. Just noise and haze and the smell of alcohol.

Perhaps it didn't work with an outsider.

She started through the crowd. She hadn't gone ten feet before they were all aware of her. They knew that she was with Max Savoie, knew she wasn't one of them. They didn't like her, didn't trust her. But there was something else in the mood swirling about her. Something uneasy and curious. The second she saw Max, she forgot about everything else.

He was at his usual table. The jacket of his elegant charcoal pinstripe suit hung on the chair back. The top three buttons of his stark white shirt were open and its sleeves rolled up to the elbows, displaying a good deal of blatantly masculine chest and forearm. The designer clothes and hard lines of his face created a contrast snarling with harsh intrigue and sensuality. Desire rolled through Cee Cee as she approached him.

Her Jack and water was on the table. Using the toe of his red Converse sneaker, he pushed out a chair.

"Detective, you look so good you've got my mouth watering."

She smiled, pleased to hear it, because she'd dressed for him in a short denim skirt and mile-high heels that bared her toes. The open weave of her baby blue shrug-on sweater revealed teasing glimpses of bronze flesh not covered by the tight, white, spaghetti-strapped tank top. She was all sleek limbs and curvy handfuls, tempting him as she stepped close.

His eyelids lowered into long slits as he breathed in.

"You smell like warm, naked skin on my sheets."

Her fingertips brushed under his chin. "And you look like hot sex, right here with me on your lap."

She sat down, close but not touching, and his lungs emptied in a shaky gust. "I thought you wanted to smack me around until you felt better," he goaded softly.

She gave his cheek a light tap, then spread her fingers to explore the lines of his face and mouth. "No, you misunderstood me. What I want is to roll around with you until we *both* feel better."

"Ahh. My mistake." His smile curved up slightly and the mood between them simmered with heat.

Dare she hope that things were back to as normal as they could be? "Not interested?" she teased.

He nipped her fingers lightly. "I am so far past interested, it's becoming embarrassing."

"Good." She sat back to sip her drink, and glanced up as Jacques LaRoche's hand settled on the back of her chair.

"I need to borrow Max for a minute."

"Just for a minute," she allowed, feeling generous because Max was smoldering so delightfully. She didn't think he'd go far.

When the two men stepped away to talk, Amber approached up to refresh their drinks. She slid a cautious look at the policewoman.

"You left your jacket here last night. I put it behind the bar."

"That's not the only thing that belongs to me that

I left here last night. But that doesn't make him any less mine."

Amber took hold of the neckline of Cee Cee's sweater, pulling it over far enough to expose the telling mark. Awe and regret flicked across her face.

"I would have done anything, given anything to have him just once, for the chance to take a part of him with me," she confessed. "But all he wanted was you. I won't ever intrude again."

"I did what I had to do to keep him. Now that I have him, I'll never share him."

"You can have his children—but they'll never be what they could have been with one of us."

She left Cee Cee considering that when Max rejoined her. His gaze followed the retreating waitress, lines furrowing his brow. Cee Cee turned his attention back to her with her quiet request. "Kiss me, Max."

He leaned forward without a word. He could taste her desperation in the way she latched onto his mouth so urgently, in the way her hands moved restlessly up and down his forearms. He didn't let up until he felt her relax, her hands sliding down to curl about his.

"I love you beyond all measure," he whispered against her soft lips. "You know that, don't you, *cher*?"

Unshed misery sparkled in her eyes. "Then why weren't you with me when I woke up this morning? Why did you push me away in the study?"

"I got a little scared for a minute."

"Of what? Us?"

He brought her hands up to his mouth for quick kisses. "No, *sha*. I have no doubts there."

"Does it have something to do with what you were discussing with LaRoche?"

He should have known better than to think her shrewd cop's brain wouldn't be alerted. "Some of it. The rest would just make you angry."

His smirk made her scowl. "What? Tell me."

"The minute I stepped in here, every one of them knew my, umm, circumstances had changed. They were betting on who I'd been with."

Her eyes narrowed. "And what did you tell them?"

"Nothing, darlin'. A gentleman doesn't discuss such things."

"Who won the bet?" When he inclined his head toward the bulky bartender, Cee Cee stood up and called LaRoche's name loudly. When he glanced up, she pulled aside her sweater to display Max's brand.

"Charlotte, sit down."

The hiss of his voice made her obey, but not before she saw LaRoche swat several of the men at the bar, then extend his palm with fingers beckoning for them to pay up.

Max quickly righted her clothing. "Don't do that."

"Why?" Defiance edged with hurt. "Are you

ashamed that you gave yourself to someone outside your own kind?"

"No. I don't care what they think."

"Then why?"

"I'm afraid of what they'll do," he snapped harshly. "I'm afraid of what they might do to *you*."

Seventeen

WHAT DO YOU mean? I'm not afraid of them."

"And that's what scares me. You should be terrified of them, Charlotte. I am, because they'll get to me through *you*. And that will kill me. I won't be able to go on if anything happens to you."

He was so earnest, so fierce. She tightened her grip on his hands. "I understand now. That's why you've been poisoning yourself with the silver. So you'll be strong enough to protect yourself."

He shook his head. "No. So I'll be strong enough to protect *you*."

Her heart turned over with a glorious shudder. Then she was all business. "So what are we looking at? Who's coming for you? This lot? You can take them easily."

"No. Something horrible. Part of what we are, but different. Cold and cunning and dangerous. They're the reason my mother force-fed fear into me to keep me safe. And the reason Tina Babineau's mother hid her among strangers to survive."

"Trackers." Icy slivers of panic prickled. "But

you can sense them, right? You'll be able to recognize them."

"No, not unless they allow me to. The same way they won't know me, unless I alert them by using energy unwisely." At her puzzled look, he explained, "Changing form, healing myself, casting off glimmers."

She went cold. "In other words, you're powerless to use anything that would help you defeat them."

"It's a game of patience and skill, waiting for the other side to make a mistake first. They're already here, Charlotte. That's what LaRoche wanted to tell me. Strangers asking questions about Oscar, about Tina. I've put several of my men on the boy, professionals that Babineau won't spot and arrest on suspicion. I'm not sure if they know about me yet. Maybe my father never got the chance to pass on any hard facts. Maybe he never planned to." His expression grew sad, then he sighed and shook it off. "I don't know who sent them or how many there are. I don't know what they can do."

"But you have something they don't."

"What's that, *sha*?"

"You have me. They won't expect you to have told a human all your secrets. They'll think their King of the Beasts is trifling with a weak, helpless female. They won't know they're wrong until it's too late. Then we'll have them, baby."

He stared at her, amazed by her fearlessness,

especially after she'd already done battle with their enemy.

"You and me, together. Not separately. We're only strong when we're together. Then we can take care of each other."

It was that simple. That outrageously complex.

"I love you, Charlotte."

"You'd better. Why do they want you so much? What's in it for them?"

"If they can catch me, they'll want to study me. I'm somehow different, more powerful, more of a threat to them. I don't know why. And they'll want to breed me, to sell the next in my line."

"Now there's something to look forward to."

Max grinned wryly. "I don't think they plan to buy me dinner and take me dancing first."

A faint smile. "And if they can't catch you and make you behave?"

"Then they'll hunt me down and kill me."

"No way that's going to happen. They're not going to find it easy to take you away from me."

Max stroked his thumb down her soft cheek. "Sometimes I forget what a warrior you are. How foolish they are, to think the children I'll share with you will have no value."

Her eyes went blank, her expression flat. And part of him went cold with despair.

"You don't want to have my children?"

The answer was there in the starkness of her reaction. He tried to take a breath but couldn't, as his dreams folded in upon one another. He'd thought she'd shared them. He'd always assumed . . . He asked again, praying he'd misunderstood.

"You don't want to have a family with me?"

"It's not that, Max." Her words were soft, weak.

"What is it, then? Because I have blood on my hands? Because I can't make you proud of who I am, because of what I've done? Because I'm a monster?"

He thrust out of his chair, making her jump to catch him. She held to him as tightly as she could, knowing he wouldn't risk harming her by shaking her off.

"Let me go, Charlotte."

"Not an option. Not until you listen to me. Please, Max."

"I'm listening." His tone was low and fierce.

"Not here. Will you walk with me?"

He nodded once and she released him, retaining his hand in case he decided to bolt. Hers was sweating.

Twilight seeped across the city, making dark shadows between the buildings, spreading deep and thick across the Mississippi. The air was ripe with the rich, muddy dankness of the river as they walked along the levee.

Max remained silent while Cee Cee struggled to tell him what she didn't want to remember, what he wasn't going to want to hear. Finally he came to a stop, looking out over the wide waters.

"Tell me."

She took a breath, studying the grim set of his profile.

"I should have said something before we got so carried away. It took me by surprise, loving you. Things were all teasing and playful, and then you kissed me and I was drowning in you. I never thought . . . I never believed I could want someone so desperately, so completely. I was selfish and greedy and excited. I never thought beyond just you and me.

"It never occurred to me that you'd want more . . . until I saw you with Tina and Ozzy. And then I didn't know how to tell you. I was so afraid I'd lose you, and I couldn't let you go. I . . . let you bind yourself to me without telling you a truth you had the right to know. I'm so sorry, Max. It wasn't fair. It wasn't right."

His arms came up around her, his voice steady. "Tell me, Charlotte. Trust me."

She gripped his shirt and forced her gaze to meet his. "There's nothing I'd like more than to make children between us. But I can't, Max. I'm sorry."

His brow crowded with puzzlement. "Because of your job? Do you think I'd demand you give up something that's so much a part of you?"

She pressed fingertips to his mouth to halt him. "No, baby. Listen to me. I can't give you children. I can't *have* them. Ever."

His expression blanked in shock, in disbelief, in objection. Finally, he murmured, "How do you know? Are you sure?"

"They did more than beat and rape me, Max. They . . . did worse things." She swallowed hard, unable to bring that horror out from where she'd locked it away so far down inside her. His arms cinched tight around her, snatching her up to him as if he could crush out the memory. From the protectiveness of his shoulder, she continued, "They told me at the hospital. Too much bleeding, too much trauma, too much damage. My father . . . my father was devastated, knowing that everything he was would end with me. Of course, he never came out and said that. He never said anything. And neither did I, to anyone. I didn't think it would matter, because I never wanted any man to touch me again. Until you, Max. And then I convinced myself that I could be everything you needed, because you were everything I wanted. But I'm not. And there's nothing I can do to change that." She shoved back and began to walk away.

He grabbed her arm and spun her to face him, his expression dark.

"So what do you expect? For me to toss you away, to say you're of no use to me now? Just because your father did? For the love of God, Charlotte, how could you think so?"

"I don't want your pity or your sense of obligation," she told him gruffly. "I don't want you to stay with me because you're so damned noble. You can walk away, Max. I won't blame you for it."

Rare fury radiated from him like a furnace blast.

"And just who would you blame, then? Yourself? Oh, that's right. *That* makes sense. You're to blame for what those bastards did to you, and it's fine that I should just stop loving you because now you're somehow imperfect and unlovable."

She said nothing, her eyes wide and luminescent. Tears made glittering trails down her pale cheeks.

Max's voice gentled. "You've looked upon the horror of what I am and called me magnificent. You've held me in your arms and wept over my pain. You've thrown yourself into mortal danger at my side. You've loved me until I'm weak-minded with gratitude. You gave yourself to me when you *knew* what it would cost you professionally and personally.

"How could you seriously think I would walk away from you? You are all I've ever wanted. You are all I'll ever want or need, in this life or the next. Do not insult me again by suggesting that I don't know how lucky I am to have you love me."

She remained silent for a long moment, her lips quivering. Then she said hoarsely, "Let's go home."

Giles drove them back to the house, saying nothing as he watched in the rearview mirror the woman he so admired quaking with silent weeping.

Max simply held her. She needed him strong and comforting and unwincingly certain. And he was those things for her, lying with her cradled to his chest in his bed, both of them still dressed, tenderly kissing her brow and her damp cheeks. When exhaustion finally claimed her, he slipped away and wandered out the front door aimlessly until his knees gave way, dropping him down hard on the porch steps.

They did worse things.

Horror surged up through his numbness. His mind went mad with imagining. He couldn't breathe. Couldn't drag air past the sickness clogging his throat. He lowered his head between his knees, swaying, rocking, struggling to keep the awful grief and anguish from howling out of him.

Worse things . . .

The pungent scent of tobacco curled about the edges of his misery. Then he heard the flat calm of Giles's voice.

"Nice night."

Sitting there in the darkness, close to weeping, his eviscerated guts figuratively strewn at his feet, his chest a huge, gaping void where his heart had been, Max couldn't speak.

Giles puffed on his cigarette and asked mildly, "What did you do to make that brave little girl cry?" The y*ou son of a bitch* was unspoken but clear.

"I failed her, Giles," he whispered hoarsely. "She needed me and I just walked away. She's blaming herself for my weakness, and I can't make it right. I can't take it back."

It came spilling out of him then. He'd been just twenty, blinded by his obedient loyalty to Jimmy Legere. He'd stumbled across two seventeen-year-old girls in the hands of cruel men ordered to hold them captive—but they did worse things. He saw them and did nothing. He'd walked away. And for hours, *hours,* he'd wrestled with a suddenly awakened conscience. The one girl's fright and desperate pleas clutched at it, tearing away the veil of his indifference. But the other girl, who spat a wad of blood and contempt at her abuser, had shocked his heart into a frantic beat. And he'd shaken off twenty years of caution and security to rescue them.

"By the time I went back for them, it was too late. I'll never have a family with Charlotte. They stole that from us—ripped it out of her while I was trying to make up my mind. *Hours,* Giles. Hours with them. I can't ever give that time back to her."

Silence, just the smell of smoke. And then Giles's snort. "You've got the most amazing ego, Max. You just have to take credit for every damned thing, don't you?"

Max turned his head slowly, his eyes glittering. "'Cuse me?"

"Exactly. Give yourself a freaking break. You were just a kid, minding your own business while these deviant sons of whores were doing their worst to these girls who were nothing to you, had nothing to do with you. You decided to risk your life playing hero, going against everything you were raised to believe in, to save complete strangers—and yet their trouble was somehow *your* fault? *You're* the one who should be punished for stepping between evil men and two innocent girls?

"I'm sure that's just what Charlotte thinks every time she remembers you carrying her from that warehouse: damn that son of a bitch for deciding my life was more important than his. How could he be so selfish?

"Boss man, sometimes you are an incredibly arrogant fool. Eat my eyes if you want, but that's the truth. Choke it down."

"She can't have children, Giles." His sorrow made the words raw. "I can't give her children."

"But you've got each other." Giles shrugged his huge shoulders. "Lots of women can give you children, Max. But how many will give you what she does?" He snubbed out his cigarette. "Was I you, I'd be upstairs loving her bowlegged, instead sitting down here sharing all these touchy-feelies with some fella. But what do I know?"

Max studied him for a long moment, the words slowly sinking in. Finally, he smiled. "Good night, Giles."

" 'Nite, Max."

THE SOFT BRUSH of his lips across her eyelids made her smile. Then his mouth was on that curve, tempting her from the glum shadows of sleep. A contented sound purred up through her as she kept her eyes shut and let him woo her. He was so good at it.

He trailed light kisses down her neck, down to the curve of her breasts, his tongue sliding over to disappear into her cleavage. His hand rested on her abdomen, its heat burning through the thin fabric of her top.

"You'll be more comfortable without this, *sha*." He lifted her to peel off her sweater and tank top. His mouth pressed above her left breast, tasting the hurried flutter of her heartbeat. She reached for him to keep her balance, her palms sliding over bare shoulders. He'd already undressed and was sleekly, invitingly naked.

"You are the most beautiful, exciting, desirable woman I've ever seen," he murmured, his voice low, seducing poetry. "I will want you madly, desperately, every day of the rest of my life."

She clutched at his dark head as he circled her nipple with his tongue, then blew lightly so it tightened into a hard, achy peak. Moaning in objection when he shifted his attention to her shoulder, arching as he licked along her collarbone, chaining kisses around her throat, then pausing when he reached the scars in her flesh. Then he kissed her there, too, very, very gently.

"The courage it took to give yourself to me drops me right to my knees. Thank you, *sha*. You're mine now. You belong to me. We belong to each other, *only* to each other, for the rest of our lives."

This was what she'd wanted to hear from him when she awoke to find him gone. Relief warred with resistance. "But I didn't tell you, Max."

He claimed her gaze tenderly. "Tell me what? You couldn't tell me anything I didn't already know.

I knew the first time I saw you that you were the one for me."

She touched his cheek. "But that wasn't real, Max. That was a fantasy. You didn't know me; you knew nothing about me. You were in love with an idea that would keep you from being so alone."

He smiled. "You're so wrong. I did know you. I saw right to the soul of you with that first glance. I saw a spirit passionate enough to love someone like me, one strong enough not to fear what I was. I knew everything about you from that single moment, and I've never wanted to look away again.

"I'm not fickle, Charlotte. When I give my loyalty, it's with every bone in my body. When I give my heart, it's to the very last drop of my blood. I will never leave you, or stop loving you. I simply can't do it. What you are is everything to me. You put your mark on my heart long before I put mine on your body."

She leaned forward to take his mouth in a slow, searing kiss. Then she said, "I seem to still have some clothes on. I expect you to do something about that right away, because I want you, Savoie. Right now. Quite desperately."

She toppled him onto his back, her mouth on his ravenously. Her hands fisted in his hair, prowled his shoulders, combed over his chest, insistent, possessive.

His attention torn between her kiss and the difficult buckle on her belt, Max finally rolled her off him.

"There's less security at the Treasury," he grumbled. He jerked the belt free with a grunt of triumph, then swatted her bottom. "Lift." She did so and he wiggled the denim over her appealing curves and down those long legs. He pitched the shirt, then picked up one of her feet. "These are some seriously sexy shoes."

"I've been meaning to speak to you about your mildly disturbing interest in my footwear." She poked his bare backside with the stiletto heel on her other foot.

He grinned at her. "I don't want to wear them. I just like the way they look on you. The way they hold your scent and your heat. And I like to take them off you," he said, slipping them free, "so I can start at the very intriguing bottom of you and work my way up every other equally delightful inch."

He licked her toes, rubbing her arch with his thumbs until she groaned at the luxury of it. His focus moved to her calves, kneading them while he watched enjoyment relax her features.

"Strong, beautiful legs," he murmured. "Sexy knees." He kissed them as his palms went higher. "You could probably crack a man's rib cage with these thighs, couldn't you?"

She smiled. "Or I could just wrap you up in them and trap you until I'm done with you."

"Ooh, yes. And then there's this tasty piece of you." His fingers played over her, slipping into her. "I could lose myself here for a day or two."

"You make it sound like you're exploring Mammoth Cave," she grumbled as her hips lifted, rocking into his touch.

His grin flashed at that while his eyes smoldered. "Oh, no. No tourist attraction here. This is my own private playground."

"Stop talking, will you?" she panted, then moaned as he gave her a hard, sucking kiss.

His voice grew quiet. "You'll let me know if you're in any discomfort after last night."

She pushed against him impatiently in answer.

"Then I'll test the waters, so to speak." When he dipped in to do just that, her first climax slammed through her. He took his time until she was wet and trembling, then said, "Speaking of natural wonders, I'd like that Grand Canyon tour again. Do I need to purchase a ticket for that?"

Her glassy eyes refocused and she returned his sly smile. "No, you just need to hang on." She flipped him and settled atop him, sinking over him with a long, glorious shiver, stealing the breath from both of them.

His hands came up to rest on her waist. "Nice to have you back in the saddle, detective."

"I plan to ride you hard, Savoie."

And she did with fierce concentration, in a race to prove something to herself. She reached it with a strangled sob of relief, then let him roll her limp body over so he could take control.

"Charlotte, look at me. You are mine—now and forever."

He began to move in a slow, strong rhythm, his fingers laced through hers, pressing them into the mattress. His gaze was riveted to hers, watching her eyes mist.

"Max, promise me you'll never regret this. Make me believe it."

"I will." And he did.

Eighteen

No. Please. Don't leave me. Please, don't leave me here alone. Please, don't leave me. Please!

She woke with a gasp, tendrils of the dream still tugging her back toward them. So strange, because she never remembered them. Except for one.

"Everything all right, *cher*?"

She turned to Max, and all other thoughts scattered.

The first rays of morning slanted across his wonderfully rough and rumpled features. His black hair stood in spiky clumps. Heavy-eyed, stubble-cheeked, his mouth sleep-softened and irresistible, he was her every waking dream.

"Now it is."

He grinned.

"You're looking rather pleased with yourself," she said. Her fingers meshed with his.

"I'm feeling rather pleased with myself. How 'boutchu, *sha*?"

She smiled and snuggled into him. "I'm feeling rather pleased with you, too." She wanted to linger for a few more minutes but, aware of the clock, she finally rolled out of bed with a sigh. "I've got to shower and go."

She didn't dare look back; imagining him there in the sheets, all sleek and hard, was bad enough. Snatching up some clothes, she decided a cold shower was what she needed.

He joined her under the spray, heating her up faster than the pelting water could cool it. He pressed her back against the slippery tiles, pinning her there with the force of his greedy plundering mouth. She grabbed at his wet hair and clung to the rock-hard slickness of his shoulders as desire surged, demanding to be satisfied.

He obeyed without hesitation, lifting her, filling her, pounding into her, rushing them both to a knee-weakening climax.

Unbalanced by Max's slack weight, Cee Cee slipped and went down, her bare flanks squeegeeing the tiles, landing with a jarring shock to the spine on the floor of the tub. Pulled down with her, Max cursed as his knees hit bottom but made no effort to move.

"Do you suppose this is how most fatal accidents happen in the home?" he chuckled.

"That's the way I want to go," she murmured contentedly. "You'll see to it for me, won't you, Savoie?"

"My pleasure, detective."

It took some cautious maneuvering to regain their footing. Since it involved some intimate handholds on each other, though, neither complained. As Max worked up luxurious suds over her most likely to be bruised posterior, Cee Cee sighed.

"I wish you had one of those big, old claw-footed tubs we could splash around in, then just soak until we turned all wrinkly."

"Charlotte, darlin', exciting images of you all wet and pruny will not get you to work on time." He turned her under the showerhead even as he kissed her, letting the soap and scent of well-enjoyed sex go down the drain. Then she was wiggling away, scrambling out of the shower, buffing herself dry as quickly as possible while he leisurely lathered up. She managed to be almost completely dressed by the time he emerged.

"What were you dreaming about this morning, Charlotte?" he asked as he dried off.

She shivered as the memory returned. "It was very strange and so real, I could smell the swamp, could feel its chill all the way to the bone. And I was so afraid. There was someone with me, a woman. I knew her, but it wasn't someone I recognized. I felt so small, so helpless and . . . Max?"

His face had gone pale.

"Baby, what is it?"

"And there was a big tree, with roots knuckling up all around it?"

"How did you know that?"

"Because it's my dream."

She stared into his eyes, into those windows to

his past, and she knew the woman in the dream was his mother. The horrible, roiling fear she'd brought back to the surface of consciousness with her was real. It was his fear. His memories.

She embraced him, hugging his dark head to her shoulder, while she wondered how this sharing of consciousness was possible. Was this the power of the bond between them, this opening of the psyche? Her intensely private nature rebelled against the intrusion, even as her tender heart cherished the idea of such intimacy. How would fiercely guarded Max view her unintentional invasion?

"So, how does it work, this thing between us?"

"I don't know. When a human male mates with one of our females, there's nothing unusual about it. Between our kind there's just a stronger glimmer, a special sharing of awareness. I've never heard of an exchange of thoughts or communication or anything like that. But then, I've never heard of a bonding between one of our males and a human female."

"And there's one other thing we have to take into account," she said. "There's never been another like you."

"Yeah. There's that." He frowned a little, then moved away to dress with a quick efficiency in jeans and her chopped-sleeve NOPD sweatshirt. Then he turned back to her.

"We don't talk of this with anyone else. No questions, no hypothesizing. Not with anyone. Agreed?"

Her look matched his for severity. "Agreed."

"We keep this strictly between the two of us until we figure it out ourselves."

"I understand."

She realized the danger as well as he did. How much more valuable would such intriguing knowledge make this man she loved, to those who would take him from her if they could?

"Can I ride into the city with you?"

Alerted by the tension in his voice, Cee Cee asked warily, "What are you up to?"

He snatched a quick taste of her lips. "Some undercover work. I have to find these men who've been asking questions. I want to get a look at what we're up against."

"Be careful. Don't let them see you, and don't try doing anything about them on your own. We're in this together. Don't you forget that."

"I love you, Charlotte."

"And don't you forget *that*, either."

THEY RODE IN silence, both caught up in the same thoughts and concerns. Finally, Cee Cee glanced at Max. He was studying her hands and feet as they worked the shift and clutch. Sensing her attention, his gaze flickered up in question. She didn't look pleased.

"You're not going to try and, like, read my mind, are you? You'd tell me if you could, right?"

He grinned at her touchy tone. "Depends. Is there anything particularly interesting on your mind that you'd prefer I not know?"

She glared at the road ahead. "I'm serious, Savoie."

"I can see that you are. Afraid I might pick up some interesting information on, say, Alain Babineau?"

She looked perplexed. "What could possibly interest you . . . oh."

"You brought it up, detective. You might say you rubbed my face in it."

"I was trying to provoke you."

"You succeeded." He waited for a patient minute or two, then demanded, "Tell me."

"He has nothing to do with us."

"I can make you tell me."

She laughed. "No, you can't. You don't scare me, and I don't think you have the self-control to go without sex for another thirty years, beast that you are."

"We'll see who has the better self-control, detective." And he leaned over to tongue her ear and tug at the small gold hoop she still wore. The low vibration he made sounded suspiciously like her engine.

"Stop it, Savoie. I'm trying to drive here." She reached up to lightly smack his head, and suddenly, the playful mood was gone. She gasped, her body bowing, her eyes rolling back. The car jerked across the lanes in a frantic zigzag before she could wrestle it under control and screech to a stop on the shoulder. She sat pressed back against the seat, eyes shut, her body shuddering.

"Charlotte? Charlotte, what's wrong?"

The sound of his voice shocked her back to awareness. She whipped around to face him, her eyes huge and glazed, breath ragged, brow and neck slick with sweat.

"Holy geez," she gasped. "Holy geez, what the *hell* was that?"

He blinked, at a loss. "What was what? Charlotte, I don't—"

She seized him by the ears, yanking him to her to devour his surprise-slackened mouth with hard, hurried bites and determined thrusts of her tongue. The blast of the horn from a passing semi snapped her frenzied state. She pushed away as abruptly as she'd grabbed him, then sat frozen, panting, staring at him as he touched fingertips to his bruised lips in baffled amazement.

"Charlotte—"

She put up a staying hand that trembled wildly. "Don't say anything. Just sit there. Don't talk to me. Don't touch me. Don't even think for a minute. Okay?"

"Okay."

She scrubbed wet palms on her pant legs, then wiped the dampness from her face. She was shivering uncontrollably as she shifted and guided the car back onto the road. They were cruising down the busy avenues before she finally pieced her fractured system back together. Max was still watching her, silent, alarmed, and uncertain.

"How did you do that?" she asked in awe.

"I wasn't aware I was doing anything. What did I do?"

What indeed? She'd never experienced . . . no, that wasn't quite true. Once, as he'd said her name, as he'd sunk his teeth into her flesh to seal their bonding. Those same sensations had rocked her and left her hot and reeling.

"Geez," she muttered to herself, her insides still quivering. "No wonder it's for life. Who'd ever walk away from that?"

"What? You're not making any sense, detective."

She slid him a speculative smile. "We'll discuss it later, Savoie. In depth and in meticulous detail. Just not while I'm driving. And here I didn't think perks got any better than frequent flyer miles." She reached over to rub the sleeve of his leather jacket, then was distracted by her cell ringing. "Caissie," she all but purred.

"Ceece, is Oscar with you?"

"Ozzy? No, why? Babs, what's going on?" The frazzled tone of her partner's voice had her gripping Max's arm. "What's happened?"

"There's something going down at his school. He's not in his classroom."

"I'll meet you there in less than five. Alain," she made her words firm and convincing, "I'm sure he's fine."

———

COLLIER ELEMENTARY WAS in chaos. Teachers tried to herd weeping, frightened children into organized groups. Parents raced wildly across the lawn and parking lot searching for the faces of their little ones. Fire trucks blocked the street, and hoses snaked across the sidewalks to doors that billowed black smoke.

Tina Babineau stood in her front yard, her hands gripped together as if in prayer, her pretty face pale as death. When Cee Cee squealed to a stop on the driveway next to her, she ran to Max as he leapt out of the car. He held her so she could see his face and hear the calm rumble of his voice as Cee Cee came up beside them.

"Tell us what you know, Tina."

"When I heard the alarm and saw the classes come outside, I thought it was a routine fire drill. Then I saw the smoke and fire trucks." She broke off when her husband's vehicle bounced up over the curb, popping a tire as it tore grooves in the grass. She rushed into his arms. Alain crushed her close, then the same competent control in Charlotte's face settled over his.

"Tina, where's Oscar?"

She took a breath. "I found his class, but he wasn't with them. He wasn't anywhere around. One of his friends said he saw some men in the hallway—not firemen or policemen, not parents. One of them had Oscar by the arm, pulling him the other way."

Max had turned toward the school building. His

eyes half closed as he stood with an eerie stillness, scenting the breeze before announcing softly, "It's not a fire. It's a ploy, a distraction. To get Oscar."

At his wife's terrified cry, Babineau demanded furiously, "How could you know that?"

Cee Cee placed a hand on his arm. "Believe him. Can you tell where he is, Max?"

"Not in the building." Max flipped open his phone to quickly dial, then asked tersely, "Nigel, where is he? Who are they? How many? Nigel—are you there? Nigel?" He swore softly. He looked to Cee Cee, mouth thinning grimly. "They took out the men I had on the boy."

That was enough for Babineau. "What the hell is going on here? Savoie, if you have anything to do with what's happened to Oscar, I'm going to shoot you where you stand."

Max's keen gaze swept the street, fixing on an unmarked Expedition with tinted windows coming way too fast, weaving between rescue vehicles and startled pedestrians. Without a word, Max charged into its path and, even as Cee Cee was screaming his name, jumped up onto the hood of the vehicle. He held to the windshield wiper with one hand while using his elbow to crack the thick glass. A quick jerk of the SUV sent him rolling, skidding off the hood to hit the pavement hard, but he was on his feet before Cee Cee, Alain, and Tina could reach him.

"Keys," he demanded of a startled Charlotte.

"You don't know how to drive," she sputtered as her gaze flew over him in search of possible damage.

"I learned on the way over. Stay here with Tina."

"The hell I will," she growled as he snatched the key ring from her hand.

Babineau looked at his flat tire in frustration, then grabbed Max's arm. "I'm with you."

"Come on then." And he was up and over the hood of the Nova, pausing when Cee Cee shouted his name. Meeting her penetrating stare as she said, softly, fiercely, "Be careful." With a nod, he was beneath the wheel and the car was in motion even before Babineau could shut the door. Gears ground, and the vehicle shuddered and lunged. Zero to sixty in a heartbeat.

EVEN BELTED IN, Babineau hung on to the dash to keep himself from being snapped side to side as Max threaded in and out of the heavy traffic. He'd thought Cee Cee was hell on wheels, but Savoie was fearless. With the timing and coordination of an Indy driver, he put the pedal to the floor, whipping through red lights, chewing up the shoulder, barreling down the oncoming lane with unflinching concentration. And no apparent knowledge of traffic laws.

"Who the hell taught you to drive? The Speed Channel?"

"Watch for them. We should be catching up to them any second."

Babineau glanced at the speedometer. Ninety plus in a residential zone. "Unless you want to catch up to tomorrow you'd better ease it down."

"Don't you want him back, detective?"

Babineau glared. "Of course I do. What I don't know is why it matters so damned much to you."

"He's my brother."

Alain could think of no reply.

"There they are."

The big vehicle was racing along an adjacent street, heading toward Highway 10. And ahead of them was a line of stalled traffic.

"Savoie, you're going to have to slow down. Max, slow *down*. Sonofabitch, *slow down!*"

The car jolted up onto the sidewalk, clipping newspaper boxes and filling the air behind them with the confettied early edition. Then he was back on the street, slicing across five lanes of blaring horns like a knife through hot corn bread, and slick as you please roared onto the highway.

Max glanced at Babineau's white face. "Charlotte will be mighty annoyed if you ruin her seats."

"I'll try to control my bodily functions if you won't be quite so determined to end them." He took a shaky breath. "Explain brother to me."

"We share the same father. I don't know any of the particulars."

"Why didn't Tina tell me?" This was said more to himself.

"I'm not sure she knows."

"So that makes you . . ." He couldn't get the word out.

Max flashed a quick grin. "Family. Yes, it does. Can I call you Daddy?" Then he was all serious business as he sent the boxy little car shuddering into a lightning-fast lane change.

"Who are these people, and what do they want with my boy?"

"They want my father's son—and failing that, they'll want me."

"Why?"

"Let's ask them."

The 427-cubic-inch big block growled up behind the slick SUV.

"Shall we knock first?"

Bumpers tapped.

No response.

"They're not taking us anyplace we want to go. It's better if we stop them here."

"On the damn overpass? With no backup? Are you crazy?"

"No more than Oscar is."

Another hard knock, metal to metal.

"I don't think they're taking us seriously." Max cut the wheel sharply and tromped down on the accelerator. The gutsy little car surged forward, flying up alongside the powerful Expedition.

Babineau drew his gun.

"That's not going to help. Let me take them. You get the boy and go. Don't look back."

"And leave you?" Alain stared, amazed, then he snorted. "Cee Cee would kill me. We're in this together, Max, whether you like it or not."

"I don't like it much. Just don't get in my way."

A barking laugh. "*Your* way? I'm the cop here."

"They're not going to care about that. And you're not going to stop them with what you're packing in that gun. Let me handle it, detective. This isn't about ego. It's about the boy."

The two vehicles paced one another for several miles. When there were miles of nothing but empty concrete and swamp ahead and behind, Max gunned it to pull ahead and cut the other off. The monstrous SUV elbowed sharply into them, flipping the lightweight vehicle and sending it skidding and sparking down the road on its black roof.

When the Nova stopped, Babineau hung upside down from his seat belt, blood running into his eyes from where he'd smacked his nose on the dash. Max crawled out of the vehicle and ran toward the maimed Expedition. The tinted driver's window rolled down to expose a lethal gun barrel. Max took hold of the shooter's wrist and didn't let go even as he took two close-range bullets in the chest. He jerked the driver out, door and all, and leapt into the vehicle.

Things greyed out for a moment as Babineau struggled to release his belt. Through blurry eyes, he saw Max Savoie round the rear of the Expedition with Oscar in his arms. He tried to pull his gun, blinking to clear his eyes so he could back Max up. The doors to the SUV were flung open.

And as Babineau watched in dismay, Max vaulted over the guardrail and disappeared, plunging with Oscar into the bog some thirty feet below.

TINA AND CEE CEE raced out of the house when the squad car dropped Alain off at the door. Both stopped when they saw his bloodstained clothes and bandaged head. And the fact that he was alone.

"I'm sorry. I'm sorry." He dropped down heavily on the front steps, head in his hands, unable to look either woman in the eye.

"Oscar? Where's Oscar?" Tina demanded.

"He's with Max."

Before Tina could release a breath of relief, Alain told her the rest of it, concluding miserably with, "We've got choppers up and men on the ground. It's only a matter of time before they're spotted."

Tina nodded, tears glittering on her lashes. "I'll get you some clean clothes. You'll want a shower and a meal before you go back out."

Babineau waited until she went inside to grip Cee Cee's hand.

"How bad?" she asked tersely.

"They shot him twice, point-blank in the chest. Didn't even stop him. He went over the rail with the boy. Chances are it's not so much a search and rescue, as it is a recovery."

Cee Cee never flinched. "Did he fall or did he jump?"

"He jumped."

She released a shaky breath. "Max will keep him safe. Don't underestimate him. Don't you *dare* give up on them."

Her partner stared up at her through weary eyes and said nothing. Not when they joined the search team for the remainder of the day. Not when the search was suspended for the night as a thick fog rolled in. He asked her to stay at their little house so they could get an early start together. And she lay in Oscar's twin bed, listening to Tina Babineau sob, her own eyes dry and her heart aching at the thought of Max and the boy out in the swamps alone.

She woke to pale darkness, her pulse pounding, her body crippled with pain and fever. She lay still, letting the sensations roll over her—the fear, the hurt, the desperation. And reached out.

I'm here, baby. Don't be afraid. You're not alone. Show me where you are.

Nineteen

"Max, can we go home yet?"

He dragged his eyes open. Oscar was crouched at his side, dirty, shivering, looking miserable but not complaining. He smiled faintly. Brave kid.

"Not yet. Soon. Just stay quiet."

"Okay. You want me to pack some more mud? You're bleeding again."

He blinked slowly and glanced down. One bullet had gone under his arm and out his back—nothing serious if he could get it to stop oozing. The other was a bit more worrisome, low below his collarbone, lodged deep where it made it difficult for him to breathe. Both bullets had been silver and probably would have killed him in minutes. That's what they'd be thinking, so maybe they weren't still following.

Maybe.

The blood was his bigger concern—keeping it from dripping in the stagnant water, from scenting the air. He knew what it would bring once it got good and dark, and he feared that more than those who'd been tracking them.

Oscar eased the leather coat from his shoulder, features tightening at Max's low groan. He moved the makeshift bandages and covered the wounds with more of the slimy muck.

"Why don't you just make them go away?"

"What?"

"Fix them. You can do that, too, can't you?" When Max just stared, he shifted uneasily and explained. "When I was little, I climbed out onto the roof to sit in the rain. I wasn't supposed to, but it was so hot and the air smelled so good. You know?"

Max returned his smile. "Yeah, I know."

"Well, I slipped on the wet tiles and fell. I broke my wrist. I couldn't tell my mama because I wasn't supposed to be up there, but it hurt really bad. And I . . . I sort of made it go away. If you tried, you could do that, too."

"I could, yeah. But they'd know, and it would bring them here before I'm ready for them."

Oscar was all attentive interest. "What are you going to do, Max?"

"Wait until morning, when it starts to get light. I'll bring them here and while you run, I'll make sure they never hurt you or scare you again."

The boy regarded him solemnly. "You're going to kill them. Alain told me sometimes that's the only way to stop really bad things from happening again. He's had to kill people, but he doesn't like it."

"Neither do I, but they have to be stopped. They

can't be allowed to tell anyone else what they've found out about us."

"Are they the ones who killed my grandparents?"

"I think so. We have to let them think they've gotten the best of us, that we're no threat to them. And then . . ."

Oscar's smile was as cool and calculated as his own. "Then we give 'em a big surprise."

"Exactly."

"But Max, I'm not going to just run off and leave you."

"You have to do what I tell you, Ozzy, or you'll ruin the surprise. You don't want to do that, do you?"

"No, Max." He finished binding the wounds and wrapped the heavy coat back up around him, noticing how badly he was shaking. "Are you cold, too?"

"Just not feeling very good. I'll be better in the morning. Don't let me go to sleep, Ozzy. You keep me awake. Can you do that?"

"Sure, Max." His voice was small and weighted with upset.

"C'mere. Sit here by me. We'll keep each other company and won't be so cold." The boy burrowed up against his good side, settling in as Max pulled part of his coat about the boy's narrow shoulders. "We'll be fine, Oscar."

"I won't be scared if you won't be."

"Okay." And he was smiling faintly as he slipped quietly away, letting the fever gobble him up. He closed his eyes and could almost hear Charlotte's voice, a cool caress across his burning mind.

I'm here, baby. Don't be afraid. You're not alone. Show me where you are.

He let himself fill up with her, with her warmth, her scent, the feel of her touch whispering over his lips.

Charlotte. Find me. Help me. I love you.

HE WOKE WITH a jerk, the creeping chill of danger all over him. Oscar lay heavily across his knees, asleep. He fit his hand gently over the boy's mouth, then gave him a slight shake.

"Shhhh."

Oscar nodded that he understood and sat up slowly once Max released him.

It was minutes to dawn. A cold mist shimmered over the bayou like sheer curtains, cloaking the surroundings in a surreal gauziness. Max closed his eyes and reached out just the softest of whispers, letting it glide on the fog, until he bumped up against a recognizable signature. He eased back before they were aware of him. Seven of them.

So many.

"Ozzy, we have to move. This isn't a good place for what I have in mind."

"Are they coming?"

"Yes."

Nothing could be worse than the momentary terror that leapt in the boy's eyes before quickly becoming sober trust. Nothing until Max tried to move, and discovered he couldn't.

He hoped it was just numbness from the cold, then he looked under his jacket, dropping it quickly to conceal the sight from Oscar. No sense in scaring the boy.

"Here's as good a place as any." Talking hurt. There was so much pressure in his chest, he could only breathe in tiny snatches. Time was up. "Ozzy, I want you to listen to me, to do what I tell you."

The boy's big eyes fixed upon his. "Okay, Max."

"You need to go, quickly and quietly as you can."

"I can't leave you here by yourself. I can help you. There's things I can do, things nobody knows about."

"I know, Oz." Dear God, like he'd want the same knowledge of killing and death hanging over the boy's head that had his own when he was too young to deal with it. "But don't show anyone except Charlotte what you can do. You can trust her with anything. I need you to go, now, and find Charlotte. Don't look back, and don't come back or you'll spoil the surprise. Okay? Promise me, Ozzy. *Promise* me."

The boy's chin quivered but his voice was strong. "I promise, Max." His thin arms whipped about Max's neck and he buried his face there.

The effort it took just to bring his hand up to rest between the quaking shoulder blades was monumental. Max turned into the boy's hair and breathed his scent in as deeply as he could. His family's scent. His brother. Then he pushed him away.

"Go now." But he found himself hanging on just a few seconds longer. "Tell Charlotte . . . tell Charlotte my thoughts were of her. She'll understand. Go."

Oscar jumped up and ran. The mists quickly swallowed him, but as Max closed his eyes, he followed the boy's progress. Just a bit farther. A bit farther. *Go on, Oscar. Don't look back.*

The waiting was harder than he expected. He kept drifting, and his fear for Oscar gnawed even more fiercely than his wounds. He had to be ready. He couldn't let them kill him too quickly. He had to give Oscar time to reach safety. Then it wouldn't matter if he no longer had the strength to shift into something that could make a decent fight of things.

He let his barriers drop. He couldn't have held them in place much longer anyway. He immediately was aware of them, just as they were of him. Close. So much closer than he'd thought.

He tried to maintain his edge, but he was cold, so cold.

Charlotte.

Hang on, baby. I'm almost there.

Take care of him, sha. *Take care of him for me.*

He could feel her. The touch of her hands on his face. The warmth of her body against him, through him, filling him up with a sweet embrace of heat.

And he was smiling slightly when they came upon him.

SHE'D BEEN RACING blindly through the trees, refusing to wait for daylight because urgency thrummed in great surging pulses, pushing her forward. She wasn't sure where she was going until awareness of Max suddenly surfaced as if he were right in front of her. She redirected her course, heading for where she knew she'd find him. But would she be in time?

They almost missed one another in the fog.

She caught a quick flash of movement. But it was the scent, the scent of Max still on him, that snagged her attention.

"Ozzy!"

Cee Cee rocked back on her heels as the boy flung himself on her. She hugged him tight while her gaze swept the mist. "Are you okay? Ozzy, are you okay?" A brisk nod. "Max. Where's Max? Is Max all right?" She knew he wasn't and was scared to the marrow.

"He told me to come find you. To not look back. To not come back. He made me promise." Tears quivered in the boy's voice. "He made me leave him there alone."

"You did the right thing, Ozzy. Max can take care of himself."

The dark head shook. "No, he can't. He's hurt. He's hurt real bad. Worse than he'd let me see." He leaned back to regard her steadily. "He told me to tell you his thoughts were of you."

The same last message Max had delivered to her

from her best friend Mary Kate Malone, when she believed she was going to die.

"No." The sound moaned from her. Then fierce anger slammed into place. "Don't you dare, Savoie. Don't you dare think I'm going to let *you* leave me, too."

She gave the boy her cell phone. "Call your dad, Ozzy. He's just minutes behind with backup. Stay *right here* until he finds you. Don't make me have to worry about you."

"I won't. I'll stay here. Max loves you, you know."

She rumpled the boy's filthy hair. "I know. But that's not going to stop me from kicking his butt."

She ran, homing in on Max like a GPS signal, Feeling it fading even as she grew closer.

Hang on, baby. I'm almost there.

Though her heart hammered frantically her mind was cool, clear, and ready.

As the fog thinned she finally saw Max, limp and bloodied as one of the sleek assassins dragged him into a seated position by the hair.

"Where's the boy?"

"You'll never take him." Even weak and thready with pain, Max's voice rippled with menacing certainty. "I'm not going to let you."

A laugh at that audacious claim. "Who's going to stop us? You? You're going to take all seven of us? All by yourself?"

"No. Not by myself. Charlotte, take 'em."

Because it was ingrained in her, she shouted, "NOPD. Freeze or I'll shoot." Of course they didn't listen; they didn't think they had anything to fear from a human female. Her silver bullets took two of them down, blowing those misconceptions right out of their skulls.

Max looked up at the one still gripping his hair, his eyes a cool green edged with golden fire. He'd taken this one's scent before from Charlotte, when the Tracker had been foolish enough to put a mark on his girl's face.

Max smiled ferociously. "Surprise."

And Max's fist was through his assailant's chest before awareness of his mistake even registered in his eyes. The other Trackers stood stunned, as did the members of Cee Cee's backup team, as Max consumed the gory object in his hand, then stood, eyes closed, shuddering slightly as if in some orgasmic trance.

Alain Babineau had his son tucked behind him. He was flanked by Joey Boucher and Junior Hammond. All three stood with jaws hanging as Max Savoie became something out of a nightmare, his features altering into a monstrous bestial form. Only Charlotte and Oscar Babineau were unfazed.

"Max," she shouted, "behind you!"

He spun about just as one of the elegant killers shifted into his own fearsome entity. They immediately locked into battle.

Cee Cee heard her partner's hushed conclusion. "Fangs and claws . . . fuck me."

After a brief, violent fight Max overpowered the other Shifter, flinging him to the ground. He straddled his opponent's chest, his shaggy head bent over the other's throat. His deep, rumbling snarl brought the hairs up on every man's arms. He sat back with a savage jerk and, for a moment, didn't move. When he turned to his petrified audience, they saw his own face covered with the other's blood. His eyes dazzled with unnatural light.

"Max, they're getting away," Oscar shouted, pointing after the two who'd disappeared quickly into the rising mists. Max was up and gone without a sound, without seeming to even move.

"Holy mother of God," Joey Boucher whispered as he instinctively crossed himself.

As she walked away from her team toward the edge of the clearing, Cee Cee surveyed the carnage and did a quick tally. Four down. Max was chasing two; that was six. Where was the seventh?

Arms wrapped about her from behind, shutting off her startled cry with a sudden crushing pressure. Her feet left the ground and she struggled to breathe as her lungs were squeezed like a balloon in a fist. She could hear her own ribs snapping, the sound brittle, surreal. She twisted frantically, seeing her own death loom over her shoulder in the gleaming red eyes and sharp, dripping teeth. She centered her pistol between those horrific features and fired.

MAX BROUGHT DOWN the first as easily as they had Tito Tibideaux, dropping him with an explosive mental surge that, until this very instant, he wasn't sure he could do. The second decided to turn and make a stand, which was fine with Max. He wanted information from this one before he killed him.

They circled each other, gauging strengths and possible weaknesses, finding plenty of the first and none of the latter.

"Who are you?" the assassin asked, professional interest piqued.

"It doesn't matter. You're not going to live to tell anyone." Max smiled chillingly.

"You're the one, aren't you? The one they talk about."

"Who talks about?"

"It doesn't matter, if I'm not going to live to get back to them." And he smiled. "You're Rollo's boy, his first one with Marie Savorie."

Savorie. So that was his name. Not Savoie.

"Knowing your genealogy isn't going to help you."

"We weren't sure you were here, too, or we would have come for you first."

"Too bad you won't be able to share that information. Or have you already?"

Max sprang and brought the other down to the soft ground, knees on the other's forearms, one hand over his defiantly beating heart, the other covering his face so only his eyes glittered hotly between the spread of his fingers.

"Who have you told? Who knows about me?"

He leaned close, his stare burning into the other's, piercing through the widening pupils to images held in recent memory. Prepared for the strangely altered perceptions this time, he didn't let them distract him from what he was looking for. The imprint of the first one he'd killed back at the tree was trapped in the other's conscious mind as he spoke on the phone in the jostling SUV.

We have the boy. We're bringing him to you. But there's another here. Stronger than we've ever felt before, but he's like a ghost. We can't get a fix on him. He might be the one. He might be the key to everything.

Max pulled back. Pain lanced through his temples, breaking a sweat on his brow.

The Tracker beneath him paled and trembled. "I don't believe it. It can't be true. You can't be a Reader. That's impossible."

"I can't be what? What does that mean? Tell me."

"I've told you too much already." And he surged up, knowing it was suicide, to save whatever else was hidden in his mind.

THE SILENT TRIO of cops stumbled back several steps, tightening their defensive huddle as Max appeared from the mists. They stared at him, eyes glassy, features slack with disbelief. They'd seen. They knew what he was now. A whispering dread urged him to run away while he could, but he ignored it to find Charlotte. The only thing he wanted was to grab her up in his arms and hold her.

She sat at that base of the tree that had sheltered him through the night, half leaning against the body of her dead attacker. His gaze did an anxious scan. No sign of injury to her slumped figure.

Her gaze met his, warming, softening, but then she caught the subtle shifts of movement at the edges of her vision. Reacting without thought, her palms outstretched in the direction of her peers.

"No! Put 'em away! You're not going to shoot him. You're not going to touch him."

Startled by her vehement cry, Max glanced at the uneasy trio who'd begun to draw their weapons but now paused in uncertainty. Then Cee Cee reached for his hand, and their threat was forgotten as he went down onto his knees next to her. Small things reached him, not making sense at first. The chill in her fingertips as they brushed his gore-soaked features. The strange sound of her shallow breaths. The pallor of her skin.

"Oh, Max, I was so worried. Did you kill both of them?"

"Yes."

"Good. That's good." Then her arm dropped limply to the ground. "I won't let them take you. I won't let them hurt you."

"Charlotte?"

A thin line of blood trickled from the corner of her mouth as he gathered her up in his arms. Her body was alarmingly lax in his embrace.

"I love you, baby."

The way she said it, like a farewell on a soft sigh, sent panic through him. Something was very, frighteningly wrong. He lurched to his feet, clutching her to his chest.

"Babineau, where's your car?"

His fierce tone brought Cee Cee's partner instantly alert. "What is it? Is she hurt?"

"We have to go—*now*."

"He—whatever the hell he is—is not leaving here," Hammond argued, his service revolver pulled and ready. "Not without my cuffs on him." When he took an aggressive step forward, Babineau shoved him back.

"Get out of the way, Junior, or I swear to God they'll have to bring a body bag for you, too."

Max carried her out of the swamp, frustrated by having to slow his steps so the others could keep up. She was so very still. He shut every part of himself down except the essentials needed to get her help. He wouldn't think about anything else.

When he eased her into the rear seat of Babineau's car, Oscar leaned over the back of the front seat, his eyes huge and anxious. "Is she going to be all right, Max?"

"Ozzy, sit down and put your belt on," Babineau snapped. Then, taking a breath to calm himself, he placed a hand on the boy's shoulder. "Sit down, son, so we can get going."

Clicking the seat belt closed, Oscar strained to see into the back where Max was holding Cee Cee across his knees.

"I want to see you," she insisted as Max positioned her carefully so her feet were up on the worn, fabric-covered seat. "I want to see your face, Savoie."

"It's not that much to look at, *sha*." But he eased her down with an arm about her shoulders to cradle her.

"It's a magnificent face," she argued with a dreamy little smile. "They both are." She reached up to touch him. He took her wandering hand and fit it to his cheek. Her eyes closed briefly as the vehicle jerked into motion and bounced along the rutted two-track.

"Careful," Max growled at the driver.

"Do you want careful or do you want speed?" Babineau's combative tone was belied by his worried glance in the rearview mirror.

"Hurry," Max told him quietly. Then he turned his attention back to Cee Cee. "How you holding up, *cher*? Any pain?"

"Just hold me, Max. Don't let go."

"I won't."

"My legs are cold. Could you cover them up for me?"

He looked down at the heavy stadium blanket

he'd tucked around her and asked without moving, "There. Is that better?"

"Ummmm, much. Thank you."

Keeping his expression relaxed, he pushed the blanket aside and pinched the underside of her knee hard. She didn't even twitch. With a shaking hand, he restored the blanket and absently rubbed her thigh. He tried not to see the way the color leached from her face, or hear the suspicious gurgle in her breaths, or note the frothy substance of the blood appearing again at her lips. He refused to believe what those signs told him.

"We'll be there soon," he assured her.

A snort. "Not with Babs behind the wheel. You scratched the paint on my car, Savoie."

He smiled. "I'll get you another one. Anything you want."

"I want you."

"You have me, Charlotte."

"Then I have everything I need." And her lips curved up as her eyes slid shut.

SHE WAS STRIPPED from his arms the second he carried her into the ER. His bullet-riddled jacket and the blood he was bathed in forced him to stop for insistent questions regarding his own condition while he watched them wheel her swiftly away. Then there was nothing to do but wait.

He stood motionless, his unblinking eyes fixed on the corridor, unaware of the whispers and attention, he drew. Hammond and Boucher arrived to confer with Babineau, watching him with wary indecision. The only thing that reached him was the feel of Oscar's small hand squeezing his before Babineau called him away.

More and more uniformed and plain-clothed officers filled the room once news spread that Charlotte Caissie was there. Even the vice team arrived, giving Max Savoie a wide berth. The mood was grave, her colleagues mostly silent in grim law-enforcement tradition. They waited.

Tina Babineau rushed in, dropping to her knees to envelop her son and bathe him with her tears. She had a quick hug for her husband, then she turned to the stoic and solitary Max. Her arms went around him without hesitation, her hand guiding his head down to her shoulder in a timeless gesture of comfort.

"Oh, Max. I'm so sorry. She'll be fine. She has to be."

Max squirmed away; it would have been too easy to fall apart within her tender care.

She touched her fingertips to his bloody face and smiled in understanding. "You look terrible. Alain said you needed a change of clothes. Here. I brought you some things."

He took the brown grocery sack from her, and because his hands were starting to shake, he simply nodded and made his way quickly to the bathroom.

Seeing his appearance in the mirror, Max understood the eddy of alarm he was spreading. He looked like the aftermath of a drive-by in a barbecue pit. And from out of the gruesome hell, his eyes shone dark and flat.

He slipped out of his coat and shirt. The bullet wounds were nearly healed, no longer paining him. Tina had folded an olive green tee shirt and zippered black sweatshirt in the bag.

Before putting them on, he splashed cold water over his face and hair, hoping the chill wouldn't wake him from his numbness. He needed to stay insulated from whatever was happening behind the doors that kept Cee Cee from him. He needed to hang on, because one little crack would open a devastating crevice all the way to his soul, one from which he'd never be able to climb.

Take it one minute at a time. Don't look ahead. Don't look back.

He could hear Jimmy Legere calmly talking him through his initiating trial by fire when he was hardly much older than Oscar.

Don't think. Just act. Thinking and feeling are for later, when you have the luxury of time. Don't let your heart or your mind get in the way of what you have to do, or it will never get done. Close those doors, Max. Close the doors and keep everything locked away. Because once you open them, everything's going to come spilling out and you won't be able to shove it back in.

And Jimmy was right. That first time when he'd

gotten into the car with the blood of his victims still on his hands and in the back of his mouth, he'd curiously, defiantly, cracked that door open to see if he could handle the knowledge of what he'd done. The scent of death and horror took him under so fast, he'd thrown up on the floor mat. After the stoic driver had cleaned it up, he'd slumped weakly across Jimmy's knees, overcome by guilty shame. Jimmy had let him howl and sob, his hand resting lightly atop Max's head until all the emotions had run dry. Lesson learned. Some doors weren't meant to be opened. Ever.

He dressed quickly and then rejoined Cee Cee's friends in the waiting room, with them, yet noticeably apart.

The first thing he saw was the tragic pain in Tina Babineau's eyes as she turned from one of the staff. He shut himself away from the knowledge shimmering there, still and emotionless, until Tina crossed the room to gently touch his shoulder.

"She's not going to make it, Max. I'm so sorry. So sorry."

Twenty

*T*HE DOOR CLICKED shut, then there was silence. Silence and the scent of Charlotte wrapping around him like a welcoming embrace. He leaned back against the door, his eyes closed, unable to move as the events of the long day came back in fractured shivers.

He didn't know how he'd gotten through the hours, through the sympathetic looks and regretful murmurs. Giles and Helen had come that afternoon. And LaRoche. And Father Furness. They'd all spoken quiet words of comfort; he didn't remember if he'd said anything to them or not. It had taken all his energy just to breathe.

Junior Hammond had cautiously approached and took the brown bag holding his blood-splattered clothing. Evidence—Max understood. Hammond had been looking for a way to crucify him, and now he'd found it. It didn't matter.

When the doctor came out to address them, he'd confirmed what Max had guessed but hadn't wanted to believe. Massive internal damage, almost as if she'd been caught between two colliding buses. Rib cage and spinal column crushed. Lungs, heart, and other organs perforated, ruptured, failing. Shock. BP so low it barely registered. Still, they'd thought they might have a chance. But before they could stabilize her, just as they'd begun a major transfusion to replace the fluids pouring out internally, a clot had raced to her brain and, for all intents and purposes, ended everything that made Charlotte Caissie unique.

As the weary surgeon explained that machines were now keeping her technically alive, Max had been distracted by a teasing whisper. *I want you, Savoie. I'm never going to let you go.* When he tried to focus on all the grim faces as they were told, "We'll run more tests and an EEG in the morning, just to be sure; then a decision should be made," an image dazzled the edges of his memory. A bold figure shimmering in bronze, wreathed in a smoky spotlight. Dark eyes daring him. *Step up, Savoie.* The feel of her fingers gliding over his. *You said there'd be dancing.*

"Who's responsible?"

The question echoed for a long moment. She had no family.

"I am," Max said. No one argued, though for a second it looked like Alain Babineau wanted to.

"There's no hurry. She's in no pain. Take your time. Think of what she would have wanted."

Then Father Furness's hand pressed over his. "We need to talk about what she'd like. Tomorrow. You need to pick out something for her to wear."

He'd blinked. Wear?

"Max, do you understand what I'm saying?"

"Yes. Of course. Thank you."

And Tina's fingers gripped his. "Come home with us, Max. You need family around you."

LaRoche's sturdy arm circled about his shoulders. "Nothing more to be done here. Let us take care of you for a change."

And Giles's somber features, his eyes swimming, unable to speak.

Helen's soft voice. "Time to go home, Max."

He'd backed away from them, from their well-intended suggestions, from their sad faces and confusing sympathy. What in God's name could any of them possibly do to make the situation better?

Tamping down the wild panic of that thought, he thanked them and said he'd be fine. He'd see them tomorrow. Tomorrow, when decisions had to be made. And then he went to the only place he'd feel safe. To the only place that would feel like home. A place filled with her.

For once, her little rodent pets didn't launch into terrified shrieks when he moved toward them. They sat still and unblinking as he opened the cage and stuffed in some food. Oscar would take good care of them.

He forced the thought away as he went into the kitchen. He had to get something to eat. His entire system was about to crash.

But what did it matter? What did he have left to

do but pick out something for the woman he loved to wear to her funeral?

He opened the refrigerator, blinking at the mostly empty shelves. What did she live on? She needed someone to take care of her. He'd promised Mary Kate. Someone to see she ate right and laughed more. One couldn't live on take-out alone.

Alone . . .

He sat down hard on the tiled floor and leaned his head back against one of the metal-edged shelves, the refrigerated air cooling the raw burning in his eyes as tears ran down his face.

The sound of the phone startled him. The sound of her voice yanked his heart to a stop.

"Caissie, leave a message."

"Savoie, pick up if you're there. Max?" Babineau.

Max tried to get his feet under him, but his strength was gone. He took a shuddering breath and let his eyes close, bracing to hear what Cee Cee's partner and onetime lover had to tell him.

"I wanted to let you know that business with your friends this morning has been taken care of. We gave them a proper send-off for you and tidied up. Least we could do." A long, awkward silence. "Yeah, well. Thanks for what you did for the boy. See you . . . tomorrow."

Huh. What do you know? He didn't think he had enough energy to feel surprise. The NOPD's finest covering his butt. He almost smiled.

Get up, Max. You will stop this right now.

Jimmy's voice, stern and necessarily cold. Automatically, he obeyed. It was that or curl up and die. And then who would pick out Charlotte's clothes? He knuckled his eyes, then jerked open the freezer door and found one frost-encased steak. He thawed it in the microwave and ate it raw.

Then, because he couldn't gather enough courage to go into her bedroom and touch her things, not yet, he laid down on the couch, tucking his knees up tight, begging for escape in sleep.

Beside the sofa were her baseball shoes, discarded when he'd iced her ankle. He picked them up to hug to his chest, breathing the history held in the scuffed leather. The scent of the Babineaus' ragged lawn, gravel from the driveway, hot sauce, perspiration, baseline chalk. But mostly, Charlotte. He closed his eyes and tried to shut down.

Think of what she would have wanted.

He let his breath out in a shiver.

"Don't leave me. Charlotte, don't leave me. Who's going to take care of me?"

The sound of his own voice shocked through his daze, opening the way for a subtle stroke of warmth along his senses. For one paralyzing moment, he heard her voice so clearly, he expected to see her when he opened his eyes.

It's all right, baby. I'm here.

He sat up, startled, as if she'd slapped him awake.

What the *hell* was he thinking?

Then he was off the couch and out the door.

MAX WALKED THROUGH the mostly deserted wing as if he belonged there.

The young nurse at the desk told him directions without thinking, then started after him in alarm as he strode down the hall.

"Sir. Sir! Visiting hours are over."

"I'm not here to visit." He heard her footsteps coming after him, but he didn't slow or look around.

The sight of Cee Cee, as white as the sheets and running with tubes knocked him back for just an instant. Then he was more certain than ever. By the time the breathless nurse scurried in, he'd turned off most of the machines that pumped artificial life into a too-vibrant soul and was gently removing the IVs and probes.

"What are you doing?" she gasped, horrified.

"The doctor told me to think about what she'd want and make a decision. I made it."

"You can't just unplug things. There are papers to sign. Liability."

"I'm not going to sue you."

"I'm going to get a security guard."

"You'd better get plenty of them."

Alone with Cee Cee, Max took his time, undoing straps, dropping the side rail, wrapping her snugly in the starchy blanket because the night was cold and she seemed so fragile.

"I'm sorry, *sha*." He spoke conversationally, as if he expected her to join in. "I betchu thought I forgot my promise."

"What promise was that, Max?"

He didn't turn at Dovion's quiet question. "Not to abandon her. Not to let her feel unloved. Then I left her here alone. How could I have done such a thing? I don't know what I was thinking."

"Are you, Max? Are you thinking now? They called me to tell me some crazy fella was up here trying to rob Charlotte of her last hours of life. Is that what you're doing?"

Max looked back over his shoulder. "Do I look crazy?"

"No." A pause. "What *are* you doing, Max?"

"Waking her up so I can take her home."

"Max, you know that's not going to happen," he said gently. "Don't you think this is a better place for her?"

Max turned toward him then, his features coldly composed, his voice a volcanic rumble. "No. And knowing her, neither do you. Is this where she'd want to be? Strapped down, pumped full of drugs, alone in the care of strangers? I am all she has, and I'm not—" His sentence broke with a sharp snap, then continued stronger, bigger. "I'm not going to disappoint her." He adopted a defensive stance when two anxious guards appeared behind the calm ME. "Don't get in my way."

"Max," Dovion coaxed gently. "Let her go peacefully."

"That's not how she wants to go. Not now, not later. She's a fighter. She'll spend her last breath cursing, her last ounce of energy clawing and scratching—not politely fading away so as not to cause any trouble. Would the Charlotte Caissie you know agree to do that?"

Dovion couldn't argue. "I want you to listen to me, Max. Will you listen?"

The aggressive posture eased slightly.

"She had a living will. She left it with Mary Kate at St. Bart's."

"I don't know what that means."

"That means she agrees with what you want to do. No drugs. No artificial means. The paperwork is already being done. She has to stay here at least for the night, but you can stay here with her. No one will bother you, except to check on her occasionally to make sure she's not in any distress. Will that be all right?"

No. None of it was all right. But he found himself nodding stiffly.

Dovion observed him for a long moment. "Max, have you considered what it's going to be like, watching someone you love die?"

"It wouldn't be the first time." His gaze glittered, then was opaque once again. "I'm not letting her go."

Dovion sighed. "I'll be on call all night if she needs anything. If you need anything, just buzz the desk. Will you do that?"

"Yes. Thank you."

"I'm going to have someone reattach the IV, just to keep her hydrated and comfortable. Would that be all right?"

Max nodded.

Dovion smiled bittersweetly. "I guess she didn't do so bad after all, picking you."

Once Dovion was gone, the nurse had reconnected the IV, and the light was turned off, the awful coil of tension began to ease from Max's chest. Trying to ignore the soft blips of sound as if they were measuring out the rhythm of her remaining seconds in his life, he sat carefully on the edge of the bed, his fingertips tracing the determined cut of her jaw. Her color was better. He wasn't imagining it. Her cheeks were slightly flushed, and her lashes curved in a gentle sweep almost as if she teetered on the edge of awakening. He sat for long moments, just watching her breathe. Then he gave himself a little shake.

"This doesn't look very comfortable, *cher*," he murmured, smoothing the bunched hospital gown at her shoulder. "That's better, isn't it?"

Turning, he reached down to tuck her feet beneath the covers, his hand folding over her cold toes. He bent, touching a kiss to the top of her foot, rubbing the cool skin between his hands to restore its warmth. He tried to block out the doctor's grim prognosis, tried to cling to the sudden burst of hope that had him hurrying back to her side. But it was hard, when he was so beaten down with fatigue he could scarcely form a rational thought. Shaky sickness unfurled in his gut, expanding steadily no matter how valiantly he tried to hold against it. He took her unresponsive hand and laid it against his cheek, holding it there.

Don't leave me. Don't leave me, he mourned.

And just as his overtaxed system began to shut down, he heard her whisper. *I've got you, Savoie. I'll keep you safe.*

His heart pounded. He *hadn't* imagined it. Not at her apartment and not now.

Charlotte was reaching out to him.

He took her hand between his and closed his eyes, struggling to attain that inner peace and power. He forced his breathing to quiet until he could hear his own pulse, let his thoughts calm and his mind narrow to a single focus.

Charlotte.

She *had* to be there. They shared a bond, a future.

Her energy drew him—a faint glow at first, then stronger, brighter, vital, and bursting with life.

Max.

Then the moment was gone, slipping away before he could grab on.

No!

He sat back in frustration, warming her still fingers between his palms. He could sense her, *feel* her, just beyond those frail human boundaries that kept them apart.

"You are the strongest, bravest woman I know," he told her with fierce conviction. "You let nothing stand in the way of what you want. I'm here, Charlotte. Come back to me."

No human female could, he understood that impossibility. But she was his mate. When they'd bonded, he'd shared with her all the marvelous gifts he possessed. He believed that. But to wake her from the finite state she'd accepted as inevitable, *she* had to believe, too. She had to fight her way back to him with all the stubborn, irrepressible courage she possessed.

He spoke out loud as if he had no doubt she could hear him. "If I'm right, why am I sitting here alone?"

No answer.

His tone roughened into a low growl, goading her famous temper. "You're a coward, detective. Grabbing at the chance to take the easy way out. You knew I wouldn't let you go any other way. And you're a liar, too—telling me I could wake up to you for the rest of my life. If that were true, you'd wake up for me now."

No flicker of her lashes. Just the slow movement of her breaths.

He made his attack on her subconscious more aggressive.

"Jimmy was right when he said you wouldn't

stick by me. And now that your cop pals have enough to lock me away forever, you're not going to even stay around to drop by for conjugals on visiting day. What am I supposed to do? You know I don't play well with others."

Still nothing. His words grew more forceful, pushing for a rebuttal that in life, she could never resist.

"And now that those of my kind have a pretty good idea of who and where I am, do you keep your promise to watch my back? You didn't even watch your own. If I'd known you couldn't handle it, I would have told you to stay safely tucked in with Babineau."

I know you're in there. Fight for me, Charlotte!

"So, where does this leave me?" he drawled with an arrogance that would have had her bristled up and spitting like a cat. "You said I was selfish but after all I've done for you, this is the thanks I get? You'll just go gently into that good night? Where's the rage, Charlotte? Are you just going to lie there and—and die?" His voice broke. His resolve quavered, but he fought back for her. He squeezed her hand between his. *Please, Charlotte.*

"I guess there's no reason for me to work at being legitimate now, is there, detective? I could have it all, you know. I could take it by force and intimidation, just like my father did. Just like Jimmy did. I'd be just like them, if not for you." His voice deepened with anger over his despair. "I took you for my mate, Charlotte. For life."

Charlotte, don't leave me.

What good were all his abilities if he couldn't do this one thing? If he couldn't hold on to the one thing that meant the most to him? What good to be king, if he had to rule alone?

He took a breath and let his consciousness fly once more, until it fixed on an unmistakable scent. *Voodoo Love.* He surrounded that essence of her, distilling all his power, all his energy, all his love.

Come back to me! Hold on to me, sha. *Hold tight.*

He pulled, and for an instant she was there with him. He could smell her, feel her touch on his face, taste her smile on his lips.

I love you, Max.

But even as he clutched frantically, she was fading.

No! Don't go! You promised you wouldn't leave me! You promised you wouldn't fail me!

He opened his eyes. Her still image blurred through his tears. Angrily, he shook them off. He could do this! They could do it together. He wasn't wrong about that. He'd never been wrong about the strength that bound them, even before he marked her.

I will not let you go!

What would it take to bring back the spark, the fiery spirit of the woman he loved?

He smiled to himself and leaned close to provoke her, rubbing his cheek against her cool one so he would fill up her senses with every faint inhalation.

"I know you can hear me, detective. So hear this. I won't have any trouble replacing you. The very tasty Amber has let me know she's ready to step in. Into your place, into my bed. She'll keep me warm at night and won't cause me near the aggravation you have. And she's strong enough to take it. The others were right about that—I was foolish to expect so much from you. So go ahead. Leave me. I won't be lonely for long.

"Too bad I can't say the same for your lover, Detective Babineau. He'll be weeping and wailing for that precious relationship that was too sacred for you to share with me."

He felt a smack against the back of his head.

"I said it was nothing, Savoie. Quit bitching about it."

The sound of her aggrieved voice put a shaky grin on his face. He lifted his head, his breath suspended, waiting for her eyes to open, for her to scowl at him.

"You bastard—the minute I look the other way, you're sniffing around that brainless pair of boobs."

"I'm sorry, detective. I didn't mean to provoke you on your deathbed."

"Yes, you did," she grumbled. Then her palms rubbed the sheets, and she looked confused. "Isn't this our bed? Who's dying?"

"Apparently no one. Not today."

Her tone mellowed as her fingers caressed over the tops of his, a sensation so sweetly sensual, emotion backed up in his chest until it ached like a heart attack about to explode. "I'm not going anywhere for another sixty or seventy years, so you're going to have to put your other plans on hold."

"With pleasure."

"Besides, I already told you how I want to go. Having sex in the shower with you."

"I'll try to keep that promise." He touched her cheek, had his hand shaking with a fierce tremor. "How are you feeling?"

"I was having such a strange dream."

He smiled. "Was I in it?"

"You were calling me. You were in my apartment, wondering who was going to take care of you. That's silly. I am, baby." Her eyes drifted shut, then snapped open again. "You'll be here when I wake up, won't you?"

"Always, *sha*."

"Good."

His hand soothed down her leg, then—

"Ow! Why'd you pinch me?"

"For scaring me. Go to sleep."

She frowned, then stopped fighting the pull at her droopy eyelids. "Don't go away." Her voice sighed like the ripple of satin sheets. "I love you, Max." And she drifted into a healthy slumber.

"Good."

All his compressed feelings finally gave way, crumpling his features. Pressing his cheek into her palm, he shook with silent sobs and laughter. He hung on to her hand, unable to let go, because he was holding his dreams, his future, his world.

He didn't have to pick out any clothes for her tomorrow. And he'd better come up with a spectacular new car, or there'd be hell to pay.

"Am I too late?" Devlin Dovion asked. Seeing Max Savoie with all defenses down could mean only one thing. His broken heart was in his eyes, when he was startled by Savoie's smile.

"She's asleep. Take a breath. They don't allow throwing up in here."

"She's been awake?" His look was stupefied.

"And talking. Scolding me, actually."

Dev stepped over to check her vitals, taking her pulse just to absorb the warmth of her skin and listen to the easy in and out of her breathing for reassurance. Clinical disbelief quickly undercut his delight. "How could that happen? How do you explain that, Max? How am I going to explain it when the hospital and her superiors ask me?"

Max protectively tucked the covers in around the sleeping figure. "You can think of something they'd believe. Something a little less . . . shocking than the truth."

"What *is* the truth?"

"I don't really know myself."

Dovion wasn't going to let him off that easily. "But you can guess. It has to do with you and what you are, doesn't it? With the bullets that put holes in your jacket but don't seem to be bothering you at all. What did you pass along to her when you bit her?"

Max ignored the speculation to insist, "You can quiet the questions. You can fix the hospital reports, lose the tests." His stare held Dovion's. "Because if you don't, and word gets out that my girlfriend came back from the dead no worse for wear, a whole lot of trouble is going to be coming this way. You have no idea how dangerous the truth can be."

Dovion studied him for a long minute, weighing his words. "I could handle the paperwork and silence the rumors." He left that comment hanging for a minute until Max nudged at it warily.

"What do you want?"

"I want you to talk to me, Max. To satisfy my curiosity. It won't go any further, but I want to know. I *have* to know. Is Charlotte's safety worth that to you?"

"Yes." No hesitation. Then he was all cool and in control again. "I need to speak to Charlotte's doctor."

MAX STOOD AT her bedside as the stunned physician did a hurried and incredulous examination. He was confused, then amazed, then intrigued, just as Dovion had been. "This isn't possible. I need to run some new tests."

"Because the first ones were faulty," Max suggested. "They exaggerated the seriousness of her condition."

"No. Not to this degree," the doctor said to himself before glancing up at the man he remembered from the previous day. The one who'd been covered in blood. "Who *are* you?"

"My name is Max Savoie. And I'm about to become a very influential patron of this hospital. And of your career."

"Welcome home, *sha*."

Max carried her into the room they shared, and deposited her gently on the big bed. While she smiled and got all misty-eyed at the arrangement of fresh flowers on the night table, Max went to the French doors and threw back the curtains.

Sunlight flooded the room and she soaked up the sight of him, so dark, so fierce, and so damned desirable. She was considering how to lure him under the covers when she glanced around, and then just stared.

In the big room where he'd lived most of his life with blank white walls and bare wood floors, startling splashes of color had bloomed. An abstract art print from her living room warmed the space above his dresser, which now held her scented candles and her favorite pictures of her father and Mary Kate. Several of her woven pillows brightened his functional chair, and a rag rug she'd purchased at a fundraiser at St. Bart's was on the floor. A half dozen pairs of sexy shoes she didn't recognize but which looked like her size toed off with his workboots, shiny leathers, and worn red Converses in the partially opened closet.

"What is all this?" she asked, fighting back the emotion building in her throat.

Max slid the closet door shut. "I picked up a few things I thought might make you feel at home. Ahh—sounds like you have company."

Oscar bounded into the room, carrying a vaguely distressed Baco. Alain Babineau followed.

"Hey, detective. Max told me I could bring them over here to stay 'cause they were lonely at your apartment. Their cage is down in the parlor."

"Did he? How thoughtful of Max." She shot a glance his way, which he met without a blink.

"How are you feeling, Ceece?" Babineau asked.

Max had faded back to stand by the balcony doors, distancing himself both in space and expression.

Confused, she looked to her partner. "I'm good."

Babineau exchanged a quick look with Max, then said carefully, "I spoke to the doctor yesterday. He said everything was on the mend and that you might be back on a desk in the next few weeks."

"Just a lot of bruising and some swelling, but no fractures. I should be as good as new in no time."

Babineau fidgeted uncomfortably for a minute, then said, "Oscar, let's get going. We don't want to overstay our welcome. Oh, another thing." His jaw clenched for a moment. "Tina wanted me to ask you both over for dinner, when you feel up to it. She wants to thank you for what you did for the boy."

Max stared at him for a moment, then his grin spread sudden and wide to acknowledge the other's discomfort. "Why, that's right nice of you, inviting us into your home for a family meal."

Oscar went over to give Max a quick hug, ignoring the pig's alarmed wheeks. "Can I come over for a visit sometime, Max?"

"Anytime you want, Oz. Anytime." As he straightened, he met Babineau's challenging stare with one of his own.

Babineau looked away first. "We know our way out." He smiled at his partner. "The guys say hey."

"Hey back."

And then it was just her and Max.

She patted the mattress. "Come here."

She didn't have to ask for his kiss. He supplied it generously, to the limit of their breath. As his fingers sifted through her hair, he spoke softly against her lips.

"You saved my life. Thank you."

"And you saved mine when you shared more than just your mark with me. I would have died, Max. I would have *died*."

They needed to talk about it, about what was going on between them, inside her. About the differences their bonding was creating in their relationship. New to them both. It was something they would have to learn about together, their circumstances so unique that there were no guidelines, no examples to follow. Just the limits of their love and the boundaries of their trust. They could approach these new sensations with a denying caution. Or they could explore them boldly and without fear.

Belonging to him was such a huge, huge step—implying a commitment and a connection of faith that scared her spitless.

But to have him. To *have* him . . .

"I seem to recall a lot of big-dog noise about me being yours, and the two of us belonging together. Have you changed your mind?"

His gaze smoldered. "No, detective. I have not."

He disappeared into the bathroom.

"Max? Where are you going?"

"A surprise for you. Just a minute," he called.

She heard water running, and her body began to simmer in anticipation as she pictured him wet and naked. He returned to scoop her up in his arms, and she smiled in delight as he carried her into the bathroom. "What's this?"

The wall between their private bath and the large one that had opened to the hall was gone, creating a huge space filled with light and scent and welcome. The half partition now separating the two rooms held a jungle of vining green plants that thrived on the humidity.

Max carried her around it to a huge, claw-footed tub filled with steamy, scented water. Beyond it, a wall of glass rose all the way to the ceiling and slanted up to form an unbroken view of trees and sky. Imagining the hedonistic pleasure of soaking beneath the stars, she gave a soft, overwhelmed laugh as he set her down carefully on the thick teal rug. Her toes curled in appreciation.

"I've been picturing you in it, all wet and slippery and pruny," he explained as he stripped her.

When he deposited her into the frothy water she moaned, sinking into bubbles up to her neck, her eyes closing in ecstasy. "Oh, Max, this is wonderful."

"And roomy."

He stepped over the rolled edge and slid in, all sleek, bare skin, behind her. She snuggled back between his knees, lounging on his hard chest as his arms curled about her waist. After a perfect moment, she repositioned his hands, one higher, one lower.

"I've been missing you, Savoie," she purred. She felt so strong, so confident and powerful, she wanted to roll over and devour him whole, starting with the delicious temptation of his mouth. Lust and love wound through her, provoked into a sultry impatience by just the scent of him.

Her man. Her mate. Her everything.

In the back of her thoughts, a fragile whisper teased. If their bonding had given her the ability to heal her wounds, could it also heal her scars? Would she be able to repair the damaging past and make all his dreams come true?

She didn't dare consider it. Not yet.

This time was just for them, and they had some long overdue business to attend to. Business that pressed full and hard along her back.

"Make me howl at the moon, Max."

She felt his smile against her throat. "The moon doesn't rise for another six hours, *sha*."

"Which leaves plenty of time for foreplay," she teased.

Her breath caught as his touch went from sensuously soothing to all-business, and his voice was a husky growl in her ear.

"Then we're going to need a *lot* more hot water."

Sometimes love needs a little help from beyond...

Bestselling Paranormal Romance from Pocket Books!

JILL MYLES
SUCCUBI LIKE IT HOT

The Succubus Diaries

Why choose between the bad boy and the nice guy...
when you can have them both?

CARA LOCKWOOD
Can't Teach an Old Demon New Tricks

She's just doing what comes supernaturally....

GWYN CREADY
FLIRTING *with* FOREVER

She tumbled through time...and into his arms.

MELISSA MAYHUE
A Highlander's Homecoming

Faerie Magic took him to the future,
but true love awaits in his Highland past.

The darkness hungers...

Bestselling Paranormal Romance from Pocket Books!

KRESLEY COLE
PLEASURE OF A DARK PRINCE

An *Immortals After Dark* Novel

Her only weakness...is his pleasure.

ALEXIS MORGAN
Defeat the Darkness

A *Paladin* Novel

Can one woman's love bring a warrior's spirit back to life?

And don't miss these sizzling novels
by *New York Times* bestselling author
Jayne Ann Krentz writing as

JAYNE CASTLE
Amaryllis Zinnia
Orchid

Discover love's magic with

a paranormal romance from Pocket Books!

Nice Girls Don't Live Forever
MOLLY HARPER

For this librarian-turned-vampire, surviving a broken heart is suddenly becoming a matter of life and undeath.

Gentlemen Prefer Succubi
The Succubus Diaries
JILL MYLES

Maybe bad girls *do* have more fun.

A Highlander's Destiny
MELISSA MAYHUE

When the worlds of Mortal and Fae collide, true love is put to the test.

Available wherever books are sold or at
www.simonandschuster.com